THE DOOMSDAY BOOK OF FAIRY TALES

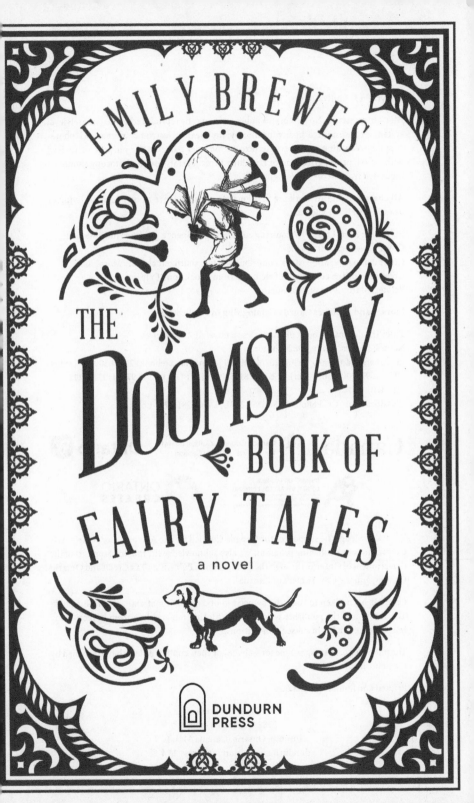

EMILY BREWES

THE

DOOMSDAY
BOOK OF
FAIRY TALES

a novel

DUNDURN
PRESS

Publisher: Scott Fraser | Acquiring editor: Rachel Spence | Editor: Julie Mannell
Cover designer: Laura Boyle
Cover composite: Man: istock.com/ilbusca; Dog: shutterstock.com/Morphart Creation; Border: comprised of elements from istock.com/Extezy
Printer: Marquis Book Printing Inc.

Library and Archives Canada Cataloguing in Publication

Title: The doomsday book of fairy tales : a novel / Emily Brewes.
Names: Brewes, Emily, 1982- author.
Identifiers: Canadiana (print) 20200300229 | Canadiana (ebook) 20200300237 | ISBN 9781459747005 (softcover) | ISBN 9781459747012 (PDF) | ISBN 9781459747029 (EPUB)
Classification: LCC PS8603.R484 D66 2021 | DDC C813/.6—dc23

We acknowledge the support of the Canada Council for the Arts and the Ontario Arts Council for our publishing program. We also acknowledge the financial support of the Government of Ontario, through the Ontario Book Publishing Tax Credit and Ontario Creates, and the Government of Canada.

Dundurn Press
1382 Queen Street East
Toronto, Ontario, Canada M4L 1C9
dundurn.com, @dundurnpress 𝕏 f ⌾

This book is dedicated to my mum, my dad, and my brother.

HAPPY BIRTHDAY, JESSE VANDERCHUCK!

IT'S BEEN FORTY YEARS since I've seen the ocean. I mark that moment, the one when I first witnessed that infamous vastness, as one of rebirth. Standing on a wet beach, as near the break of day as makes no difference, I felt no larger than a mote. And hanging there, weightless, waiting for the sea to speak, I knew that one day I was going to die.

We were on a rare cross-country trip to visit my mother's family. A three-hour drive down to Toronto, followed by a four-hour flight to B.C. From our little patch outside of Trout Creek to a commuter town east of Vancouver. My sister, Olivia, having just turned one, spent much of the journey letting us all know her displeasure, her volume turned to eleven.

I remember a lot of tension: my father constantly cracking his loud farmer's knuckles. My mother's company laugh — the one she did reflexively when burdened with keeping the peace. It was less like fakery and more like camouflage.

There were unfamiliar foods I was expected to try and, more importantly, to like. Big Hungarian-style dishes like cabbage rolls and sour cream and sweet pierogies. I mean, who'd ever heard of a sweet pierogi? I heard a litany of cajoling that trip. There was the *try it, you'll like it*; the *just a bite, for Grandma*; and the final concession, *you don't know what you're missing*. Perhaps I didn't, but that was for me to decide, wasn't it?

I did my best — less out of familial obligation and more out of my understanding of social rules. Not to mention the certainty that I'd bear the brunt of my dad's frustrations should I be too resistant. My father was not a violent man. I don't want to give that impression. He was a man easily irritated, and he was known to lack discretion when it came to venting his ire. I found it best to keep my head down and avoid catching friendly fire.

Anyway, the trip to the ocean. Dad had bundled us all into the car before sunrise, groggy and confused. Our soundtrack was the warm drone of CBC morning radio, the perfectly smooth diction of trained voices punctuated by interludes of indie rock or Inuit throat singing.

Dad was beaming with excitement, rare enough to begin with and historically fragile. As sleepy as I was, I had a tingle at the back of my mind that signalled caution. Not enthusiastic enough and he'd be disappointed. Too over the top and he'd suss I was faking. Whatever we were up for, I needed to craft an appropriate response, lest the ornament of his enthusiasm be carelessly crushed.

My mother, in many ways, was too honest for my kind of calculated behaviour. As much as she loathed conflict, she just as frequently waded into it as avoided it. Brave faces only took her so far. In any pantomime, she inevitably hit some kind of wall, beyond which there was no room for dishonesty. She was especially vulnerable at times when her guard was naturally low. Like then, as dawn broke wide against the horizon, at the very crack of creation.

When we left the main road to take a rutted dirt track between a pair of high grassy dunes, she muttered something like, "Where are we?"

Innocent enough. Reasonable, certainly. Perhaps her tone was slightly too sharp, or maybe the words hit some particular structural defect in Dad's buoyant mood. An underlying pessimism kept him expecting negativity, so he might've reacted the same way regardless of what was said or by whom. The air in the car seemed to seize up like stricken oobleck. I knew that the calm was over. Time for the storm.

I was in the back seat on the driver's side. In the rear-view mirror, I could see Dad's mild smile wrench into a deep frown. From the top of his plaid-flannel collar, a line of sunrise-red crept up the nape of his neck. He bounced his palm off the top of the steering wheel before replying.

"I thought," he said, voice drawn taut with careful control, "we would all enjoy going for a little drive to the ocean."

On the radio, *DNTO* signed off, thanking its producers and contributors. Mum squinted at the dashboard clock. "We're on vacation. Why so early?"

Now the steering wheel was squeezed, thick fingers squeaking as they rotated over the leatherette. Dad's habit of intermittently clicking from halfway down his throat intensified, a sure signal he was about to boil over.

"Well, we're here now, but if you want, we can just turn around and go home."

Mum sighed, resigning herself to the familiar situation. We passed a sign that told us we were Now Entering Porteau Cove Provincial Park, and that swimming in the ocean was forbidden here. Barely glimpsed small print specified acidification, plastic pollution, and hordes of Humboldt squid as reasons to stay out of the water. As I breathed relief that I wasn't the one who had set Dad off this time, I wondered if the squid mentioned were the ones that had developed venom sacs filled with liquefied PVC.

"Don't be like that," Mum said. "It's a bad example for the children."

No, I begged silently. *Don't drag me into this!*

I watched Dad's eyes flash up in the rear-view, their distinct blue hue gone hard and icy, and felt a pang of sorrow. As much as I was in for self-preservation, I felt bad for him. It's hard for a kid to see a parent unhappy, and my father was rarely happy. The only place that kept him pleased for any length of time was his woodshop. For him, the meticulous tuning of tools, the cleaning and maintaining of machines, were akin to raking a Zen garden. If only he could've found that meditative calm at times like this. Maybe I should have carried around a set of oily socket wrenches as a preventative measure, dosing them out as needed.

The car stopped. Outside the sky was a shade paler than the smoked salmon frequently splayed across a long white plate on Grandma's breakfast table. Gulls wheeled like shreds of paper being juggled on competing breezes, their gurgling laughter bouncing between sea and sky.

Back home, beside the creek formerly laden with trout, early mornings were nearly silent. Silvered snakes of mist coiled out from between trees along the face of the distant forest. Ghosts of blue jay and chickadee calls drifted across hushed fields, and the whole world felt painted onto the inside of a blown-glass bulb: frail and ready to shatter at the first loud sound.

Here there was no shortage of noise. Instead the swelling roar of what turned out to be the ocean itself permeated the stillness of the car. There were the gulls calling down to the fleets of sandpipers, and the sandpipers chirping amongst themselves as they ran stiff-legged, weaving in and out of the surf.

The instant the engine went still, I was out the door, so glad to be free of the stifling tension that I nearly leapt into the sky. The sand was wet and dense underfoot, more like semi-set concrete than the gravelly lake beaches I was used to. It slapped beneath my sneakers as I ran toward the great shifting roar, away from what was almost certainly now a full-blown argument between my parents. I imagined I could hear Olivia's rising cry from her car seat, as much from being woken up as from any situational distress. Given her status as the beloved baby, her upset might well have quelled my parents' ire, redirecting their energies to sooth her. I couldn't know, because I was close enough to the waves that their noise was all-consuming.

And the winds — one blew out from across the land, the great bellowing breath of the rising sun, flattening the fields of sea grasses and thrusting fists of warm air into my lower back. Another gust crashed boisterously from the water itself, its clammy, salt-crusted arms wide and sweeping, forcing me to brace against being knocked over.

It really was too bad that Dad didn't get to see my reaction when I first set eyes on the ocean. He'd have been so pleased to see my ten-year-old mouth gaped in utter wonder. My instinct was to head directly for the water's edge, to place my feet along the shifting join where it met the land, the way I did at Wolf Lake. Thankfully, I had enough sense to hang back. Even so, about every fifth wave came in so hard I was misted by spray. The smell was overwhelming and alien — fishy and salty and ancient. It assaulted the senses until, just as suddenly, it disappeared. Deep in the oldest part of my brain, it was understood as familiar. Beyond familiar even, if such a thing exists. It was huge and terrifying and unmistakably vital.

For some time, I stood there mesmerized, in a state of profound oneness beneath the paling pink sky of the rising day. The fact of my own mortality appeared before me like a reflection made of solid shadow. I closed my eyes and leaned forward. The shadow must've done the same, because we met in the middle, nose to nose. A sensation not quite like cold — not quite like anything, really — suffused the skin where we touched. It spread across my face and down my scalp. Without fear, I understood that should that not-feeling reach my heart, I would drop dead.

Then my dad yelled from the car window, "Get in! We're leaving!"

Just like that, it was over. The shadow disappeared like a popped soap bubble. My senses were roused by an overwhelming stink. I was standing on a dead fish. I did my best to rub it off on the sand as I returned to the car. Despite my efforts, my mother's nose crinkled the moment after I closed the door.

"What's that smell?"

"Stepped on a dead fish," I mumbled.

As a result, the first fifteen minutes of the return trip focused on this error in my judgment. I should've looked where I was going. I shouldn't have gotten out of the car, gone out alone. Didn't I know how terribly dangerous the ocean was? And so on. We travelled with the windows cracked, which was uncomfortably chilly in the early autumn morning. Both of my parents complained about it ceaselessly. I was impressed they had enough remaining energy to give me heck, as much as I was annoyed by getting it. Sinking sullenly in my seat, I glanced over at Olivia. Her cheeks were red and blotchy from crying, though at that moment she was peacefully gnawing on a plastic maraca as she watched the scenery pass by the window.

Maybe their voices got tired, or maybe just for a change, Dad turned the radio back on. Over the chattering of my teeth, I heard the top-of-the-hour national news bulletin.

"Today we are hearing more reports out of Winnipeg, where nearby communities are being evacuated due to severe flooding of the Red River. The mayor of the city, as well as several MLAs from the surrounding region, claim they don't know how many more refugees they can support. Seasonal droughts and a severe blight that wiped out two-thirds of last year's crops have left the area short on supplies. They are asking the premiers of neighbouring provinces for assistance in taking in those affected by the rising waters, but the leaders are dealing with crises of their own. New outbreaks of rabies-B are being reported throughout Northern Ontario, with seven fatalities at the Central Algoma Health Centre in the past month. Wildfires continue to burn much of the farmland across the prairies. From Regina, Saskatchewan's premier said there is little help they can offer …"

Dad reached over to the radio and pushed the seek button. The first sound to break the static was a fuzzy oldies rock station. They were playing a song I recognized from the rare times Mum drove and therefore selected what we listened to. It was something about raising hell.

Dad's eyes glanced up to check the mirror before locking back onto the highway. Mum's cheeks were wet, a pair of clear streams running into the laugh-line channels bracketing her mouth. Some degree of awareness dawned on me, that perhaps this visit was more than simple courtesy. I couldn't know then that it was a farewell trip, saying goodbye to family we were unlikely to see again.

When we got back to my grandparents' place, they were just getting up. Grandma was wearing a faded pink terrycloth robe. Grandpa was settling into his armchair in the living room, sporting his uniform of tan slacks and a white undershirt. Later on, if we went out, he would deign to cover up with a short-sleeved button-up in some variation of a checkered pattern.

Barely glancing from the TV screen, he offered me a terse nod. On catching sight of Olivia, finally back to sleep, he reached out his arms to receive her. She woke, but it only took a few bounces on his knee for her to settle into goggling baby silence, one fist most of the way in her mouth.

"Where were you off to so early?" asked Grandma, stirring her first tea of the day.

Nobody answered.

I crossed the kitchen and hugged her, then excused myself back to bed.

"What's gotten into Jesse?" I heard her query as I pulled the chenille bedspread up to my chin.

There was a brief silence that was broken by the opening and closing of drawers and cupboards.

"It's nothing, Mum. We took a drive to the shore. Go sit down. I'll make some pancakes."

"Oh, I can help …"

The troubles we had heard about on the radio weren't new. My life until that point had been liberally peppered by news of similar tragedies. What worried me was that they were getting more frequent and growing in number. It was getting to the point that environmental collapse was the only thing being reported on at all.

I was hollered at to come to the table. I ate everything put in front of me in silence.

It was about that time that I started to make more of an effort. You know, like pitching in without being asked to. If I had to put a finger on why, I can only say what I see in hindsight: that I was utterly terrified of being alone. My tiny ten-year-old brain must've cranked itself into high gear to make sure I was indispensable to my family. I had no reason to think that they'd abandon me. In fact, the possible dissolution of our nuclear unit never even crossed my mind.

Until my mother took us away to live Underground — and left my father behind.

PAYING THE TICKTOCK MAN

MORE THAN THIRTY YEARS of being buried alive in the Underground, there's a routine that has become second nature. On waking, make your bleary way to the water pump by the sink. Count fifty pumps; unless it's a wash day, then count one hundred pumps. If it's wash day, light a few scraps in the tray beneath the tank so it won't be icy to the touch. Any other day, don't waste the fuel.

Open the bathroom cupboard and do your business. Experience the same moment of panic every damn day when you think you've accidentally peed in the poop hole, or vice versa. It happened once shortly after the reclamation system was installed more than twenty years ago, but you still have nightmares about it. Check you've done it right about seven times before activating the vacuum lever that sucks it away.

If there's food, make breakfast.

If there's no food, wait until supper. Don't go looking for breakfast. Eating right away means waking up at midnight with pangs from an empty belly. Better to have the pangs during the day when you can do things to distract yourself. Like salvage.

Head over to the Heap: a huge pile of wasted, discarded, and forgotten things us poors dig through on the off chance of finding something valuable. Something useful in our brave new world. The path from the humble custodial closet of Union Station that I call home is two lefts, a right, and thirty metres of damp subway tunnel. Nod at the familiar faces who arrive from other passages, collecting into the stream heading for one of the only jobs left. Leastways for those of us who've not lucked into a prenticeship or family business that miraculously remained viable once society collapsed. The unskilled, the elderly, and the antisocial must still pay their way.

Spend most of your day at the Heap doing salvage, sifting through the leavings from the rich folk who live in fortified towers. Use the tools you've cobbled together — a shovel and a kind of rake-headed glove — to dig and scratch away at one of a dozen hills that rise out of hip-deep detritus, compacted over the years into a mass of what could not be saved. Some of it I can identify, like CD players, computing devices with their shells cracked open, skateboards, various examples of recorded media, dismembered mannequins, and vacuum cleaners. The original uses of other things are unsolvable mysteries. Nearly everyone who could provide answers is dead.

Find yourself constantly mystified at the array of nonsense that clatters down enormous corrugated pipes, landing at the crest of the hill and tumbling down. Develop a sixth sense for knowing when a new batch is on its way, long before it can be heard, so you can get out of the way. More than one salvager has been rendered out of commission by such an impact, in some cases permanently.

Become an expert at sorting junk by type so you spend as little time as possible at the trade desk at the end of the day. It's bad enough standing in line for hours to get half a handful of tokens, most of which you're saving to get your shoes repaired; you don't need to make it worse by being unprepared for your turn at the front. Make a stop at the commissary and pay one token from your hoard for some mushroom jerky and algae supplements. Go home.

By midevening, start feeling the crushing depression of the life you've been relegated to. If you're especially maudlin, sneak another token from your stash and use it to buy a mickey of high-octane hooch from the old woman down the hall who distills it from who-knows-what. Drink yourself into oblivion, halfway hoping you won't wake up in the morning.

Wake up, anyway, and do it all again.

FOR A WHILE, there were three of us. Mum, Olivia, and I lived all together in a neighbourhood to the southeast of here, under a place called De Grassi Street. Mum was teaching kids at a little school, until someone decided learning to read was maybe a lower priority down here. That notion spread among the parents. The school was shut down in a week. So, we started making our living at salvage. Mum went first, then started bringing my sister and me to show us the ropes.

Olivia took off one midsummer night about five years in (I think it was summer, though it's hard to know for sure down here). She was twelve, at most. Mum kept going like nothing had happened, only she refused to acknowledge her daughter's existence. If I made some mention of my sister, it was brushed off or else outright ignored. Without Olivia, Mum made everything at least twice as difficult as it needed to be, antagonizing neighbours, alienating friends, and clawing what small living she was able from the corpse of what had been, until she died in her bed about twenty years ago.

It was two weeks before her fiftieth birthday.

I wish I could say I miss my mother. That sounds awful, but she seemed so put out by most aspects of life that her death was a relief. There are certainly moments when I miss her deeply — I'm not a monster — but there are many more moments when what I actually miss is the distraction from my own thoughts. In those moments, it's less that I miss her as a person than as an object: a warm body, living and taking up space, making all the little noises that go along with that. The worst part about living alone is being trapped inside your head, ceaselessly thinking, as though one moment's rest would be like dying.

It's easier when there's someone else, to talk to or to care for. Then the thoughts can reach outward instead of turning on themselves. The lonely brain is a special kind of nightmare. It gets to the point when, even with other people around, there's no attempt at comfort. They may as well not even be there. You don't start conversations, and you tend to finish those started with you by grunting monosyllables. Or ignoring them completely.

It's habit — like pumping water into the tank every morning. The momentum of the treadmill you're on prevents dismounting. Slowly and steadily, you march your weary way toward your grave until it's all over and you die.

Or until you rise once more into the land of the living.

I FOUND DOGGO nosing around the Heap on a particularly bad day. Water supply was offline, so the routine was thrown completely out of whack. No pumping. No rhythm. No beat to move to. I was so off my game that I'd already bounced my forehead against the low point of the tunnel — you know, the part I was always warning others about and even got the jerry-rigged local council to paint yellow — then had my heels stepped on in the march through the main tunnel. Twice. If my shoes weren't already about falling off my feet, they were in dire straits now.

Doggo was the scrawniest mutt I'd ever seen, with wiry hair in nearly every colour a dog comes in. His waist was so thin, it was virtually a spine with skin draped over it, which made his stubby legs seem longer than they were. His coat was patchy with mange, and his wonky, mismatched ears lent him a particularly pathetic air.

Something inside lit up when I saw him, as if moments earlier I'd lacked an essential electricity. I pictured my mind as a rabid rat trapped in a racing wheel before heroically hurling itself toward freedom. I'd discovered an emotional accelerant by nearly tripping over it.

Doggo looked up with guarded caution. I carefully lowered myself to the ground and sat very still. When it became clear that I wasn't interested in whatever food-stained packaging he was sniffing, he went back to licking it, keeping his eyes fixed on me.

Mid-lick, he had a thought. I know this because I saw it happen: his head raised and tilted to one side, and a tiny spark dawned in his eyes. He stood, looked at me, tail wagging with hope.

"Got a biscuit?"

The fact that he spoke in any human language, let alone in Canadian English, didn't sink in right then. I must have forgotten it was abnormal for a dog to speak like a person. I couldn't think clearly through the dizzy happiness I felt upon discovering an animal, a real-life lovely canine. Here was a friend, a companion, someone to save me from my wretched existence! I collected

Doggo in my arms and gave him some enthusiastic ear scritches before confessing my biscuit-less state.

"Oh" was his reply, gently easing his way from my embrace. Then he plonked his butt down and began to thoroughly, and thoughtfully, lick his furry little wiener.

If I'd left him to his own devices, I knew he'd surely die. Though he'd survived some time on his own, he was near enough to our small settlement that he'd likely be caught for meat, despite what little was on him. On the other hand, keeping pets wasn't entirely legal. At best, it meant banishment from this neighbourhood. Wandering the Underground, hoping another neighbourhood would take you in, didn't exactly appeal. That was if one of the Underground's many fabled dangers, like man-eating giants, didn't snatch you first.

At worst, it meant asset forfeiture. The thought sent a chill up my spine.

I spent some time watching Doggo. Once he was done with his nethers, he perched back on his butt and twisted his long, little body in a desperate contortion to put tongue to asshole. When this was complete, he lay down so his body formed a circle, nose to tail. And in that moment, I knew I couldn't leave him.

So I brought him home.

RABBIT, RUN!

AS A SPECIES, we knew it was over years before we finally turned tail for Underground. A generation before I was even born, environmental Cassandras were prophesying the end of days. People like David Suzuki, at once lauded by those in power while his increasingly desperate pleas for action were callously ignored. Or Wangari Maathai. Jane Goodall. Pick a name. Anyone who spoke up got either polite nods or caught heck in the papers as a "fearmonger."

They told us the end would be brought by the oily hand of fossil fuels, unleashed from beneath the Earth to sweep the unfit from its surface. Foul weather, they cried, plague winds. Droughts, floods, crop decimation, and more. It all came to pass, as did some things we could not predict. Unknown unknowns, knocked into existence by the progressing fall of ecological dominoes.

The decision to flee didn't make much sense — as Earthbound beings, where could we go? — but it was an act of desperation. It was something to do once there were no other options. Staring into the face of certain destruction, we hightailed it. Kind of like the way burrowing animals beeline for their warrens instead of for the hills when a wildfire comes sweeping through. Kill or cure. It was far too late, and it was absolutely too little.

While those of us who were able dove for cover, so many more of us had nowhere to go. Sure, most cities had sewers, stormwater systems, but few had the extensive subterranean network of structures boasted by places like Toronto, better known these days as the Underground. What became of Winnipeg or St. John's or Fredericton is anybody's guess.

It didn't take much beyond political will to install a system of sumps to pump away flood waters, to shore up the walls with a kind of spray-on rubber laced with carbon fibre. Budgetary limitations or risk of financial collapse didn't hold the same sway when it seemed the age of money was coming to a close. It's just a shame nobody had that mindset until it was too late.

By the time people began moving to the Underground, there hadn't been broadcast news for about a year, not even CBC. If there had been, it would have been exclusively negative.

Even as humanity ran — to the tunnels, into mountain bunkers, or onto vast floating cities made by welding together a bunch of liberated Carnival cruise ships — we insisted it was our idea. It was our human volition that sparked the move. As though we were saying to the planet that had birthed us, "Well, you're clearly being unreasonable. We'll just wait downstairs until you're ready to talk."

It was an attempt to gaslight a super organism that isn't sentient in any way we understand. Who was this deception really for if not ourselves? We accused Mother Earth of betrayal when She stopped loving us, refusing to acknowledge that She'd never loved anyone in the first place. This was the dying breath of deistic thinking. I don't think I've met one God-fearing person down in the Underground, not in thirty-five years. If there are any, they surely keep it to themselves. Perhaps out of shame that their prayers and good living didn't pay off, or out of fear of reprisal from those who have a bone to pick with the Man Upstairs.

For all intents and purposes, there is nothing quite like us. In all the world, the prevailing theories go, humanity is unique. We have close evolutionary relatives, but they're more like second cousins once removed — about as related to us as a species as I am to any given stranger. And perhaps, once we're gone, there will never again be anything like us on Earth.

If I say that's for the best, it can only come off as cynicism of the highest order. Yet, I would only make that claim based on personal experience. We were monkeys given the top spot on the evolutionary ladder, and all we did was take delight in pooping on all the creatures clinging to the rungs beneath us.

It's also possible that we aren't so unique as all that. Perhaps if we'd recognized that everything on our little blue dot was like us, at least inasmuch as possessing a desire to keep living, we'd have acted with more care. With empathy. If only we'd had as much faith in the end of the world as so many placed in the existence of a benevolent, omnipotent, and invisible man.

A god.

So it goes.

MY FAMILY HELD out for some time before we made the move Underground. After all, we lived in the country, where "these things" don't happen. Never mind the decade of steadily worsening winters that tried to bury us alive in snow, when they weren't trying to freeze the life from our bodies. And ignore the increasing frequency of summer storms that included tornadoes in their bags of tricks. Month-long power outages that dragged on because one disaster was overlapped by another. Alternating droughts and floods replaced plenty with scarcity.

But "these things" don't happen outside of the city — that urban den of iniquity. This wasn't a moral judgment based on any religious belief (though we were ostensibly some stripe of Christian). This was the mistrust, the tribalism, of the small town. The attitude of bib-overalls and straw-chewers who drawl, "Yer not from 'round here, are yas? We do things a mite differently in these parts."

These things, the extreme weather, the epidemics, did happen to us. We lived in the sticks, not on Mars! Yet during every disaster, there would be some old timer telling the group holed up in the church basement, "I remember a storm like this'un, back in aught-six. We survived it then, we'll get by now. Sometimes the weather jes' takes a turn. Those of us with longer memories won't let a little rain scare us."

That year, our small herd of a half-dozen goats was washed away by a deluge that dumped a metre of water in an hour.

Year on year, it grew worse and worse. True terror set in. The kind that settles as a cold puddle in the very bottom of your stomach and doesn't go away; that no amount of homemade stew and a mother's love can warm.

And then in singles and couples, folk started moving away. They used every excuse in the book to retain their small-towner cred. An ailing relative who can't travel needs them to come help with the kids. It was getting too hard for old bones to till the field, so they were taking retirement. The Good Lord told them to take mission to the urban heathens.

It all amounted to the same thing: we're getting the heck out of Dodge.

My father, typically pragmatic, was unusually stiff-necked about the whole thing. The merest mention of the city or Underground was grounds for being sent to bed without supper. Then again, it was a bit of a toss-up whether there was any supper to be denied on a given night.

Mum had been putting up any and all surplus, canning, drying, pickling, and preserving. When there was no surplus to be had from our small patch, she sent us into the woods with foraging baskets and the imperative to only come home with them full. Berries, nuts, greens, roots, even the occasional mushroom. Whatever might have come up in the neighbour's patch, abandoned since they lit out, if the harvest in the woods fell short. She worked some kind of miracle, and we ate nearly as well as always for longer than seemed feasible.

It wasn't till the stores were running frighteningly dry that she started to broach the subject of moving away.

"We don't have to go to the city, but we do need to find food."

Dad grunted into his bowl. "What's this? Food, isn't it?"

"Christ, you are so stubborn!"

His response was to slurp up his dregs and mop out the rest with two fingers, the bread having run out more than a year past.

"I'll be in the shop," he announced, letting his bowl rattle on the table as he stood up from his chair.

Mum hit the table hard enough to clatter the silverware against the dishes.

"Get back here, Gord. We need to talk about this!"

There was a rattle of keys being taken off the hook, followed by the back door slamming closed and the creaking of floorboards from the closed-in porch.

At the time, his attitude pissed me off. To a kid, his avoidance looked a hell of a lot like not giving a damn. He didn't care about us, and he made Mum so upset I found her crying more often than not. Olivia wasn't any help, either, as sullen and silent as Dad. She sat at the table pushing lima beans around her plate and frowning.

Looking back, I think I understand. He was afraid, like all of us were, but not of the weather. At least not directly. This was a thing too big to fathom — a thing he had no way to fix — and he feared how afraid it made him. It became a kind of paralytic, so the only way he could carry on was to behave as though nothing was wrong. He was like a windup toy set on a track, ticking along in the most familiar ways. To do otherwise was literally impossible.

Then came the night we left. Hushed and moonless, the chill of late spring just warming so that the wet air felt like stepping into freshly drawn bath. The air was dense with the smell of lilac and pollinating birch trees, and it was utterly, eerily silent.

It was past midnight. Mum roused us, told us to be quiet. She'd packed bags for us and helped us get them on, but only after we were out of the house. We went on foot. Even if we'd had more than a whisper of fuel for the biodiesel pickup, Mum didn't like to drive.

"Besides," she said, "we're leaving it for Dad. He's staying behind to close up the farm, then coming along later."

And we were coming back, too, just as soon as the bad weather stopped. Then we'd all be a family again. I think it was the most lying she'd done in her whole life, and she'd gone and dropped a couple of whoppers. If the guilt of it hadn't killed her, I'd almost be proud.

GETTING DOWN

WE TRAVELLED AT NIGHT. Summer was arriving with a vengeance, so the daytime temperatures were rapidly becoming intolerable. We'd walk until the first rays of sun peeked over the horizon, then find a shady place to hole up for the day. There were basements aplenty to either side of the highway, so we never wanted for shelter. With a tarp stretched across one corner, we were set in minutes.

Sleep evaded me those days for the most part. I'd sit in the slightly stuffy blue-tinted light of our transient home and wait for sheer boredom to weigh down my eyelids. There was no way to know how long I slept in any one stretch this way, but it was far from restful. I woke often, jolting as though shocked, only to find Mum and Olivia blissfully unaware of my suffering.

At least the weather held. Previous ante-summers had been like monsoons. Skies opening up, dumping deluges as though teleporting oceans before ending just as suddenly. We were lucky enough to only catch one big storm that whole month of travel.

Our backs were bent double by the downpour as we ran down one of the old highway off-ramps to an abandoned downtown. We made it to a multistorey building at the edge of the town centre, beige bricks and mirrored glass. Mum led us up several flights of stairs until we found a spot still intact enough to shelter us. It was maybe the third or fourth floor, an old corner office. The windows were spiderwebbed with cracks but not broken. She sent us to find anything that would burn, then built a fire in a metal trashcan to warm and dry us off.

Midday was as dark as night. Though we weren't terribly high up, the clouds looked low enough to reach out of the window and touch. Thunder rattled, its deep bass shaking everything that could be shaken. Lightning whipped across and through the charcoal blanket of cloud, occasionally lashing toward the ground.

As we watched the storm's progress across the land, a big buck bolted out from someplace down on the street and went running. It could only be seen in fits and starts, as the curtain of rain rippled out of the way, shoved by intermittent gusts of wind. The fascinating rotoscope came to a sudden end when lightning stabbed down, directly into the head of the beast. The accompanying crack of thunder was harmonized by the dull thud of the buck's skull exploding.

By the beginning of our fifth day on the road, we made it to the farthest reaches of the Underground network. A line of people snaked away from a low concrete building that looked the way a shoebox would if the lid had been stepped on before being put back: each end kicked up from a central depression. The place was mostly roof, its windows long since shattered and swept away.

It took the better part of two days to make it to the front of the line. Once there, we were briefly separated — me alone, Mum with Olivia — into curtained-off cubicles to be inspected for disease. Eyes, ears, nose, and throat. Temperature, blood pressure, reflexes. Say "ah," turn and cough, breathe in … and breathe out. The woman doing my exam was greying blond, perfunctory but not cold. Something about the practiced way she moved was deeply reassuring.

"Age?"

"Fifteen, I think."

She raised an eyebrow at that. My only reply was "We used our last calendar for kindling."

With an accepting shrug, she wrote it down on her clipboard.

"Put your clothes back on and toss the robe in the hamper," she said, pointing with the end of her pen but not looking up from the paperwork. "Down here," pointing, "first left and have a seat."

Suddenly feeling very alone, even rejected, I did as I was told.

Mum and Olivia were already there. My sister looked like she'd been crying.

"Whassa matter, kiddo?" I tried to ruffle her hair but she ducked away.

"She got a booster shot," Mum explained. "And she's not impressed."

"I wanna go home," Olivia complained, her voice taking on that especially grating tone she employed when she was really trying to be a pest. "I want Daddy!"

Mum motioned to comfort her but was likewise rebuffed. Olivia squirmed down from her lap and went to the corner for a good old-fashioned sulk.

As stressful as things had been these past weeks, months, years, in that moment my mother looked as tired as she ever had. Defeated. Her eyes were empty and flat, like she'd cried all the tears her body could make, leaving her hollow. Like Dad, she was running on automatic. Some primitive instinct told her to bring us here, to protect us, even though I think most of her would have rather given up long before this point.

A man in a blue work shirt that was nearly black around the collar with sweat and dirt entered through the curtain on the other side of a brown picture-wood desk. In his hands were several sheets of paper that he set down before taking his seat. He was here to question our intent.

This inquiry went on a torturously long time, though the questions were pretty predictable. Why move Underground now? What had taken us so long? Some settlements in the Underground had been established for years, which meant a tougher time integrating newcomers. Did we have any special skills to offer?

My mother lied as though the floodgates of her dishonesty had been opened wide. She claimed Dad had kept us prisoner and prevented us from leaving before, when everyone else had. She painted him in the image of a monster as tears streamed openly from her eyes. God knows where she found them, but she did. Our querant seemed less moved by the waterworks than by the presence of my sister and myself. Maybe he was a parent, too.

Or maybe he had been.

When Mum's intricate tapestry of falsehood was near to completion, Olivia offered the protest I was too indifferent to give.

"No, no, no! We left him, we left Daddy and now he doesn't know where we are, and he can't get us, and I wanna go-o ho-o-ome!"

The man strolled over to her corner and crouched down beside her.

"Hey, I know this is all pretty scary, but it's okay. You are home. This is your new home. It's safe here, and we'll take care of you."

Olivia looked about to protest, but weariness and hunger had taken much of her fight. Besides, she was clearly too young to understand. The warden of the Underground nodded sagely, patting her shoulder. Then he stood and returned to his desk.

"I'm approving your application," he said, signing three sheets of paper. "Take these to the lift station to get your official documentation."

"Thank you," Mum managed through her crocodile tears, sweeping them away with the heel of her thumb.

At the lift station, they gave us identification papers and a couple of tokens — just enough to get started — then herded us over to an elevator already full to groaning with other refugees. A pair of burly guards pulled the gates closed and latched them. There were several loud ticks, then the grumble of a combustion engine coughing to life. With a grating squeal of metal on metal, the elevator descended.

Before the topside world disappeared completely, I saw a sheet of pink light stab over the eastern horizon, candy coating the world. It was the first and only time I cried for the state of things, and the last time I saw the sun for a long, long time.

FRIENDS LIKE THESE

IT TOOK A GOOD night's sleep before I fully internalized that Doggo had spoken.

Even then, it wasn't as surprising as it maybe should have been. It was post-apocalypse after all, so such oddities were surely to be expected. Then again, it could have just been a teenager's overdose of science fiction long fermented in an aging brain.

It was maybe two days after I brought him home. I took those days off work, dipping into my shoe-repair fund for rations and some extra fuel. Doggo was in desperate need of a bath, but he was so thin I couldn't conscience washing him in cold water. We got to know each other in silence. I watched as he sniffed everything his nose could reach, and as he dug and burrowed in my one and only blanket before rolling on his back and kicking his little legs in the air.

That morning, Doggo was sitting up by the water tank, staring at me as I slept. As soon as my eyes opened, his bony tail went to wagging, hitting every surface in his vicinity with a force that sounded painful. I had to reach out to stop him ringing the water tank like a bell.

"I'm so happy you're awake," he declared. "Because it means you're not dead and that there will be food."

I groaned, rubbing my face with work-roughened hands. That texture still startled me, even all these years on. It was the texture of my father's hands somehow affixed to my body.

To Doggo, I said, "Well, I'm definitely awake, but the food situation is less sure. Don't get your hopes up."

His head canted to the side, his lopsided ears thrust forward. "You are the Food Bringer. You brought me food before. You will do so again."

I snorted, shuffling into my pants. "Either there's food or there isn't. It's not like I'm God; I can't make food appear."

The tail fell still. "What is 'God'?"

Yesterday's shirt smelled like mushrooms and BO, so I took the other one down from its hook by the door and shrugged it on.

"You know, God? Like miracle worker? Water into wine? Something from nothing?"

The tail kicked into full force again. "Yes, yes! The Food Bringer does this. There is no food, and then there is food. The Food Bringer makes a miracle. The Food Bringer is God."

I crossed the tiny room in two stunted strides and wrapped my hand around his muzzle. He struggled a bit before whining.

I hushed him. "Not so loud. I've got neighbours who might not be so thrilled you're here, okay? Maybe who'd see you more like meat than man's best friend. So, keep it quiet, yeah?"

It'd been years since I'd said more than two words in a row.

I was briefly debilitated by a coughing fit, which freed Doggo to slip away and jump onto the bed. He cast a worried, guilt-ridden glance over his shoulder before he did it, which was equal parts annoying and hilarious. I coughed some more. Doggo laid down so his head hung over the bed's edge, tail thumping on the blanket.

When I caught my breath, I said, "Besides, I don't make food appear. I get it out of the bucket over there."

On gesturing to the very bucket, I saw it was on its side, with the lid halfway across the room. Well, part of the lid. Smaller pieces were spread around in orbit. All looked suspiciously chewed. Closer inspection also revealed scratches and tooth marks on the bucket. The little bastard had eaten tokens of food. And ruined a perfectly good bucket!

"Doggo," I began, trying my best to keep my voice low and level, "did you eat the food out of this bucket?"

The thumping increased in volume and quickened in pace. When I gazed directly at him, he rolled over on his side with his front leg raised.

"Please don't kill me," he whimpered.

He was so small and pathetic and helpless that it dispelled my rage like a lit match to a fart. I was still pretty annoyed, so I didn't want to, but I burst out laughing.

"Jesus, I'm not gonna kill you!"

"Keep it down, Vanderchuck! Some of us need our sleep."

The voice of Karl Metzler, the neighbour across the hall, bellered to all and sundry. His shout was followed by a calling conversation between him and others who had now been disturbed. Leave it to Karl to fix a situation by really stepping in it.

"Aw, hell," I hissed. "See? I moved here on account of the quiet, and now you're fuckin' it up …"

Doggo flopped back on his belly, looked at me side-eyed. "You want me to go?"

I hadn't known him long, but already Doggo was the most pathetic creature I could've imagined, let alone invited into my company. For all he was skinny and diseased, and kind of like a furry goblin more than a cute dog, he elicited sympathy. He was so poorly built for the world that his very existence begged to be protected.

I scooted across the floor to the bed and scritched the hollows behind his ears. His eyes closed in bliss and tiny piggy grunts rose from his throat.

"Don't go," I said. "But also don't shout. And don't steal the food. I need to eat, too, you know."

"Food Bringers eat? Who knew?"

We sat like that for a few minutes, me scratching Doggo's ears and back and hindquarters, Doggo stretching and making little grunts of pleasure. Then I had to leave.

"Okay. You stay here and be quiet. I'll come back later with food."

"What's later?"

I stood up, brushing down my pants. "You know, not now. I've gotta sort some scrap, get some tokens, then go to the commissary and get food. Then I'll come back."

"Back here?"

I nodded. "Yep. I'll be back in no time. Just keep quiet and don't let the neighbours catch you here. Maybe hide or something."

"Is on the bed hiding?"

I shook my head, grabbed the edge of the blanket, and tossed it over him. "That's hiding," I said.

"Hiding is very dark and very warm," replied Doggo.

"If you get too hot, hide under the bed instead. Go someplace where you can't be seen." I put on my hat and went for the door.

"See you later!"

His voice muffled by wood and wool, Doggo recited the morning's lessons. "Later's not now. When Food Bringer returns is later, with food."

At least he was being quiet.

THAT MORNING WAS a long slog. I was plagued with sharp bursts of worry, imagining one of the neighbours breaking into my place and taking Doggo away. There wasn't enough on him to eat, which meant they were more likely to kill him in frustration. Then they'd report me for housing a non-human animal. Instead of simply taking him away or booting me out into the wild, unsettled tunnels, I'd be euthanized and inoculated for chitin farming. I felt waves of sickness picturing the broad sheets of hybridized fungus mushrooming from my decaying corpse.

My concern made it hard to concentrate.

Pets weren't really a thing anymore, since long before we took the deep dive. In the Underground, there were a number of feral cats, but their population depended on whatever rats or snakes or frogs they could catch. Nobody kept them. In fact, no one went near them. If they didn't run away, they attacked, and infections Underground were deadly.

Before Doggo, I hadn't even seen a dog for years. There used to be a kind of farm of them down by the lake, mostly to supply the rich folk in their towers — the ones who insisted on eating meat or wearing fur — but I don't think they kept it up. It was too much water and food to raise them, and they never really got fat like farm animals used to. Soon enough, everyone was eating cultured mushroom protein and wearing tanned chitin sheet leather.

The very idea of a pet was so foreign, I felt giddy when I thought about it too hard. I was going to spend rations on a non-human animal. It seemed insane, but at the same time it felt entirely correct. I was already deeply attached to Doggo. It wasn't rational; it was instinctual.

I knew about humanity's relationship with dogs from long hours spent trying to convince my parents we should get one. Even now, I could probably name a dozen breeds without thinking overly hard. I had learned about obedience training and canine behaviour, become versed in the different kinds of collars, harnesses, and leashes; brushes and nail clippers; dry foods, wet foods, and raw foods.

It was all for nothing. Despite living on a farm, as many did in Trout Creek, my family just weren't dog people. Not even a yard dog as the country dweller's version of a home security system. For one thing, I was the only one remotely interested, and I wasn't considered old enough or responsible enough to care for a dog. Most days, I could barely be bothered to collect eggs from our trio of aging hens or to milk our single ornery nanny goat.

For another thing, it was going out of fashion, even then. Resources were drying up at alarming rates. The province, and then the country, encouraged people to stop keeping "non-productive animal companions." They offered a one-time benefit for anyone who voluntarily brought existing pets to euthanasia centres: a bag of flour for a cat and a sack of corn for a dog.

Then there were epidemics of rabies-B — a mutation of rabies, which had come from animals, that was more universally transmittable. And as with most diseases that hopped species, infection was typically fatal. Human fluid contact. Mosquito vectorized. It killed thousands, and we blamed dogs instead of ourselves.

I guess some folks were too soft-hearted and let their animals go instead of euthanizing them. The cats disappeared into the woodwork, as cats do, and the dogs formed packs. A lot of them starved or drowned, but I suppose enough of them survived to be penned up on that farm.

And then there was Doggo.

Where had he come from, anyway? I was pretty sure they wouldn't let anyone bring a dog with them down the chute. I heard there was a time when they weren't even letting human babies in. It's anybody's guess what they did with the ones denied entry. It was possible he'd weaseled in through some kind of air exchange, though that would only get him so far. Doggo didn't strike me as an especially clever example of his species, so that seemed unlikely. Then again he was smart enough to get into the food bucket …

"Hey, Vanderchuck!" Karl Metzler waved from across the scrap heap. He got closer before continuing, though his volume remained about the same. "Heard you talkin' to someone this morning. You got a friend over? Hiding some little pigeon in your bed?"

"What? No. No pigeons." The briefest pause. "Why would I talk to a pigeon?"

He scoffed and slapped my shoulder. "Naw! You know what I mean. You got a piece of tail, yeah? Where'd you find it? I'll give you a week's tokens for a share."

When it dawned on me what he was talking about, I took a step back. "Jesus, you've a filthy mind. Aren't you married?"

Metzler shrugged. "There's marriage, and there's marriage," he explained. "That kinda union don't mean what it used ta, right? Besides, I'm just DTF. Ain't lookin' for a commitment, ya know?"

Apparently, this was the funniest thing he'd heard in some time, and the sentiment was best shared by brash guffawing and follow-up assaults to my shoulder. He hit me hard enough my arm went numb. When he noticed I wasn't laughing along, he wiped the tears from his eyes and looked at me meaningfully.

"So?"

"So what?" I snapped, rubbing my throbbing shoulder.

"A week's tokens! I've been saving to get the wife a set of crutch-es, but I'll give you the whole boodle for fifteen minutes."

"Fuck me!" I shook my head, which he mistook for an invita-tion to haggle.

"Ten minutes?"

"No minutes! There's no one at my place. I was talking to myself."

That shut him up for ten entire seconds.

"Serious?" His tone was concerned, at least as much for himself as me.

I dug around the heap in front of me for a minute or so, working up a bit of pathos. If I could get him to buy that I was losing it, he'd back off enough to keep Doggo from getting found. I was slightly unsure of my skill at bullshitting, given how long it had been since I really spoke with anyone. Maybe a talking dog was a good influence.

"Yeah, well, you know. I'm alone now since Mum died, and Olivia lit out. Who've I got to talk to? Guess I just reached, like, a breaking point. Started babbling to myself this morning. Laughing even." I paused to look up, directly into his beady brown peepers. "Sorry if I got a bit carried away. I'll try to keep it down."

With precision timing, I looked away again, feigning shame. I could feel Metzler's rising discomfort like the spread of warm pee in a cold lake. It was all I could do to stop myself from cracking up.

He shifted foot to foot, crunching matted dross under ancient hobnails. "Well, shit," he mumbled. "Well, shit, kid," he repeated a bit louder. "You need ta talk, you could just come over our way. Stella'd be happy to share a chin wag. You know how she likes ta gab. Used ta do with your mum. Fact of it is, I'd be grateful if you would. She's not had a good chat since ... you know."

Karl poked the scrap a few times with the sharpened broom handle he used to dig.

"Come on by tonight. I've put by some tokens, like I say. We'll share a meal." He reached out and squeezed my shoulder with one broad, gloved hand. "It'll be good. Come on by, yeah?"

No one was generous anymore, and Metzler was stingy by post-apocalypse standards. I nodded, too stunned to speak.

"Good, good. See you tonight."

He hoisted his broom handle over one shoulder and took off for an unexplored portion of the heap that was thankfully out of my eyeline. A saying of my mother's sprang into my head, drew me into speaking it aloud. "Will wonders never cease?" I asked nobody in particular.

Then I wondered if giving my portion of ration to Doggo would be enough to bribe him to stay home. And stay quiet.

THE METZLER PLACE was bigger than mine — more than thrice the size, easily. There was a whole kitchenette that took up most of one wall and a private bathroom behind a full-height door. The space had once been the break room for people who worked maintaining the subway tracks and tunnels.

One of the walls curved to meet an arc of ceiling, and every surface from the floor upward was covered in tiny circular tiles glazed tomato-soup red. Most of the walls were hung with quilts or blankets to keep out the chill. There was even an ancient bear skin hanging on the wall by the bed. It gazed balefully at an uncaring world through one heavily scratched glass eye.

The whole house was alive with cooking. The air was warm and humid and laced with mouth-watering aroma, and the light was invitingly yellow. Karl was stirring a pot on the boil and flipping the sizzling contents of a cast-iron skillet, all according to Stella's instruction from her chair.

"No, use the spatula. Else you'll burn your fingers. That's the way now. Gently but firmly ... Oh, hello! Hello! Come in, child, come in," she beckoned, noticing me in the doorway.

Out of some half-remembered habit, I took off my hat and ducked my head. Stella reached both her arms as far as she could. When I got near enough, she folded me into an embrace, with my face pressed to her deflated bosom. She carried the reassuring scent of floral body powder.

"Good to see you," she whispered in my ear. "So good!" Then she held me at arm's length for a thorough inspection. Frowning slightly, she said, "Skinny. You eating?"

I nodded. "When I can. Tryna save up to get my shoes fixed." One foot was held aloft for her to see.

Stella sputtered, her mouth agape in horror. "Shoes? Those aren't hardly shoes anymore — there's nothing could be done to fix 'em! Karl, where're Joey's old runners? The blue ones with the orange stripe?"

"Dunno," replied Karl, his voice tense with concentration. "What am I doing with these fritters?"

I was gently pushed to one side so Stella could get a view of the kitchen. She donned her glasses and squinted into them while Karl held up the pan.

"They're done. Fish them out and put them on that plate with the cloth, then pull the corners up and over to keep them warm."

Karl nodded, clearly happy to put the pan down at last. His face was reddened by heat and by effort, and a small rivulet of sweat ran from his temple to his jowl.

To me, but at least as much to herself, Stella muttered, "Now, where are those runners?"

Her legs, or what was left of them, shifted beneath the blanket that covered them. Stella was about as far from vain as was possible to get. Nevertheless, she was somewhat shamed by the state of her legs. She'd lost the use of them, only to have much of what remained rot away by a bad infection from a tiny scratch. I still remember that reek. Everyone nearby thought for sure there was a drowned rats' nest behind a wall, tiny bloated bodies festering and unreachable. Then my mother had come to visit Stella, who was suffering from a fever. She went to pat Stella's knee and the whole thing collapsed.

The sawbones — a mean, lean old fella who also cut hair and pulled black teeth — was called in, at some fair expense. He suspected gangrene, but it turned out to be a leg-sized colony of mushrooms. They'd eaten Stella's flesh as though she were an old oak log rotting on the forest floor. On the plus side, some of those cultures went on to breed chitin for the whole Underground colony. It was one of the reasons the Metzlers had such a cherry place to live.

"Maybe they're in that bin under the bed," said Stella, pointing a lacquer-nailed finger to a curtained area across the way. "If you'd be a dear?"

Obediently, I went to the bed and pulled a worn plastic tub from underneath. There was no lid, and it was crammed edge to edge with shoes.

"That's the one! You see a pair, bright blue with an orange stripe up the sides?"

They were easy to spot among the dull assortment of brown and black and grey. I pulled them out, catching a glimpse of a smaller pink shoe underneath. There was only one. I didn't remember the Metzlers having a daughter — only a horde of strapping sons.

"These them?" I held the shoes aloft for Stella to see, though they were obviously the pair she had described. Beyond a bit of wear and the dinge of dirt, they were virtually new. They were worth a fortune in trade.

Squinting through her glasses, Stella nodded. "Oh yes! The very ones. Take them, if you've need. They're only going to waste sitting 'round here."

I got a bit choked up, in spite of myself. They were only shoes, but it had been a long time since I'd been given anything — since well before my mother died. It suddenly made me miss her terribly. And Olivia. Even my father.

"Everything alright, dear?"

I coughed into the crook of my elbow to dispel the tension in my throat and to secretly wipe the standing tears from my eyes. "Yep," I eventually managed. "Oh yeah, fine. You sure I can't give you a few tokens for these? You're already feeding me. I feel like a mooch."

From the kitchen, Karl piped, "Well, if you insist —" But he was cut off by Stella scoffing.

"Oh, please! He didn't even know we had those till just now. And you're welcome to them. Joey grew out of the things about five minutes after we bought them, and shoes that don't get worn are no good to anybody."

Karl cleared his throat with a grumble but offered no contradiction.

"Are we eating tonight, or what?" He picked up the plate of fritters and clapped it roughly on the table.

"Is the stew done?"

"How the hell should I know?" Karl demanded. "Come over and try it."

Stella pursed her lips. "There's no call to be mean." After a pause, she added, "If you can put a fork through the potato, it's done."

Potato! Who knew my neighbours were so well off? Here I was, scrounging for the barest scraps, while they were living like royalty just ten feet away. My mother died for lack of medicine while they'd a trove of goods for trade. Just one pair of those shoes, the ones made of real leather, might have saved her life. It was galling enough to set my teeth on edge.

I looked at the shoes in my hand and swallowed my bitterness. They were being so kind when they didn't have to. And there was no way to know whether medicine would have saved my mother. In the end, it was probably more down to will than pills. Like she'd had enough, maybe, and just gave up. I was certainly no help on that account.

"Sit, sit, sit!" Stella waved me toward a crate with a cushion on it that was pulled up beside her chair. She was beaming at me like I was one of her own children. Even Karl, across the table, stole glances that were at least as contented as they were cranky. He pulled back a corner of the cloth on the plate of fritters and offered it to me.

"Guests first," he muttered.

The Metzlers didn't eat chitin, though by the looks of things they could have afforded it. Moral objections about eating the dead, which I shared but were sadly above my paygrade. The fritters were steaming hot and golden, a mix of cabbage and carrot and potato. I took one, along with a fragrant ladle of stew that was made with largely the same ingredients. Still, it was a most welcome change from pressed krill and bonemeal cakes. I did my best to eat slowly, to savour every bite. It was about the hardest thing I'd ever done, but from the look on Stella's face, I could tell the effort was appreciated.

When plates were emptied, I was filled to bursting. Karl gathered up the dishes and took them to the sink. Stella leaned over and put an arm around my shoulders. There were tears quivering in the corners of her tired eyes.

"I'm so glad you came," she managed. "It's been nice to have company, what with the boys gone and all. Nice change!"

"It was good to be here, Mrs. M. Can't recall the last time I was so full!" I patted her hand and stood up to leave.

"Off so soon?"

I heard the hurt in her voice and hesitated. Then I thought about Doggo. He'd done a good job of keeping quiet, but surely that would only last so long. My mind raced to come up with an excuse while Karl gave me the dirty eyeball from the kitchen.

"Sorry. It was a real long day, and I don't think I'll be such good company after a meal like that. If I don't get home, I might just konk out in the corridor."

Karl nodded and looked away, satisfied. Stella did the same, clearly chuffed to have fed me so well.

"Well, dear. Whenever you next need a good feed, just catch Karl at the scraps so he can pick up extra on the way home."

It was tempting — so tempting! — to stay, to curl up on their floor and give up on any pretension of having my own life. I could be their talking dog, and Doggo could … There was no place for him here. Maybe that's when I had the first inkling that I wasn't long for the Underground. It certainly wasn't the last.

"Sure thing, Mrs. M. Thanks again, so very much. And you, Karl!" I called over the clank of washing dishes, but he gave no indication that he'd heard me. On impulse, I kissed Stella on the cheek as I hugged her goodbye. "And thanks again for the shoes. You're a real saint!"

I made it all the way home before I realized there were tears streaming from my eyes. Doggo crept out from under the bed, his tail wagging so hard his whole back end bent back and forth with the force of it.

"You're back! Food Bringer came back later, which isn't now, but it is. Now." Noticing my tears, he tilted his head. "Food Bringer, why are you leaking?"

THE TIPPING POINT

WE WASTED A LOT OF TIME before going Underground.
Humans, I mean. Some denied it was happening at all, like those
in government, like my father. They said it was a conspiracy but
could neither agree who was behind it, nor explain how that secret
cabal might benefit.

There were those who insisted we decide who was to blame
rather than taking steps to fix what seemed to be the problems.
Some of these said it was God's judgment for any number of sins:
abortion, homosexuality, decadence, and degeneracy. Not one
could rationalize, assuming the existence of such a being, why
God waited so long to take exception and wipe us off the planet.
They advocated prayer. Unsurprisingly, this did nothing beyond
self-soothe.

There were those who acknowledged the problems early on, who were desperate to begin treatment, who harangued the powerful for decades to take action. Sadly, short-sightedness won the day. And many argued amongst themselves which remedy ought to be tried first.

In the meantime, we all sickened. Families were pried apart by disagreement. The conceptual distance between members of communities, between neighbours, opened into gulfs too wide to see the opposite side. Little kids defined themselves by the party lines of their parents, and schoolyard arguments became full-blown gang fights.

I went to school for a while. First to a run-down elementary by the highway, with its combination auditorium-cafeteria-gymnasium that perpetually smelled strongly of floor wax. Single grades taught by single teachers became combination grades taught by single teachers. Those in turn became an entire school taught by a harried man who had been the principal. Classes moved to the audi-caf-gym and largely consisted of silently reading or practising sheets of times tables.

When the total number of students in the entire area dropped to a few dozen, they moved us into a room in the basement of the public library. I don't recall many high-schoolers there for long. The ones who continued to show up were more like teaching assistants than students, helping out with the youngsters, leading sing-alongs when the ever-present tension got to be too much.

I remember one day very clearly, maybe because it was near the end of my school career. Class had been taken over by Mrs. Barfoot after the former principal, Mr. McCullough, couldn't be found. She was a warm older woman from town who made gingersnaps by the bucket and who didn't sing but always clapped to the beat with a sad smile on her face.

Anyway, some bickering had come to blows, which Mrs. Barfoot and an older girl whose name I never knew were having trouble pulling apart. I was standing back, trying not to get sucked into the vortex of violence, when I was shocked by icy water splashing against my shins. Everyone was stunned into stillness, panting to overcome the shock of the cold on their skin.

Looking up, I saw Constable Ferris holding a yellow janitor's bucket. Just behind him were Mrs. Barfoot and the girl, who had clearly been warned the water was incoming, since neither of them were wet. On the floor, a soaking tangle of skinny limbs painted with threads of watery nose blood coughed and shivered and sniffled. I think Jeremy was one of them. He was okay, most of the time. I remember wondering who'd got his goat enough to pull him into the fray.

Constable Ferris had that very serious square jaw that is commonly associated with law enforcement. Yet he wasn't the bully archetype who seemed pulled to the occupation like filings to a magnet. He had no swagger but moved with quiet competence. A peacekeeper in every sense.

He put down the bucket and started pulling the tangle of children apart. As he got one free, he handed them over to Mrs. Barfoot, who seemed to have conjured a stack of towels out of thin air. Each one was wrapped around the shoulders and set into a chair, one after another. The older girl was handing out tea and gingersnaps. When everyone was up, the constable asked us all to have a seat.

"Mind the wet spot," he said, pointing to the place where the carpet was dark and a few ice cubes continued their slow dissolution.

I sat on one of the reading chairs. It was a curved shape made of foam and upholstered in green vinyl the colour of Slimer from *Ghostbusters*. The material squeaked against my bare skin where my shorts ended. I hoped nobody thought I'd farted. Seated and in expectant silence, we turned our eyes to the constable.

"Well, I was coming to tell this to your teacher, but since you all seem grown-up enough to bring politics to the classroom, I'll tell all of you." He took the kind of deep breath, ending in a sigh, that was common to adults at the time. "Mr. McCullough was taking a bit of a walk in the woods near here, 'bout a week ago they say. He was attacked by an animal. Coroner said maybe a mountain lion."

A hand was raised. Const. Ferris acknowledged it. "Question?"

"What's a coroner?"

Ferris frowned and glanced over at Mrs. Barfoot. She provided the answer. "A coroner is a kind of doctor who looks at people's bodies to see how they died."

The word was allowed to sink in. Died. That meant dead. It meant Mr. McCullough was …

That train of thought was interrupted by the constable continuing. "He had his phone on him. Even had time to dial in to 911. Trouble is that the cell tower on Ski Hill was damaged in that last storm, so the call didn't go through."

He had to take a moment. I've never been sure if it was just sympathy for the plight of a fellow human being or something else. For a man who had seen worse in his tenure, like the time the Jamieson's eldest ate his twelve-gauge on the way back from a turkey hunt or the transient man who got drunk and fell asleep on the railroad tracks, he seemed especially choked up. When he got himself together, he swept his gaze across the group, ensuring he made brief-yet-meaningful eye contact with everybody.

"Point is, be extra careful out there. I think you all know things are changing. If you're walking, don't go alone. Stay away from the woods, 'specially at dawn and dusk. And don't rely on cellphones to save you." He turned to Mrs. Barfoot, touching the bill of his cap. "Thank you for your time."

My mum told me much later that she heard Mr. McCullough had managed to make another call that went through, to Constable Ferris's office. He'd left a message on the machine, his voice slow and slurred. She said they figured he made the call as he was going into shock from his injuries, which involved a significant part of his body being consumed by his feline assailant.

For years after that, I had nightmares about such a situation. My last words would be delivered to my parents' voice mail, wavering with pain as I was eaten by a large predator. I begged Mum or Dad to pick up the phone, to tell me it would all be alright and that they were coming to find me. Every time, it ended the same way. The message time elapsed. I heard the beep and let the phone fall from my hand. Then my mind turned to the farmhouse, where it found my dad listening to the message. The voice mail robot was rhyming off available options.

"To erase this message, press seven. To save it, press nine."

And every time, I imagined him pressing seven right before he hung up.

ENEMY MINE

WHEN OLIVIA WAS BORN, I was asked to stay home. I was just shy of nine then, really getting into the swing of the whole school thing. The routine of it, the occasional civil conversation with someone my own age. Jeremy's family left shortly after the scuffle he'd found himself in. He had told me, "Jesse, it was like I woke up getting punched in the face, so I just kept swinging."

Actually, I'm not sure they lit out for the Underground. Now that I think on it, there was talk of going someplace by boat. Mum made note of how dangerous such a trip was sure to be, with the storms and acid water. Dad said, "At least they've no more sharks to worry about."

For a while, I hated Olivia for ruining things. She made our house loud and smelly. The routine became her routine. With the density of a tiny star, she pulled us all into her orbit. Even

Dad — especially Dad. Nearly every moment he wasn't repairing something in the shop, he was building something for her. I'm not sure what bothered me more: the jealousy I felt or the hypocrisy I saw in his behaviour. He'd built my bed when I got big enough to need one (the crib was a loaner from another much larger family), but this eventually became Olivia's, too.

I hated my mum for having Olivia. She wasn't an especially doting mother at the best of times, seemingly wrapped in the cocoon of her own troubles, but there were moments. I remember making modelling dough with her, from flour and water and salt. We shaped it and baked it, watching through the grime shadow of the oven window as it swelled and solidified. Then we painted it. It was a nativity scene, with a donkey splotched in primary colours that was my creation. Dad's only comment was to point out that donkeys were brown. At that point in my life, I hadn't been informed of my father's role in baby-making, or I would have hated him, too. More than I already did, anyway.

The following year, the local school was disbanded for good. Mrs. Barfoot was ailing, and there were only a handful of students. With families itching to get gone, whatever their excuses, it didn't make sense to waste time on old-world skills like reading. The future we were facing looked bleaker by the day.

There was little point hating anyone anymore, not that there had been any to begin with. Whatever friends I might have had were moved away by their families. Most went Underground. Some went north. It wasn't as cold there as it had been, and the government was giving away land to families willing to farm there.

We stayed. We rooted in place, until we were the epicentre of absolutely nothing in all directions. Not a neighbour, not a public servant, not a bandit. Quiet, even for Trout Creek. We were like the meteorite that cleared out the dinosaurs.

Meanwhile, far above our heads on Parliament Hill, debates raged on about what was to be done. Whose role was it to correct the damage? How much should be invested? And where? On and on and on, as the seas rose, as the rain clouds gathered densely, as the immune system of the Earth prepared to purge its illness for good.

When we'd gone out west, it was one of the first and only times I'd been to a city of any size. Our wee town had about five metres of sidewalk that lasted until they didn't. This place had sidewalks along both sides of every street! We were just strolling along when we came across a square patch of asphalt, ringed by radiating cut lines. I pointed and asked what it was all about.

"Why'd they do that to the sidewalk?" As though those pristine slabs of concrete, glowing in the midday sun, were holy relics.

Dad shrugged and said, "See that valve there? Probably had to repair it, or replace it. So they needed to cut the concrete into pieces to break it out of there — that's those saw marks. Cut it up, bust 'em out, put in the new valve. Then they had to fill in the hole, but new concrete doesn't stick to the old stuff. Cheaper to fill it in with asphalt till the whole stretch needs replacing."

To me, narrating this from the future, the process sounds a lot like what the higher-ups did to the rest of us. Carelessly splitting us up, breaking us apart, then offering one flimsy plastic bandage for our wounds.

DODGING JOHNNY LAW

MY ILLNESS STARTED SMALL. Just a cough. Maybe allergic to
Doggo? Who could know. Doctors cost their weight in gold down
here, and I wasn't about to spend my last tokens on a sawbones so
I could keep sticking around here, working the Heap till I keeled
over. Dressing Doggo in a trench coat and teaching him to walk
upright to fool my fellow Underground denizens.

There was a time when I would have barely noticed a cough,
let alone would it have set off alarm bells for the neighbours. But
everything was different now. After the epidemics on the surface — rabies-B, sporecemia, septo-sclerosis — quarantines locked
down most entrances to the Underground. Things relaxed a bit as
immigration thinned out, as people became reluctant to guard the
borders. Some clever so-and-so whipped up an easy and accurate

blood test that could be done with a drinking straw pipette, some glow-stick fluid, and a low-voltage jolt from a cellphone battery.

In the Underground was a different story. Everything was close and closed. Citizens were watched for signs of sickness the way agricultural inspectors used to check for hints of hoof-and-mouth in everyone's herd. Friends and family ratted each other out on the regular.

Herd immunity was what we had on the surface. Vaccines protected most of us from the most virulent diseases. Diseases that had crippled my own grandparents, great-grandparents, were unheard of when I was growing up. Turns out they were just waiting for us to trip over our own pride and fall down a hole. Well after we were buried, when we thought we were safe, they all came creeping back: polio, measles, mumps, rubella. It was one of the many reasons there weren't a lot of little kids crowding up the place, if you see what I mean.

Anyway, I wasn't planning on sticking around. Doggo was getting itchy, too, being cooped up all day, which was making it tricky to keep his presence secret. Plus, much as that secret privately thrilled me when I thought about it, the stress of keeping it was winning out. With Metzler nosing about like I had the map to some buried treasure, that tiny thrill was hampered by fear.

Just a few more tokens, I kept telling myself. Another day of rations to keep us going. Where we were going was undecided. Ostensibly the surface, but in the decades since I'd been near the lift, the way there had become faint, garbled. I had only the vaguest idea how to find it again. And all of that bother was on top of the very real possibility that the way I'd come in had changed, become blocked off or sealed up altogether. People in the Underground weren't much for filing building permits with the appropriate authorities.

The scrap supervisor noticed it first. Before I did, even. Just a tickle in the throat that bubbled up through the day into a series of barks. Out of reflex, I covered up with the crook of my elbow.

If I thought about it at all, it was as a dry throat. Maybe thought about getting a drink of water.

"Vanderchuck!" The supervisor hollered loud enough to get everyone's attention, not just mine. When I looked up, she waved me over. Everyone else went back to work with an ear perked toward the action. In a world without television or radio, and that valued books for their flammable qualities over their contents, gossip was nearly as valuable as tokens.

The supervisor was a stocky woman who was wrapped year-round in woollen scarves. The top-most one covered her face up to her eyes, so that they looked like a pair of glittering stones stitched to the top of a mound of yarn. Broom-straw blond hair stuck out from beneath a grimy Maple Leafs toque.

Her job at the scrap was to see that new loads were spread out evenly, and that any fights that broke out were short-lived. It was an unofficial position (which ones weren't, these days), so we all chipped in a few tokens per week to keep her around. Maybe we could've gotten by without her, but it wasn't unheard of for her to make cheapskates regret their refusal to pay. The scrappers all called her Big Ethel. She didn't stop them, so it's the only name I knew to call her.

On my trip up the heap to her seat of office, I took sudden notice of how deeply tired I was. My climb wasn't steep, nor especially hard. I ended up out of breath, anyway.

Big Ethel got to the point. "You're sick."

I shook my head. "No, I'm n—" I managed before being interrupted by a longer, deeper fit of coughing. These weren't tickles but came from the very base of my lungs and left my chest and head tingling.

"Sick," she repeated from her woolly keep of mufflers. "Oughta call the doc ta section you out to a hospital. Gimme a month's pay an' I'll let you go home, see if you heal up."

"Jesus wept! A month? I don't have it. Even if I did, I'd need it to keep myself fed and watered, else I'd just end up a different kind of dead."

When she shrugged, it was like an earthquake rolled through Yarn Barn. For a moment, the sliver of her face normally visible was obscured as the bottom of her toque and top of her scarves came together. Then they parted again, revealing eyes as unmoved by my plight as a boulder is unmoved by a wailing wind.

I looked out across the scrap, a burning knot of emotion swelling in my throat. Metzler was on his usual patch, poking through the loose top layer with his broom handle. When his eyes caught mine for the briefest moment, he turned away to stump downhill.

Underground, sickness was serious. One person with a cough could turn into thirty people with plague. Everyone knew at least one story of someplace Underground that had to be closed off, decontaminated. Whole neighbourhoods lost.

Come up sick, and you may as well already be dead.

"Maybe you could take and sell those fancy new shoes of yours. Sure to fetch some tokens, those."

"But I just got 'em!" I could hear the plaint in my voice — childish petulance — and hated it. Over-forties oughta know life's not fair, but I guess I've yet to get the memo.

"How much you spend on those, anyhow? A month? Two?"

I glared up into Big Ethel's beady eyes and it was all I could do not to cough in her face. Being sick was bad enough, though. If I got done for incitement of illness, I'd get banished for sure. And Doggo ...

Shit, Doggo!

"None of your beeswax, Ethel," I spat, then turned for home. Inklings of a plan were coming together in my mind, much of it based around the notion that maybe being banished wasn't the worst thing after all. At least we'd find ourselves topside in a hurry.

Before I got far, I felt a heavy hand land on my shoulder.

"Hold up, kiddo. I'm gonna need your weekly in advance. Who knows when you'll be well enough to come back."

Ethel was pretty big, but she was round, too. When I made to turn back around, I got the blade of my shovel between her feet and twisted. There was enough new scrap so it shifted out from under her. She grunted and fell backward, rolling all the way down the heap and into a group of folk trying to lever out a whole washing machine.

No one was gonna stop me on her behalf, but I wanted to be well away before she could get after me herself. I half ran, half skidded down the front face of the slope and took off down the trunk tunnel that led back home. Behind me, I could hear a cacophony of shouts mixed with the clank and clamour of a fresh scrap dump. That'd keep 'em busy.

First, I'd grab up every token I had saved that wasn't already on my person, plus every scrap in my place that wasn't nailed down, and cash in for all the supplies I could carry. Then me and Doggo would light out. Head for the surface. The thought made me giddy, so I pushed it aside for later. I needed to concentrate.

Tokens.

Supplies.

Doggo.

Gone.

THE FIRST FEW STEPS of my plan went off pretty smoothly. I piled up anything I thought was worth taking onto the bed frame: woollen blanket, some clothes, a canvas duffle I could pull on like a backpack, and my small pantry of dry goods, matches, fuel tablets. The rest went onto the mattress, which I pulled down the hall like a really awkward, inefficient sled.

At the trading post, I ended up handing over my new shoes for a humbler pair, plus a warm coat. Then to the commissary to fill a dingy TVO tote bag with as much as I could afford in dried krill — which wasn't as much as I'd hoped for but would get us on our way — and a supply of purifying tablets for water.

But before that, while I was still sorting, Doggo was very curious about what I was doing the whole time.

"Food Bringer, why you borking?" he asked, jumping up on the naked bedsprings, getting startled by their creaking, jumping down, then getting onto the mattress-sled. "Borking is my job."

"Please don't! And I'm not borking. Barking. It's coughing."

He trotted around my feet as I crossed and re-crossed the room, packing things as they came to mind, relegating others to the selling pile.

"Coughing. Did you eat your food too fast? When I cough, this is why. Sometimes it makes food happen again, so I may eat twice. Will you make food this way?"

The coughing and pacing were making me tired. So were Doggo's unending questions.

"Could you shut up for two seconds?" I demanded, rubbing my closed eyes with my palms.

When he didn't reply, I glared at him. "Well?"

"You demanded silence, which I have provided. Now will you make food?"

"Jesus, if this is what dogs were like before? It's a wonder we waited for doomsday to stop keeping them as pets."

I rubbed my eyes with the heels of my hands again, willing the ache in my chest to subside long enough to finish clearing out. When I started seeing stars, I stopped and looked at Doggo. The moment my attention was on him, his ears shot forward and his tail took up its tattoo against the floor.

"Yes, Food Bringer. I am ready!"

I shook my head. "Even if I could, I'm not gonna barf so you can eat it."

He looked as crestfallen as he could, which was still the near side of hopeful, which made me laugh. I picked up a stack of stuff, and the laugh became a cough. Just then, for a second, I was ready for the authorities to come. To break down the door and haul me away to die behind a curtain made from an old bedsheet. Adventures were exciting in the planning, but actually doing them was for the young. And I am many things — young is no longer one of them.

In the place where a pile of terracotta pot shards had been waiting to be glued together, I caught a glimpse of gold. Its colour and texture rang a bell of nostalgia deep in the recesses of my mind. Reaching down, I found it was lodged under a corner of the bed, impaled by a broken leg. It was a book of fairy tales my dad used to read to me when I was very small.

The writing on the cover was illegible, and as I uncovered it, an absolute swarm of silverfish wriggled out and away. Yet I knew it was from *Reader's Digest*, just as I knew the inside cover was that special kind of seventies orange and that my aunt's name was printed in all lower-case pencil beneath the words "This book belongs to."

My father's sister. I don't think I ever met her, and I'm not sure why.

I felt my resolve return. The hero doesn't give up in the middle of a story. Not Prince Lir. Not Atreyu (who I thought for the longest time was played by a girl, his voice was so sweet). In spite of everything, the quest goes on.

I left the book and turned to Doggo. "How about a story?"

So I kept packing and sorting, with Doggo finally still and listening to what I could remember of one of the stories in the book.

"Once upon a time, there was a boy and a girl. They lived next door to each other in Copenhagen and loved each other dearly. Every day when the weather was fine, they opened their windows and spoke to each other across the alley that separated them. And when the weather was cold their windows froze shut, so they would write messages to one another in the frost on the glass or melt peepholes with coins warmed on the stove."

As I packed, Doggo watched my every move, lopsided ears held at attention. Before the story ended, I'd loaded the last necessity into my overfilled bag and fell silent. There was a beat before someone asked, "Well, what happened next?"

It took me a moment to realize it wasn't Doggo speaking. It was Mr. Metzler.

He was altogether too big for the broom cupboard I lived in, so he stood hunched in the doorway.

"Made quite the impression at the heap today. Don't expect you're welcome back there anytime soon."

Shouldering my bag, I replied, "Wasn't planning on going back."

He nodded. "I see that. Sold the shoes, did you?"

"For the coat."

Another nod, then he reached into the vest under his jacket. He pulled out an envelope gone grey with dirt and fuzzy with wear. He handed it to me with one hand, clapping my shoulder with the other. The letter was addressed To Jesse, in Olivia's handwriting.

"How did you get this?"

Metzler ignored the question and ploughed on.

"Stel's gonna miss you somethin' fierce. All our boys gone, now you. She was planning to throw you a birthday party next month."

"But it's not my birthday."

"Yeah, I know. It's the thought, isn't it?"

He was gone before I could reply.

Doggo poked his nose out from under the bed. "I was hiding," he explained.

"Good boy, Doggo. Let's get out of here."

WHAT IS THE LAW?

IF ONE POSITIVE THING came out of the end of the world, it was the final death of kings. Nobody was really in charge of the Underground the way they had been on the surface. There were constables in the towers who were pretty much bouncers: well-fed and muscle-bound folks who could be called on to turf the unruly, or haul some poor soul to asset forfeiture. And a given neighbourhood might have a reeve or sheriff or steward, usually the oldest person around who was able and willing to pass judgment.

Neither of these positions meant making new rules or advocating on behalf of the populace. They were abdications of responsibility. Jobs that were looked on in much the way of a butcher, a handler of the dead, or an executioner, depending on where you're from. Not quite untouchable themselves, but certainly doing things nobody else wanted to.

It takes a special kind of conscience to let you drag another human being, kicking and screaming usually, to the final stage of asset forfeiture. After they've redistributed what stuff you had, they shut you up, tie you down, and inoculate your body with chitin sheet spores. Soon enough, everything you were is going to feed families, or get tanned into the leather of the future.

At least these man-eating giants we'd been dodging had the excuse of incest combined with cannibalism to explain their lack of conscience. Me 'n' Doggo were holed up in a buried silo, holding our breath while a troupe of ogres stalked by. And here was me thinking, bad as our patch of the Underground was, it's so much worse elsewhere.

I could feel an agitation in my lungs: a cough itching to break free. The noise would get us killed. Part of me wanted to let go and cough my stupid head off. But poor Doggo, his head buried in my armpit to muffle his whimpering, was just so pathetic. Everything I did then was for his benefit. He was like a little kid, except he would never get any smarter.

The ogres moved in perfect silence. Their limbs were long and well muscled, and their eyes possessed piercing sharpness. The young ones, anyway. Some of their elders juddered and shook as they walked. They looked like marionettes moved by an unsteady hand. None of them were as old as me. And that was weird because wouldn't it take generations for regular human beings to breed and eat their way to such monstrosity? Yet there they were. Plain as the nose on my face.

That same nose was squished so I could hold my eye to the smallest crack, where the silo's rusted skin has flaked away. I was able to see them, but more as collections of movement than whole figures — a striding leg, a swinging arm, a head bopping to the un-heard music of spongiform encephalopathy. I couldn't tell if they were actively hunting or only moving through the area. I couldn't see any children with them, which would suggest a hunt over mi-gration, but they could've just been sterile.

Back in the day, as the end approached, I had become a bit ob-sessed with apocalypses. When the library still had power, and the internet, I watched movies and read articles. Once that was gone, I stretched out fuel-gathering visits to hole up in the library, reading novels that took place after the end of the world. Lots of grimdark descriptions of the true cost of cannibalism.

They took forever to pass by. The pain of holding in my coughs was getting bad, and all I really wanted to do was go to sleep. As hidden as we were, I feared closing my eyes, only to open them again and look into one of those faces rubbed white with bone ash. So I kept my vigil.

For Doggo's sake.

It only took minutes for the last of them to walk out of sight. Even so, the muscles in my neck were seized by cramps that gripped my upper back and head with fiery fingers. My whispered groan became a gasp, which triggered the coughing fit I'd been fighting for what seemed like my whole life.

Doggo's head shot up from a deep sleep. Half his face was all smooshed in and slack, like he'd had a stroke. It happened sometimes and was temporary but hilarious nonetheless. He shook his head with vigour, his ears slapping my hand and face hard enough to sting.

"Jeez!"

"Are they gone?"

I spared a glance through the crack. With all the noise we'd just made, it wouldn't have surprised me if they'd come running back down the path in a slavering lather.

One breath, two …

"Yeah, they're all gone. If they didn't come running for that dinner bell we just rang, they must not be hungry."

"I am hungry, Food Bringer."

"Witness my complete lack of surprise."

Silence for a second or two while Doggo looked at me, his tongue lolling in a grin. "It is witnessed. Now may we eat?"

I ruffled his ears and tried to stretch out my neck. Bars of iron relaxed into mere blocks of wood. When I stood, a bad head rush made me sit down again. My hands and head shook, and I couldn't speak until it had its way with me. I wondered if the sensation was similar to how those old ogres saw the world.

"I want to get as far from here as we can, then we eat."

Having said that, I dug deep into an inner pocket of my coat. We'd found an old store of vacuum-sealed agricultural feed near a week ago. Couldn't carry a whole bag, so I'd stuffed as much as I could in my coat pockets. I found a few crumbs to fish out, which I let Doggo lick off my fingers.

"Thank you, Food Bringer! Thank you, thank you!" he said between sounds like Cookie Monster devouring a plate of double chocolate chip.

"Okay, okay — keep it down. We've gotta motor."

I picked him up, the better to climb over the rubble that'd been jammed in there. The mix of objects made even less sense than the usual fare. Hunks of concrete and stone were mixed in with tangles of wire, old shopping carts, and ancient bags of garbage. Usually, buried structures were converted to usable spaces, like living quarters or trading posts. Why bury the thing only to fill it with nonsense?

Together, we picked our way toward what would have been the silo's top. My hope was that the hatch in the roof led somewhere, maybe even outside. Up, at any rate. At this point, though, I'd have been just as glad for the hatch to lead anywhere at all. It could've been lodged shut, buried like the rest of the silo, or it could've been underneath a mountain of refuse — another settlement's equivalent of the Heap.

We found the hatch all right. It was above us, about two or three feet higher than I could touch with my fingers outstretched. I sighed and slumped to the rubble, putting Doggo down as gently as I could. My arm was numb from carrying him, so I sat and took a minute to rub life back into it. Doggo rested his front feet on my leg.

"We eat now?"

I looked up at the hatch. Craning my neck triggered another round of coughing. This one dislodged a hard hunk of phlegm that crawled up my throat and stuck to the back of my tongue. Gagging, I pulled it out with my fingers. Yellow, no blood. Could've been worse. I flicked it off my hand before Doggo tried to eat it.

It was a bad place to camp: rough ground in dangerous territory. But looking around, I couldn't find an excuse not to have a small bite right then. It was dry rations instead of cooking, was all. I slipped out of the duffle bag straps and hauled it 'round to see what was left in the larder. Supplies weren't low, but the bag was noticeably less full. I came away with a flat can of some kind of fish and a box of crackers containing three sleeves of silvered plastic. I pulled one out and opened it. There was blue-green mould on the crackers I'd been around enough to know wouldn't kill us.

Doggo got a larger share of the fish, along with all the oil from the bottom of the can. I crushed up a few crackers into the liquid to make a paste and spread it on another cracker for him so he wouldn't cut his tongue licking directly from the can. Eating made him so happy, I just enjoyed watching him. He tried to grin while chomping and licking his chops, and it made me laugh.

It occurred to me that I might've been dead by then if not for that furry little goblin. I'd have stayed in the neighbourhood, unable to work, maybe getting sicker. Maybe Mr. Metzler would've been sent over with a few bowls of soup. And my only company in my dying hour would've been a pair of blue shoes with orange stripes.

Gratitude is a stranger in these times, but I felt it strongly in that moment. It was a warming sensation that rose from the ground, enveloping limbs like bathwater. I felt as though I could die and regret nothing more than leaving this helpless mutt to his fate. Overwhelmed by emotion, I wrapped my arms around him. He licked my ear and wiggled free.

"Food Bringer, you're leaking again."

"Yeah. Sorry. It's okay."

Easily reassured, Doggo replied, "Okay. Oh, good. Is there more food?"

I dusted my palms together then spread my hands to show they were empty. "Sorry, guy. It's all gone."

He dropped to his belly, front feet still on my leg, and rolled his eyes to look up at me. His tail wagged hopefully. "Am I a good boy?"

"Of course you are," I told him.

Doggo raised one front paw, exposing his chest for scritches. I obliged.

"And good boys are good dogs?" he asked, licking his nose.

"Yes, Doggo."

"Then can I have more food?"

I gave him a good, deep scritch under both front legs, then all down the length of his back to his flanks and back up to his ears. He licked his teeth and made tiny grunting sounds. No matter how many times we went through this routine, he acted like it was the first. I could never tell if it was because he lacked intelligence or possessed a surplus of hope.

"Doggo, I just told you. There is no more food. It's all gone. You ate it."

"Oh." He sat up and gave the inside of his ear a thorough and thoughtful scratch with the long middle claw of his back foot. This done, he held up the foot so he could lick off whatever he'd found. He paused in the midst of his dessert of earwax as though struck by an idea. Foot aloft, Doggo looked up at me and asked, "When can I eat it again?"

I sighed and scritched his head, "How 'bout I tell you a story instead?"

The Girl and the Tiger

here was a young girl, and she loved her father dearly. Her mother and brother had both been carried off by a fever, the same one that had left her with terrible scars all over her body. Against her dark skin, the scars stood out white. As she grew, they stretched into long stripes, earning her the nickname Little Tigerskin.

Little Tigerskin's father was a poor man, a farmer who scratched away at their dusty patch of land at the jungle's edge. He grew what he could — some corn, some wheat, some millet — and after the harvest, he would take it into town to sell it. With the money, he paid the rent on their land and bought what was needed with the little that was left. Patching for the cooking pot, sharpening for the cleaver or the hoe blade or the axe head. The next day, he would return, trudging wearily along the faint track that trailed from the road to their farm.

But the day came when Little Tigerskin's father went to market and did not return. She waited another day, and another. After a week, she gave up hope of his return. Perhaps he'd died along the way, for he was quite old, and they were so very poor.

So, being a determined young woman, she set about planting the seeds they'd saved. If the rains didn't come to wash them all away, she might manage another harvest before the rent came due. Sadly, the hoe blade had gone with her father, so Little Tigerskin was left to set the furrows with her hands.

At the end of the day, washing the cuts and sores from digging in the hard ground, she sang a song to nobody in particular:

> They say I am a tiger
> with these stripes upon my skin
> But if I were a tiger
> I'd never starve again
> Hunting through the jungles
> and villages at night
> they'd come to fear my tiger stripes
> as I gulped them out of sight

No sooner had she finished than Little Tigerskin looked up to see an actual tiger before her. Fangs as large and curved as sickles peeked out from his black-lipped grin.

"Well met, Little Tigerskin! And how is your father, then?"

"Missing, sir," admitted the girl.

The great cat stretched his limbs, exposing claws as long and sharp as kukris. On seeing them, Little Tigerskin shivered and looked away.

"And your mother? How goes her health?"

Little Tigerskin ducked her head. "Only the Gods know, sir. She stayed long enough to give me suck, then was carried away on the back of Death's pale horse, with my brother in her company."

Lord Tiger looked at his mighty claws and caressed his great teeth with his tongue. "Then there is no one to miss you should I gobble you up," he declared.

The girl sighed. Her day had been long and hot, and her future looked bleak. Her best luck would be to marry one of the landlord's sons, which was truly no luck at all. Jackals and layabouts, the lot of them! So thinking, she raised her eyes to meet the golden discs of the tiger's.

"Sir, I wish you would, that all my troubles get eaten also. My father is surely dead, and with him went the only person who would protect me from the evils of the world. Therefore, I ask only that you make my death swift."

So saying, Little Tigerskin closed her eyes tightly, prepared for the killing blow.

Instead, the tiger laid his paw gently on her head.

"You are a noble girl, and too thin to eat besides. Therefore will I save your life this day. Also, I have no children of my own, yet here you are: a human girl in a tiger's skin. Prove to me your mettle, and I shall make you a tiger like me. Only bring me the men who mean you harm. I will eat them, sating my hungers and proving your worth in one. From that day forward, you will fear no man. What say you?"

Little Tigerskin readily agreed to this, for it seemed to her the only solution to her troubles.

"Excellent!" Lord Tiger clapped his forepaws together. "Do you know the ruin of the jungle temple?"

"I do, sir."

"Lure these men to that place with whatever promises you might. You will run away and fetch me, then I will gobble them up. What say you?"

Blushing some, Little Tigerskin replied, "The soonest I may, I will meet you there."

WE WERE PICKING our way out of the rubble-filled silo. Doggo did his best but was getting stuck on some of the higher pieces. I heard his whimper and paused the story to go back and help him.

With my arms around his hindquarters and chest, his stubby legs began reflexively kicking me in the belly.

"Hey, watch it!" I warned. "You keep kicking me like that and I might drop you."

Once we were on the flatter ground of the corridor and past the first couple of turns, Doggo asked, "Are men made of food?"

"What the hell kind of question is that?" I asked, completely forgetting for the moment that I was in the middle of a story.

"The tiger-cat wants to eat men. I did not know that men are made of food."

I went silent for a minute, trying to come up with an answer that wouldn't see me waking up to a half-devoured face.

"Well," I began carefully, "they are only food to tigers. For anyone else, men are poisonous. Especially dogs."

The conversation dropped off again until I found a dryish niche behind a rusted grille that was quilted with fungus. Not an edible kind, the kind that eats metal. That also meant it wasn't interested in my decidedly non-metallic body. And the niche would provide some protection from the open tunnel and the wet.

"C'mon, bud. In here."

Doggo hesitated only because the opening was narrow. I'd concluded that he couldn't see all that well out of his left eye based on previous observations, so I crawled in first.

"See? If I can fit, so can you."

He hopped inside and curled himself up between my legs. I was thinking about continuing the story when his question came back to my mind.

"Hey, Doggo. When you asked if men were made of food … I mean, you weren't thinking about eating me, were you?"

He snuffled, then snorted. "You are no man. You are the Food Bringer!"

"Right, right," I replied. "Almost forgot."

 ith the road being so dangerous, Little Tigerskin decided the best plan was to wait at home. Sooner or later, one of the landlord's clan would come looking for the rent. Which happened sooner than later, as it turned out. Not three days after holding council with the tiger, the landlord's eldest son came riding into her forecourt. He was tall, with the well-fed look that all

wealthy men had. The smugness of his station radiated through the beard surrounding his sneer.

"It is Enkil! Here for the rent. Where are you, farmer?"

Little Tigerskin, dressed in her best sari, entered the yard from the kitchen doorway. She kept her eyes low and her head bowed as she said, "The farmer lives here no longer. Only I remain."

Enkil dismounted and strode to loom over her. She obliged him by cowering.

"And can you till these lands? Can you sow and reap the crop? Not on your own, surely. Begone, that we may install a worthier family here."

He was turning on his heel when Little Tigerskin threw herself to the ground at his feet.

"Oh, sir! I beg you not to turn me out so. Only let me be your wife that I may keep a roof above my head."

The landlord's son scoffed. "You think I would marry you? And with no dowry nor father to sign the contract? That fever which scarred you so made you mad, to boot." He kicked her roughly and made to mount his horse.

"Oh, sir!" cried Little Tigerskin. "But I have a dowry. If you know the jungle temple, meet me there at midnight and I will show you such riches as you've never seen!"

Enkil was not a stupid man. Yet greed does strange things to us all. At the mention of riches, he stopped and turned to face the girl.

"What manner of riches?" he asked.

"The kind that may only be shown," she replied.

She watched from hooded eyes as his avarice overcame his wisdom. He mounted his horse and turned it 'round, saying, "Be warned, farmer's daughter, that if you intend trickery, you will re-gret it most sharply." So saying, he rode back up the road to the inn to wait on the appointed time.

And so it went that at midnight Enkil rode into the clearing that was once the temple yard. From the way he swayed in the saddle, it was clear he was more than a bit drunk. Little Tigerskin watched him from the top of the temple steps where she lay hidden. She had told the tiger when to meet his supper but had not seen him yet.

Enkil dismounted and began striding about the clearing, calling for his betrothed. It was clear the liquor had somewhat softened his attitude toward her, for he cried most needfully.

"Little Tigerskin! I am here! The night is cold, so come and embrace your husband."

The girl rose from her hiding place. When Enkil's eyes lit upon her, they became bright as two stars. But no sooner was this done than the tiger sprang from his own hiding place, landing on the man and killing him in one blow. In a trice, there was little more on the ground than a pile of bones and the blood-soaked rags that were his clothes.

The tiger licked his lips and said, "I can only hope they all taste so well as that one. Take his horse and use it as your own."

This the girl did. She sold the fine saddle for a set of hempen traces and a dented plowshare. She used it to till and sow her fields just in time for the rains to start.

Within a fortnight, the next son came looking for the rent and for his elder brother. This was the middle child, clean-shaven and wary. He had no time for a woman's wiles. Luckily, Little Tigerskin had Enkil's horse, which his brother Ahmet recognized.

"Here now! How did you come to have this horse?"

"Oh, sir! I found it wandering near the ruined jungle temple. With no saddle and no markings, I could not tell from whence it had come. I thought it a gift from the Gods, for my father is gone and the fields needed tilling."

"Show me the place where you found it," demanded Ahmet.

"I will, sir. Only give me the day to make sure the way is not flooded. Stay here if you like. I haven't much, but what I do have is yours."

Ahmet was not a stupid man, but he appreciated her manners and her hospitality. And so he obliged her request.

"If you are not back by sunset," he warned, "I will have you hunted down by the raja's army."

Little Tigerskin ran to forewarn the tiger, then returned to the landlord's second-born.

"The way is clear, sir. Come with me that we may be back before the rain begins anew."

To save her legs, Ahmet let her ride next to him on his horse. They arrived at the clearing in record time. At once, Little Tigerskin slid to the ground and went to stand at the top of the temple steps.

"Here is where I found the beast, and thus did I think it divine," she told him.

Meanwhile, Ahmet had spied the shreds of his brother's clothes and bent down to look at them. No sooner had he done this than he, too, was slain and eaten. Another pile of bones and rags was left for the jackals to have at.

"Well done, well done," crooned the tiger. "Another sweet supper like that and I can die a happy creature. Go now; take this horse also and use it as you may."

Less than a week passed before the exercise was repeated, only this time with the landlord himself. Being a naturally suspicious man, he said to his youngest son, "I will go and see what has become of your brothers and of our money. Should I not return, you must not follow. Instead, call down the raja's army and tell them there is witchcraft afoot. They will avenge our family."

Lord Ranjosh arrived in the dusty forecourt on the finest horse Little Tigerskin had ever seen. He called out for someone to greet him, which the girl obliged.

"Where are my sons, for those are their horses?" he inquired, pointing to the hitching post.

Little Tigerskin ducked her head, saying, "They came by, one after the other, and asked me to keep their mounts while they attended some business at the ruined temple in the jungle. Neither one has returned since."

"Show me where you mean that I may find some clue as to their fate."

"Oh, sir! I dare not enter the jungle, for that temple is haunted. If you do not know the way, it is merely a matter of following the trail of sweet amaranth that grows along the path." So saying, she pointed to a low-lying plant crowned by dusty purple flowers. "They flourish nowhere else around here."

Lord Ranjosh nodded curtly before spurring his mount away to the wood. Once he was out of sight, Little Tigerskin mounted one of her own horses and took off at speed to find the tiger. Breathlessly, she told him to make haste for the clearing.

"If the landlord sees his sons' remains and leaves this place alive, he will surely send for the raja's army, and they in turn will burn this jungle to a cinder to kill you."

Away went the tiger, and home went Little Tigerskin, walking the lathered horse. She did not see the landlord die but heard one cry of alarm from the distance. Then she heard only the stony silence that surrounds a predator in the jungle.

DOGGO FELL ASLEEP before I finished, so I was just telling the story to myself at that point. I felt like the tale wanted to be told. I felt it like a presence in my mind. Or like a crouching tiger, waiting to pounce if I could no longer soothe it.

The story, the story, the story! It demanded telling, but who knew how it ought to end? Perhaps a happy reunion between father and daughter. Or maybe a tragedy where everybody dies and no one is redeemed. I looked inside, playing for time. The tiger's eye glinted like gold in dark water and it smiled at my struggle.

"If you want a story so bad," I informed the tiger, "you finish it!"

Silently, the tiger began grooming its paws. Great pink tongue covered in tiny pink knives, combing the deceptive softness of its front feet. With the totality that only a cat can muster, it ignored my very existence.

Fuck.

Back at her home, Little Tigerskin fell to the floor and wept. She did not mourn the landlord, nor his sons. She wept to quench the fire of guilt at her part in their deaths. She wept for the barren, stony plain of loneliness her life looked onto. No father, no mother, no sibling, no spouse.

"Why do you weep, Little Tigerskin?"

Thinking the voice was the tiger's, she confessed her guilt. "I fear my soul is so laden with karma that I'll never escape. I haven't the heart, nor the mind, of a tiger. Gobble me up and have done with it — save your gift for one who is worthier of it."

Then a gentle hand touched her shoulder, causing her a fright.

"You're not the tiger," she exclaimed.

It was true. No tiger but the landlord's youngest son stood before her. He was a slender boy, beautiful in aspect, with dark eyes that shone like beads of pitch.

"I'm not. My name is Vilesh. And while I do not condone what has been done to my family, I likewise lay no blame at your feet. Clearly, the tiger used you to fill his belly. Come with me and stay in my house. Be wed if it pleases you, or remain in leisure if it does not."

Little Tigerskin leapt up from the floor and embraced Vilesh tightly. Then together, they made their way back to the lord's manor, there to live out their days.

Several days passed before Little Tigerskin's father returned to his farm. He'd had quite the set of adventures himself and was grateful to have made it back to his own door. Within, instead of a thankful daughter, he found a sleeping tiger.

"Ah, me! This beast has eaten my only child and now thinks to reside in my home. Devil take him, for he has thought wrong."

So saying, he clubbed the beast on the head with the handle of his shovel (which was his only remaining possession), then slit its throat with the blade. Going to the shed for tools to flay the tiger and tan its hide, he found two fine horses. They were hungry and thirsty but otherwise fit.

"What the Gods take, they give again," he concluded.

THICKER THAN WATER, THINNER THAN MILK

OLIVIA NEVER WANTED to leave Dad. From the moment we departed, she kept trying to sneak back to the house in Trout Creek. Trailing behind until she was out of sight. Or waiting until we were asleep for the day and just outright heading for the hills. It might have been funny if we weren't so aware of the peril. Little arms pumping, the look of grim determination on her tiny face. Hair plaited in pigtails with ends clipped into tiny plastic butterflies.

About the third or fourth time she took off, Mum went ballistic. It took us hours to find her, because she turned out to be hiding in a culvert full of thick, foul-smelling mud. Screaming, in tears, Mum gave Olivia the business about how dangerous it was and how irresponsible she was for sneaking away.

My sister just glared up at her, a six-year-old pillar of defiance. She was Dad's kid, always following him around the woodshop or traipsing through the woods for hours, going nowhere in particular. That stare was like a wall that needed to be broken down before Olivia would do as she was told.

So Mum hit her.

Jaw set, she threw one cold crack across her daughter's face. Olivia was knocked off balance. Mum caught her, but Olivia wrestled free and ran over to hide behind me. I was nearly knocked over by the stink she brought with her. They stared at each other for one tense moment, then Mum turned away to sit by the fire, back to us.

I didn't want to get involved, but as usual I didn't get a choice in the matter. Jesse Vanderchuck: eternal monkey in the middle. Parking Olivia on the edge of what had been a concrete fountain in somebody's backyard, I gathered up a wash rag, a towel, and a set of clean, dry clothes. While I helped clean the muck off her, I did what I could to patch things up.

"Hey, kid. It's okay. Mum's just tryna keep us safe, you know?"

Olivia glowered at me, rubbing the slap on her face that was starting to glow it was so red.

"You leave on your own," I went on, "we can't go back for you. You could get attacked by bad people, by a bear."

"What about Dad?" she shot back. "He's on his own. He's not safe!"

"Well, that's no call to put yourself in harm's way. Think it's smart to rescue somebody by jumping off a cliff?"

Her chin started to quiver some, but she just clenched her jaw and turned her glare on the ground. Looking at her was like looking at a reflection of our mother. The same set on the same jaw, only smaller.

"Maybe Dad's not safe on his own," I conceded. "There's nothing you can do about that. Besides, think about this: what if he's on his way here now, and you take off and get yourself killed. Or worse. How's he gonna feel then?"

One fat tear struck the dirt with a wet splat. Olivia sniffled and snirked as the dam of her resolve broke into a flood. Tiny hands swiped at her cheeks in a hopeless attempt to staunch the flow. There was nothing to do but let her cry it out.

It took a bit for her to wrestle enough control to ask, "Doesn't he miss us?" Instead of looking up, she continued staring at the ground.

I put an arm around her and pulled my sister close. "'Course he does," I assured her.

She looked up at me. The tears in her lashes made them dark. "Then where is he? Why hasn't he come to find us?" Some thought occurred to her then. She didn't voice it, nor did I, but I saw it flare in her eyes like the proverbial lightbulb. Maybe the worst had already happened to Dad, at home or on the road to reach us. The mortar adhering the bricks of her defiance crumbled in response. The wall inside fell. She collapsed, hugging her knees and wailing.

I tried my best to comfort her, but I felt removed from any sense of tragedy. It wasn't that I didn't care about Dad. There was danger in the land and in the weather, though if there was one man who could survive it, it was our father. As for us, it didn't feel like we were escaping to the Underground. We were like a trio of ants scurrying from an approaching thunderstorm to a hill that was destined to be flooded.

Besides, leaving Dad seemed something of a mixed blessing. I loved him, but I can't say I liked him very much. He was hard to like if you were different from him, and I might as well have been a Martian as his kid. I enjoyed ideas, while he was enormously practical. High-falootin' versus hands-on. There were a couple of attempts made to bridge the gap. To take some lofty ideas and give them physical shape; to conjure their objects from the thin air of thought. I was frustrated that he misunderstood me so thoroughly, and he was put out that I wouldn't even try.

In the end, we arrived at a live-and-let-live stalemate that included avoiding all but the most cursory of contact. Nods and monosyllables at the breakfast table, punctuated by the occasional row over chores or whatnot.

Now he was gone and all I felt was a space. Not sorrow, not joy, just vastness. An ocean of distance between here and home. A hollow shape where he used to go in the puzzle of daily life.

I rubbed the spot between Olivia's shoulder blades that helped her relax. When her tears were calmed, she lay down with her back to the fire, and to Mum, and pulled the blanket over her head. I went to sit beside Mum.

She was staring into the fire, wringing her hands hard enough to look painful. "Jesus, what's wrong with me?" she asked after a long silence.

With calculated detachment, I told myself I ought to put an arm around my mother's shoulders but some kind of teen awkwardness held me back.

"It's not you," I tried to reassure her. "Everyone's stressed."

She laughed. I'd never heard her utter a sound so bitter as that. The floating sensation I felt was suddenly jolted by a tether of worry.

"Your father," she began but bit off whatever else she had to say about him. She picked up a stick and stoked the fire.

I took her hesitation for worry. The stubborn man she'd married had stuck his feet into the mud of the land and wouldn't see sense. Same as Olivia, from a different angle.

"He'll be fine, Mum. He's gonna find us when he's ready."

Now it was her turn to cry. Silent tears slithered down a face growing more careworn by the day. She pushed them away with shaking hands. All these tears weren't helping the surplus of rain.

"Okay!" Mum declared, standing sharply. "Let's get some food in us and get going."

As I helped her prepare a thin meal of broth and crackers, I wondered if the ability to switch emotional gears like that was an adult thing, or solely the domain of those who became parents.

Olivia was coaxed over by the smell of cooking. She hovered by the edge of the firelight until Mum strode over to press her in a tight hug that lasted several minutes. Then they both came to sit and eat.

We didn't talk about Dad after that. He may as well have been dead. At least the dead are remembered. And Olivia stopped running away, at least until she grew old enough and wily enough to do it properly.

I GUESS IT TOOK a week to remember the envelope Mr. Metzler had given me. I'd been tired, and my thoughts were scattered. Doggo and I had angled northward, looking for the lift my family had taken into the Underground. It was a tough journey, made no easier by my decision to skirt around the larger settlements. One thing that struck me was how few people we saw. Sure, the Underground was extensive, but thousands of people had come to live here. Where were they? Why was there so much unsettled, empty space?

As though in answer, we found what we were looking for.

We arrived to find the whole of the lift-shaft area derelict, piled high with the kind of sleeping pallets homeless people used to make — a sight I only knew from the movies. There were murmurs punctuated by the occasional rumbling cough, the shifting of an ailing body under piles of filth-crusted blankets and crumbling tarpaulins. This was a place where people came to die.

The lift itself had been dismantled, replaced with a large scaffold-cum-bunkbed. Sheets of milky plastic hung like curtains around much of it. Light filtered in from above where the lift-shaft had been roughly boarded over.

I hustled us out of there as quickly as I could, moving at a speed fast enough to stay ahead of my fear but not so fast that Doggo couldn't keep up. I took us far enough away that guilt began to overwhelm terror. Sure, they were dying — probably infectious — but they were people, weren't they? Once part of a family, or at least of the human family. It felt wrong to abandon them, but then there was nothing else I could think to do. If this dreadful hospice existed in the Underground, it did so under the watch of the authorities. Who could I tell? More to the point, who would care? Life was hard enough down here. No need to complicate it with death.

We headed east. There was another northern trunk tunnel we could try for, though it had been more heavily guarded back in the day. There were lots of towers that way, so immigration was strictly controlled. And we didn't exactly have papers of passage.

We settled down to camp in the open. Not ideal, but I desperately needed to rest. The nightmare at the lift had exhausted me, and that was on top of walking all day. I sat and dug through pockets and my backpack for something to burn. There wasn't anything that needed cooking. I just wanted to drive the chill from my bones that lingered from our encounter with that tower of death.

I found the envelope. It had my name on it, written by my sister. Inside were pages and pages of her wide, loopy half-script. Much of it was dripping with angst, but the gist was that she had gone to find Dad. We weren't to come looking for her, unless we wanted to help her in her search. It was important that our family be reunited. A second envelope, inside the first, was addressed to Mum. After reading its contents, I used that as my kindling. It was just as well Mum wasn't around to read it, and if I ever found Olivia, it would probably just embarrass her. Teenagers say such careless and hurtful things.

Doggo went about his routine, blissfully unaware of the world around him — which, I suppose, was also part of his routine. He scarfed his food, licking his chops when it was gone all too quickly. Then he gave his genitals and asshole a thorough licking, which he followed by taking a short walk away from the fire to relieve himself, presumably so he could enjoy cleaning himself again.

Not for the first time, I felt a stab of jealousy. Doggo wasn't bothered by most of life, save the moments when life denied him food on demand. He'd told me as much as he could recall of his past, which wasn't much. He'd had siblings, with whom he'd run in a kind of pack. It was not clear to me if they'd lived above or below ground. Considering Doggo's confusion when I tried to get a straight answer, I guessed it must have been down here. He didn't seem to understand what I meant by "the surface." Then he'd matter-of-factly described the terrible things that had befallen his packmates. One was killed by a pike to the head. Another drowned in a cesspit trying to reach a morsel of food.

It wasn't that he was unfeeling; he didn't know any better. He had no expectations from life. Even when he'd gone hungry, seemingly the greatest betrayal that could ever be, it was just another thing that had happened. A lack of judgment, I guess. It wasn't good, it wasn't bad, it just was.

As he settled in for a thorough ear scratching, I wondered if we might find Olivia. I had kind of planned on heading back to the farm once we got out. Not necessarily to stay. Maybe I felt obligated to make peace with the place.

If it had been me who'd gone looking for Dad, that's the first place I'd have checked. She could've gone that way, too. Even if she hadn't stayed, maybe she'd left some clue as to which way she'd gone next. I didn't dare hope. Still I felt a small flicker of something very much like hope tickle deep in my gut. I'd gone so long without any sort of family, and now it seemed to be finding me everywhere.

First, Doggo. Then the Metzlers. Now this letter. Were I superstitious, I'd have suspected Fate was trying to prepare me for whatever it had in store.

I leaned back to rest my head against the wall. One hand went to find the warm curl of Doggo, nose tucked under his tail. He wasn't much of a watchdog, so I only let myself fall into a light doze in an open corridor like this. With my eyes closed, I started to tell another story.

The Wishing Fish

Once upon a time, there was a young fisherman. He was poor and lived on his own in a hut near a river. The river was wide and slow and brown. In the river, the young man often caught lazy salmon and fat catfish. He didn't have much, but he always had enough to eat.

One evening, walking down to the river, the young man passed the cooper's cottage. The cooper was in his yard, splitting staves by fading daylight, and called to the fisherman,

"Ho! Are you not married yet?"

The lad blushed and tipped his cap. "Not yet, Uncle, but I shall be by and by."

His elder nodded sagely and went back to his work.

All night, fishing by the river's edge, the young fisherman recalled the cooper's question and thought about his own answer.

Every evening, I come by the river to fish. Each morning, I return home, passing through the town to sell my fish to the monger. Where and when should I come across a girl to marry? What a foolish thing I have promised!

As morning began to dawn, the young man made one final cast. He closed his eyes and threw his line deep into the middle of the river. No sooner had the hook hit the water than it was taken. With a quick jerk of the rod, the hook was set, and the fisherman pulled in his line.

Whatever had he caught? The beast fought and lashed, pulling like a cart horse against the line. It cut into the fisherman's fingers so they bled, and still he pulled. Calmly, one hand over the other, the line and the fish were landed. He stepped up on shore to gaze upon his hearty catch.

It wasn't a salmon, with its fat and silver belly. It wasn't a slick black-and-brown catfish, with its sage's whiskers. This fish was small for all its fight, and a dull, drab grey green. Each fin was tipped with a golden gleam, and across its back was a pair of red streaks. The fish flopped on the wet sand, gasping. It looked so pathetic, and its markings so rare, the fisherman decided he would not sell it. He would keep it against finding another like it, then he could try to breed them. If they tasted well, he might never need to fish again — he could farm the fish and have the time to go a-courting.

How splendid a thought!

The fish went into the creel with the others, and off the lad trotted to the town fishmonger. To not arouse suspicion, he claimed the new fish as his supper.

"I've not seen one like that before," said the monger.

"Neither me," replied the lad. "All the better I take it for myself then, in case it tastes poorly."

To this the monger nodded and gave the lad his few coins.

Off shot the lad to the cooper's cottage. It being early yet, the cooper and his wife were not roused. He had to bang on their door quite loudly.

"What do you want?" demanded the cooper.

The fisherman thrust the coins into the cooper's rough palm. "I have need of a barrel for to make my fortune."

The cooper raised an eyebrow but got a barrel, anyway. The fisherman thanked him and took off for his own abode. Once there, he swiftly pumped the barrel full of water at the well and put the strange fish inside it.

One moment, then two, his breath bated, the lad watched the fish sink motionless into the water. When he'd all but given up, believing the creature had died from waiting in the creel, there was a splash and shimmer, and there was the fish looking up at him from just beneath the surface of the water. The fisherman's grateful laughter was cut short when the fish began to speak.

"You have caught me but spared my life. In return, I will now grant you three wishes."

He'd never heard a fish speak, let alone have one offer to grant him wishes. The fisherman sat on the ground, too stunned to speak, and was only roused by the grumble of his belly.

To himself, he muttered, "Oh, I wish I had kept another fish for my supper!"

From the barrel, there was a splash and a flick. A drop of water flew from the barrel's top and landed in his lap, whereupon it became the finest, fattest salmon he'd ever seen. He was overjoyed until he realized he'd used up one of his wishes.

Deep in the barrel, the fish intoned:

> Two wishes left
> and use them well.
> Remember the finest fish
> often still smell.

The salmon was so fat and so fine that the fisherman took care in preparing it. With a well-whetted knife, he trimmed and carved and filleted. The meat he put over the fire to smoke, the skin he salted to cure, while the head and bones went into a pot to be boiled for soup. This last he drank thoughtfully as he considered his next two wishes.

He continued to think as he moved the barrel under the eave of his back door. He thought as he washed himself and his clothing, preparing for bed, and as he hung his clothing over his windows to dry. And he went to bed, still thinking and unable to land on what to wish for next.

The fish came to him in his dream, only it was in the guise of a beautiful woman with hair of golden flax and lips of scarlet. Her gown of green and grey shimmered in the light of ten thousand candles that adorned a ballroom of marble and glass.

"If you wish it," she whispered in his ear, "I will be your wife."

He was so overcome by her beauty and the grandeur of their surroundings that he leaned in to kiss her. At the last moment he opened his eyes and saw that she truly was a fish. Startled and disgusted, he ran away.

On the floor of his hut, the fisherman woke up. A voice by the back door was singing:

> Though you would wish
> for someone to wed,

if she were a fish
you'd spurn her instead.

The lad blushed and felt he was being mocked. "I wish that fish would be silent," he hissed.

It was late afternoon by the light, so the fisherman got a start on his day. He dressed in his clean clothes, dried by the breeze and warmed by the sun. He rolled away his bed and swept out his hut. Then he took a piece of newly smoked fish meat from where it hung over the firepit. He savoured the taste of fat on his tongue as he went out the back door to check on his magical fish.

It swam round and round, just beneath the surface of the water. But surely this wasn't his fish. Where were its red markings? Where was the flick of gold tipping its fins?

"Fish! Fish! What has happened to you?"

The fish swam and swam but said nothing.

His first thought was that the fishmonger had come and stolen the fish, swapping it for another in the hope he wouldn't notice. In an instant, the lad was off down the road to the town, where the fishmonger was cleaning out his stall.

"Where is my fish?" demanded the lad.

The monger shrugged, thinking he meant yesterday's catch. "It's all sold, my boy. Went quick as a wish, that lot."

What a poor choice of words! At hearing "wish," the young man fell upon the monger with his fishing club and beat him to a standstill.

"Now tell me what you've done with my magical fish, or I will deal you a killing blow."

"Had I a magical fish, do you think I'd still be here, cleaning out a reeking stall?" the monger managed through split and bleeding lips. "Begone, lest I call the constable and have you put in the stocks, you cheeky imp!"

The lad made his apologies and was off, back down the road, this time to the cooper's. Surely the man had wondered what the barrel was for and, finding the fine fish, had swapped it out for another.

The cooper was again in his foreyard, splitting staves in the failing light of day. On his approach, he nodded to the lad. "Ho, my young friend! Are you not married yet?"

The fisherman leapt over the cooper's front fence and shouted into his beard, "What have you done with my fish?"

Thinking the boy meant the salmon he'd been smoking, which the cooper had smelled all through the day, he only laughed. "Why, if I had even a taste of that fish, I'd have given you my own daughter to wed! The smell alone has filled my dreams with nothing but fish."

Another fatal choice of words! Hearing the word "dream" sent the fisherman into a jealous rage. The cooper, being somewhat younger and fitter than the monger and armed besides, managed to stave off most of the blows. As he fought, he demanded, "What have I said to provoke such ire? Did I tease you too strongly about being unwed?"

"My fish! My fish! My fish!" was the lad's only reply.

They fought until the fisherman collapsed with exhaustion. By this time, the sun was set. There was no light to see the road by, so the fisherman would not make it to the river to fish. The cooper's wife came into the yard, holding up an oil lantern to see by. The pair of men, bruised and tired, looked at nothing but each other.

"Come inside," she insisted, "and eat a hot meal. Then we'll make some sense of all this."

Over a bowl of stew and a crust of ash-baked bread, the fisherman told the cooper and his wife about the magical fish and everything that had befallen him since catching it. When he was finished, the generous couple nearly fell over laughing.

"What is so funny? I've lost my magical fish and my last two wishes. Now I'll never be wed!"

"Last one wish, you mean," chided the cooper's wife. "Foolish boy! You wished for silence, and so you got it. For aught you know, you wished the magic right out of that selfsame fish." She stood and gathered the plates. "I simply do not know how you survive without the wisdom of a woman," she added, winking at her husband.

After supper, the cooper walked the lad home with the aid of his oil lantern. At the door, the fisherman apologized to the cooper for his rudeness.

"Make no apologies to me, only to that poor, fine fish who's all but told you what your third wish should be. Just be sure to invite us to the wedding feast."

The lad lit a fire, then went to the back door and pulled the barrel inside. The fish still swam listlessly, round and round and round. Ever so gently, he lifted the creature from the water. He looked into its helpless, gasping face and said, "I wish for you to be my wife!"

So saying, he put his mouth against the fish's in a kind of kiss. The fish in his hands dissolved into nothing more than smoke, which joined the smoke from the fire and floated up through the roof of the hut. Feeling chagrined and foolish as ever, the fisherman sat by the fire and began to weep.

No fish! No wishes! No wife!

At the stroke of midnight, bells tolled from the abbey that overlooked the town from a tall hill. The young fisherman had cried himself to sleep beside the fire, which had burned itself to cold ashes.He was roused from this sound doze by a knock at his front door.

He staggered to his feet. Every inch of him ached from his brawling with the monger and the cooper. His skin and clothes stank with sweat and smoke. Even so, he opened the door to greet whomever was visiting so late in the night.

Standing on the road in the moonlight was the woman from his dreams. Her gossamer gown was now a practical linen frock and pinafore. Her shining hair was brushed and braided down her back. And her lips were less scarlet than they were the deep pink of glowing health. She smiled and held her arms wide, inviting his embrace.

The fisherman ran to clasp his wife, lonesome no more. And together, they lived happily the rest of their days.

WHEN I FINISHED, I fell asleep. I had a dream of being told a similar story by my father. Or maybe it was a sleeping memory. It was before Olivia was born, so perhaps he was more indulgent of me. There was no other child to compare me to, no hollering baby to demand attention.

He had the book of fairy tales he read from sometimes, but just as often he made up the stories. There was one about a group of giants who tried to play baseball, only they didn't understand the rules and ended up using bedsprings in place of bats. Another involved some elves making breakfast using a stone and a spinning wheel. The tales seemed all the more out of character for him. Maybe I was misremembering out of my own wish for a father more like myself. Maybe I'd seen it in a movie once. Surely this was not my own father of practical hands and practical heart.

Yet there were so many details that shot up from that morass of memory. A teddy bear held against his forehead suddenly became part of the tale. Silly bits and pieces shoved into the lines of well-worn stories, eliciting an avalanche of giggles. Mum poking her head in the room to remind the pair of us that this was supposed to be bedtime, not getting-riled-up time. They were moments so happy that it was painful to recall. I felt a choking knot in my throat, which woke me up in a fit of coughing.

Doggo shot awake, ears forward, his face half-slack with sleep.

"What is it? Is it terrible? Should I do hiding?" He crawled into my lap and put his front paws on my solar plexus so he could stare directly into my face. "Or shall I save you?"

Lifting him off my diaphragm so I could breathe again, I scratched him behind the ears, then helped rub some life back into his goblin mug.

"It's nothing, Doggo. Don't worry about it." Before he could ask, I added, somewhat hesitantly, "Here, let me get you a snack. Want some fish?"

IN SICKNESS, UNTIL DEATH

THE COUGH WAS GETTING WORSE. I could hardly draw breath without falling into a fit. My lungs felt like a pair of beat-up cardboard boxes: stiff, with crunched-up sides that were reluctant to move. It occurred to me that I was approaching the same age my mum was when she died. Maybe if I'd just given in, that would've classed it a family tradition.

Whenever I coughed, Doggo would look up at me with concern. He wagged his tail and scrunched his eyebrows together, shifting his weight between his paws. He was no spring chicken, either, but he seemed in far better shape than me. I told myself, *I've gotta hang on at least long enough to get him out of here.* Back to the surface or, as I was starting to think of it, the land of the living.

We stumbled on a slice of civilization, spilling through an access panel from a maintenance room into something that looked like a kind of subterranean shopping centre. The storefronts remained as market stalls but families crammed into ad hoc housing behind the counters.

I panicked, looking around like a maniac to see if anyone had noticed us — if they'd noticed Doggo. In the clear for the moment, I stashed him behind the access panel. We had our usual back and forth about "later" and "waiting," then I closed the panel door most of the way and headed into the open.

One stall was frying reconstituted krill pressed into fishy shapes. It was a little macabre for me but appeared popular with the locals. Apart from anything else, it smelled amazing. Mouth welled with drool, I sidled up and bartered one in exchange for one of my shoelaces. Between how hot it was and the speed with which I ate, it could've tasted like shit on a shingle for all I knew.

A few furtive chats with some of these locals helped me understand what had happened to the lift. Years ago, when the stream of refugees fell to a trickle, the powers that be decided to lock down the Underground. No one getting in, and no one going out. The price of safety, they insisted. Not just to prevent the transmission of diseases, either. The surface had been taken over by those who refused to see sense: marauders and bandits, religious zealots and madmen. Killing and being killed by the terrible storms and other terrors. Better to keep Them outside and Us in.

Of course, there was word of emergency egress. Up through the towers. Past levels of security and immigration controls. I was unlikely to be let through on account of my cough.

"Unless you wanna sell someone that mutt of yours. Tower-folk gotta high value on any critters, but 'specially one that size."

I almost had a heart attack, because I could not understand how this person could possibly know about Doggo. I'd been so careful, and he was hiding … Then I looked down to find Doggo lying across my feet. Tail wagging, tongue lolling, he declared, "Now is later, and I have found the Food Bringer, for I am a clever and good boy!"

With apprehension, I looked back up at the man I was speaking with. He hadn't reacted to hearing Doggo, but he looked a bit of a hard case. He had one of everything except a nose, of which he had half. I hadn't inquired where the rest of him had gone.

Even with only one eye, he saw my fear well enough. Looking around at his neighbours, he said, "Bit of an easier attitude 'round these parts toward such things. He might be novel, but he ain't illegal."

I asked, "What do the tower-folk want dogs for? Eating?"

He shook his head and seemed deeply saddened to answer. "Ah, naw. Worse'n that. Best you don't think on it too hard."

I left it there, nodding sagely. He was entirely right. If they wanted to do anything worse than eat a dog, I really didn't want to know. That didn't stop my busy mind from trying to figure it out. In thanks, I offered the man our last silver sleeve of crackers. I explained, "They're mouldy, but it's an edible kind. Blue green."

He accepted the package with gratitude. Smiling sent me into a coughing fit that attracted more attention than Doggo. The man looked me once over before he handed the package back, laying his lone grizzled hand over mine. "You need these more'n I do, but thanks for the offer. You're a dying breed down here."

Our conversation was interrupted by another coughing fit, which I ended by spitting into a rag I pulled from my back pocket.

"In my case, that's literal." I tried to smile but stopped short of triggering a third fit. Some were staring openly now. Some were skirting well around vicinity of the krill stall.

"Blue-green mould might help you get over that cough. Take those down the second corridor to the left, away at the end. There's a woman there can make a tincture — antibiotic, we used ta call it — might help you out."

I teared up at the least kindness those days. It made me painfully nostalgic for older days and reminded me how much had been lost. Maybe that's why everyone had stopped treating each other kindly — so we didn't all drown in each other's tears.

"Why?" The question was a loaded one. Why help me? Why be kind? Why not knock me out, rifle my pockets, then drag me to the lift-shaft hospice and leave me to my fate?

The man shrugged as well as a one-armed man could. "Supposing you get out of here and find a young man named Casey Turkle. You tell him he was right. Tell him his big brother Asa said he was right. He'll know what you mean."

I closed my eyes and nodded fiercely. My foot shifted, I guess, because Doggo lifted his head to see what was happening. I reached down and gave him a reassuring scritch.

"You got family up there?" Asa asked me.

"Maybe. My dad stayed behind, but he'd be in his seventies now. And my sister left, about thirty-five years ago. Just got a letter said she went to find him."

The man nodded again. "Better late than never," he said, then pivoted on his crutch and continued his limping march up the avenue. So much for good-byes.

I roused Doggo and we headed to the medicine woman. It was important to keep hope in check, but if she really could cure me … No, bury it. There was no reason to set myself up for disappointment.

A short line of folk waiting to see her snaked from an aluminum door frame patched with spray-painted plywood, so we took our place at the end and sat down. It was cold being on the floor of this wide-open space with no fire nearby. I got Doggo to crawl into my lap so we could keep each other warm. As the line moved up, I figured out a way to shuffle forward without unfolding my legs or disturbing Doggo too much, since he was already snoring with his snout shoved in my coat's inside pocket.

The nearer we came, the harder it was to manage my expectations. Surely this line wouldn't exist if she made medicine that didn't work. I dared to dream the smallest dream of surviving long enough to reach the surface. No more than that. Even if I died the moment after clapping eyes on the sky, it would be worth near any price she cared to name.

It was strange to be driven by something so powerfully, so late in life. Passion and purpose was always something other people had. I suppose that was another barrier between my father and me. He simply knew, without one shadow of doubt, what he was for and did that. He had a purpose, which he fulfilled dispassionately. Olivia was passionate, but unfocused, without any particular purpose. She had drive but in no particular direction. Or in a direction that simply didn't exist in the Underground. Perhaps if the world hadn't ended, she'd have become an artist of some stripe. She had that kind of power.

After an hour or two of waiting, we were next in line. As I took the previous leader's place, I heard the crinkle of the package in my pocket. Another small thrill of hope shot up my spine. I tried to wrangle it, to sit quietly and wait to be told my condition was incurable, or that the mould on the crackers was the wrong kind to make medicine from.

In my lap, Doggo shoved his face deeper into my pocket. A distinctly wet noise emanating from my coat indicated he was no longer sleeping but instead licking the crumbs from the pocket's lining. Fair enough, since I'd nothing else to feed him at the moment.

It'd been more than two weeks since we left the neighbourhood, by my best count. I found my mind drifting back to old Mr. Metzler and Stella, then I thought about what the man on the promenade had said about his brother. Tell Casey Turkle that Asa said he was right.

What was he right about, I wondered. That we should never have hidden ourselves Underground? That we should have stayed above and taken our lumps? Or that we should have done more when we had the chance? We should have taken every opportunity to make the world better instead of doing our best to ruin it. Maybe Casey was just right about the scoring in a contentious game of Yahtzee. Whatever it was, it was far too late for regret. Still, I thought, should I come across Casey on this quixotic quest of mine, I'd give him the message.

Our turn arrived, and we moved inside.

There wasn't much more space than could fit a narrow examination couch and a couple of human bodies, so it was a bit close. The woman was small and dark and wizened, with a scarf tied around her head. I had Doggo in my arms. He sniffed the air with a sleepy look on his face, but the crumbs dotted on his nose gave lie to his act of innocence.

"Is this a food place?" he inquired.

"Quiet, Doggo. It's a doctor's office."

The woman smiled politely and shook her head. "Not exactly." With no further explanation about what made this not exactly a doctor's office, she asked, "What seems to be the trouble?"

On cue, a deep rumble crawled up my throat and became the kind of coughing fit that left me dizzy. When it subsided, I looked up at the woman.

"Ya see, Doc. It's my feet —" I grinned to emphasize the punchline of my hilarious joke. The woman's expression didn't change.

"Please sit here" — she indicated the exam couch — "and take off your coat, shirt, what-have-you to bare chest."

I set Doggo on the couch beside me, where he immediately began licking his crotch. I was mortified, but the woman didn't seem to notice, let alone care. Still I jostled him until he stopped and curled up with his tail across his nose.

I hadn't taken my clothing off since before we left, and the innermost layer was difficult to peel away from my skin. Already embarrassed by my dog's behaviour, I became more humiliated by my own smell. Not the fresh reek of a lather of sweat but the thin reek of foregone hygiene. It was baked right into my body and seemed to come from everywhere. I reddened.

The woman only smiled, tightly and with closed lips. "Okay. Relax and take a deep breath when I say." She got in so close, I couldn't understand how she wasn't gagging. She pressed her ear against my chest. In that moment, I realized how thin I was, how frail. My torso looked like a picked chicken carcass.

"Breathe in," she instructed. I did my best to breathe into every spot of my lungs except the part where the coughing lived. "And breathe out." The breath ended on a tickle, but it fizzled quickly. She repeated the exercise a couple of times, tapping my chest in between commands for inhalation or exhalation. Her dark eyes were serious when she informed me, "You need medicine."

"I know." I rifled the pockets of my piled-up clothing for the crinkle of the crackers. "The man in the street told me to bring you these. They're mouldy." I handed over the package, gleaming in the underwater light of half-powered fluorescents like an ingot of precious metal.

She took it with a nod and turned her chair to the right, to a tray on a shelf that served as a desk. The crackers, which were almost entirely crumbs, tumbled everywhere once free. Some larger chunks showed spots of dusty blue green. The woman scrutinized the mould. She scratched some off and tasted it from her fingernail. Then she shrugged. "Maybe, maybe" was all she said.

She scooted to a cabinet hung on the opposite wall. There sat a clunky object made of wood and glass and wire, which she wrestled free and took back to the desk. A flake of mould was scraped off with a thin blade, then wiped onto a sliver of scratch-clouded acetate. This was placed in the device, which I realized was a jerry-rigged microscope. Its various limbs and lenses were manipulated as she looked through a set of eye pieces, until she found whatever she was looking for. The discovery was announced with a grunt.

"Well, it's the right kind of mould, but it will need to be cultured. Then I'll have to make an extract and compound it into pills. Expensive."

She looked up, her small face intensely serious. Any trace of her clinician's smile was tucked safely away. The face of a doctor preparing to deliver bad news. The worst news.

"Medicine may work if we begin treatment as soon as possible. You will need money to pay for the medicine." Her eyes flicked to Doggo, then back to me. "Many people place high value on such animals. Enough to pay for treatment, maybe."

I put a protective hand on Doggo's head. He stretched his legs but didn't appear to wake.

"Why does everybody down here wanna kill my dog?" It felt like I was choking. Like a fist had reached into my throat and grabbed tight, squeezing in its rage.

"Is his life worth sacrificing your own?"

There was no judgment to her question, only genuine inquiry. She sat back, hands folded across her lap, and waited.

I looked down at Doggo. His tiny, dumb face was empty in sleep, slack and blissful. He wouldn't really know better if I just handed him over to the butcher, not until it was too late. How long would it've taken me to forget his screams of betrayal, chasing me as I walked away?

Then I heard myself saying something not entirely unexpected but nonetheless surprising. "Maybe."

She nodded. "Maybe. The medicine may not be enough. The money may not be enough. Who can say?"

"How much for one pill?"

The medic drew straight up, like a doll on a string. Her tone was one of disbelief. "One?"

"If I leave you with the mould, and you make as many pills as you can, how much would I owe you for one of those pills?"

"One pill won't do anyth—"

"How much?"

The woman sat back and sighed. She pulled away her scarf to scratch a scalp heavily ridged with scars and largely bald as a result. The few wisps of hair that poked through the hardened tissue were shockingly white against her dark skin. It looked as though she'd been mauled by a tiger. She looked at Doggo, scowled, and shook her head. "Come back in three days. I'll give you two."

I scooped Doggo up from the couch, as much to embrace him as anything. His half-hearted growl at me for waking him dissolved into a yawn.

"Three days," I repeated. "Here. Two pills. Thank you!"

"It won't cure you," she insisted, pointedly.

"I don't need a cure," I told her as we left. "I just need a bit of time."

DOGGO AND I FOUND ourselves back on the promenade, this time with nothing to trade and no food besides. I found us an alcove out of the way of the main drag to huddle in and wait. Three days? No problem. I could last three days with nothing. After falling into a doze of boredom, I was roused by the thump and scrape of Asa coming back from wherever he'd been with a load of goods. He stopped in front of us, a satchel over his good shoulder. Must've had it earlier, too, only it was empty then.

A scrapper.

He dropped the satchel at my feet and pointed to the end of the square with his chin.

"Carry that to my place, I'll let you stay the night. Take my place at the scrap while you're here, you're welcome to stay as long as you like."

I picked up the satchel and roused Doggo. He was less than pleased but brightened when I told him we were going to find food. Asa's place was about the size of my closet, though it had a pair of deep cubbies punched into one wall, each big enough to sleep in. Not having a separate bed saved precious floor space, making his place seem like a palace. Asa parked himself in a much-patched recliner upholstered in dusty blue-checked felt.

"Soup's in the pot. Been cooking for twelve years now, so it ort be done."

I dished us out some soup, which Doggo polished off in record time before dropping back to sleep. I decided the best way to pay back our host was with a story, if he wanted one.

"Go on then," said Asa, closing his eye and pulling the handle on the recliner.

So I did.

By the Mane of BardyJin

Once upon a time, a girl rode her father's horse across a snowy mountainside. The horse's flank shone polished chestnut in the sharp light of high-altitude dawn, nearly the same colour as the girl's curling tresses. They were fleeing the only home they'd known, pursued by agents of the king.

They had come in the night to take the girl as a bride for the king. Any girl in the kingdom could be selected for such a privilege. But this girl's village was so far from the capital that none of the king's agents had ever been there. It was only bad luck that their cadre had become lost in a heavy fog, blown over the foothills from the sea. And worse luck that they had fetched up at the door of her father's small patch of farm.

"Kind sir, as agents of your king, we ask your hospitality this night. In return for serving us well, you will receive three gold crowns."

Her father had never seen such wealth before, let alone been offered it. He was so dizzied by his good fortune, he could only nod in agreement.

"First, you will curry and feed our horses that they will be ready to travel come morning. Then you will serve us the finest food you have, along with a measure of wine to warm us. You will give us your best beds, pillows, and blankets to sleep on, and you will keep the fire well-stoked all night. Should we be well pleased with all of this, only then will we pay you what is owed."

What her father could not know was that they had no intention of paying him. The king's agents were little more than bandits in livery. Overcome by even a modest man's avarice, he did as he was told.

Or rather he commanded his daughter do as he was told. She led the horses to the barn (for they had no stable) that was built beneath the back eave of their house. She curried them well, rubbing their flanks and their legs so they wouldn't get stiff, then fed them new oats and corn that were to do their winter's porridge. Surely that was no matter in the face of three gold crowns!

Next she fixed a supper of stew and ash cakes, accompanied by generous helpings of small beer (for they had no wine) warmed through with mulling spices. It ruddied the men's cheeks all the same, which was surely enough to earn their due.

And then she piled every mattress in the house onto the wide rope-strapped frame in her father's room — hers and her father's, and the one that had been granny's until last winter. She stoked up the hearth well to make coals for the bed warmers and even got in the bed herself to lend her warmth to every nook and cranny. It was as she was climbing free of the bedclothes that the captain of the king's agents first saw her well. Her pinafore was folded over a chair to keep it from creasing, and her hair had come half-loose from its plait. When she saw him, she blushed deep crimson and curtsied nearly to the floor.

He waved away such formality. "No need to bow to me thus, chicken. Not when you're to be a king's wife."

"Surely not, my lord. I'm too homely by half and stupid besides. Father said I'm hardly good enough to do for him and curses me for a son." This was only partly true, and most often said when her father was deep in his cups.

"Then come, my duck, and be honoured as you deserve. A king's wife has no worries and no wants. Only bear the king a son and you'll live a life of carefree leisure."

The girl was not so much a fool as she made out. She said nothing more save to bid the captain good-night and then, taking up her pinafore from the chair back, took her leave.

Before her father sat himself by the bedroom hearth (the better to keep the fire stoked all night through), she brought him aside and whispered, "Father, these men mean to steal me from you. And I suspect they may mean you harm."

"Nonsense," her father replied with a chuckle. He'd shared a mug or two of beer with the agents and was more than a little ruddy himself. "These are men of honour, and we have done well in our service."

"Even so," she insisted, "please do me this favour. As you sit by the fire, mark the passing of each hour by exclaiming,

> How pleased is a man
> to serve well his lord?
> How pleased is a lord
> to serve well his folk?
> Another hour struck,
> how well pleased are we all?"

Her father refused. "Surely that would wake the king's men and set them on me for disturbing their sleep. Worse still, we'd not be paid at all."

The girl bowed her head. "I understand, Father. Good-night and good-bye."

Kissing his cheek, she went out to sleep with the horses. She lay down on the bed of straw and began to weep. Her father's only horse came near and nuzzled her hair with his nose. She brushed him away. "I've nothing for you. Leave me be."

"Master's daughter, why do you cry?"

"I cry because my father does not know the ill the king's agents wish him, and because he does not believe when I tell him they will steal me away come morning."

"Climb on my back," said the horse, "and I will take you to a place of safety beyond the mountains."

So they had fled, and now the harsh dawn cast blades of light across the mountain's flank, driving shadows into deep hollows. The horse drove tirelessly across the blank field of snow until they came within sight of the pass. There he faltered for the first time.

"Master's daughter," he said, "I will falter twice more before we reach our destination. Each time, only tell me you love me more than your own life, and it will give me strength to go on."

The girl leaned forward and whispered in the horse's ear, "I love you more than life itself."

In an instant, the beast was spurred as though chased by all the hounds in the village. Up to the ridge they sped and through the narrow pass. Looking over her shoulder, the girl thought she could just see the purple livery of the king's agents as distant specks on their back trail.

As morning gave way to afternoon, the horse faltered again, worse than before. The girl fell forward onto his neck and called breathlessly into his ear, "I love you, horse, more deeply than my own heart."

Again, he was spurred, this time as though harried by a pack of slavering wolves. They raced and chased down the mountain's far side, flashing through the wide-spaced trees of a pine forest. When she glanced behind, the girl did not see the king's men but knew they followed still. She remembered the look in the captain's eye; it was not the look of a man easily cowed.

As the sun crept low on the horizon, they reached the flat land of a valley's bottom. There the horse faltered a third time. He tripped so badly and so suddenly, the girl was pitched from his back. There was a sharp, wet crack, and when she turned to look, she saw the horse standing on a leg from which protruded a shard of bloodied bone.

She pulled his head down beside her own and told him, "I love you more than God and all the saints in heaven!" Her hands shook and her legs trembled, but whether from cold or fear could not be said.

"Climb on, climb on!" insisted the horse. "I can delay no longer!"

The girl did as she was told. This time, the horse galloped as though all the hordes of hell dogged his heels. She cringed to think of his pain, running on a broken leg, and buried her face in his mane.

At the valley's far edge stood a house, neither humble nor ornate. A comfortable house whose windows glowed warmly in the frigid night. The nearer they came, the lamer grew the horse, until he fell to his knees before the garden path.

"Here is the place of safety, and here is where I leave you. Go to the door and beg leave to enter in the name of BardyJin, for that is my name and those inside know it well."

The girl hugged the horse's neck and wept into his mane. "If I leave you here, I fear you will die. And I do love you, for you have surely saved my life."

The horse bowed his head. "If you love me as you say, go now to the house and speak my name. Only do it quickly, for the king's men come!"

She dried her tears and went to the door. There she lifted a bronze knocker shaped like a cherub-faced boy crowned with roses and knocked three times.

"Let me in, let me in! In the name of BardyJin, let me in!"

The door was opened by a wizened old woman, whose silver hair was shorn nearly to the scalp. Her head bowed so low, her chin touched her chest, and her eyes were reddened from crying.

"Who comes to my door and demands entry in my son's name?"

"Grandmother," replied the girl, "I make such a demand. Though I only do as my horse has commanded me."

"What horse?" asked the old woman, peering into the yard. "I see no horse, but a young man on a crutch."

The girl turned, surprised to see exactly that. The young man limped forward into the yard, favouring what was clearly a broken leg. As he came into the light, he was tall and handsome, with chestnut hair that fell to his shoulders.

"Who are you?" cried the girl. "And what have you done to my beloved horse?"

As though in reply, the old woman pushed past her and ran into the young man's arms. "My son, my son!" she cried. "My beautiful BardyJin! You've come home at last!"

When the man spoke, it was with the horse's voice. "I was out gathering pitch in the pine forest. There I was cursed by an old gnome whose tree I wounded. He made me a horse, and so I wandered far and wide in search of a cure. Then I was captured by my master, and though he whipped me betimes, he gave me food and a place to sleep. And I fell in love with his daughter. Little did I know she would prove the cure to my curse as well."

At that moment, the king's men pulled up at the garden path. The captain squinted and stared, certain that he'd seen a house glowing warmly in the winter darkness.

"It must be past this stand of trees. Some trick of the eye made it appear nearer. Come men! Ride on! We shall not let the girl escape her fate."

The pack of them took off, none the wiser that the girl stood no more than an arm's length from their capture.

In explanation, the old woman said, "This cottage was built by my sister, who was a witch. It cannot be seen save by those bound to it by blood or marriage."

The women stepped to either side of BardyJin and carried him inside. Beside the fire, his mother set and bound his leg, while the girl, whose name was Falada, stroked his chestnut hair. In the morning, they were properly wed by the priest in the nearby town.

As for the king's men, they were never seen the more.

WITH A LIFE LIKE THIS, WHO NEEDS A BOAT?

THE WEEKS WE HAD SPENT traipsing through the tunnels and passages and intermittently crowded avenues of the Underground were nothing compared to that three days' waiting. Travel possesses at least a sense of moving forward, even when little progress or discovery is made. Waiting is the essence of stagnation. For the first time in recent memory, we remained in one place, unmoving.

I did a bit of work for food. Asa was the local scrap dealer in a former shopping concourse called Cumberland Terrace. Doggo and I made short daily jaunts into stubs of tunnels that branched from either end of the central promenade, as well as to the more formal scrap heap in what used to be a Whole Foods. There was little enough of value, but we got by.

Because the locals had a disturbing habit of eyeing Doggo with a range of hungry expressions, I kept him close by at all times. He meandered cluelessly around my feet, either happily wagging or studiously licking. So long as the food kept coming, he remained unbothered.

First thing in the morning on the third day, I was back in line at the clinic. I'd been expected that early, because a note on the door instructed me to come back later in the day. I swallowed my dejection as I led Doggo back to Asa's. On our way, I stopped by the fried krill stand to barter for our lunch. When I told the fella I was staying with Asa, he cut his price down to a novelty button I'd scrapped the day before: bright blue punctuated by a multi-coloured diamond shape with the legend "Go fly a kite!"

During downtime from scrapping, I had enjoyed watching Asa clean and repair found objects, transforming junk into useful things. It was a painstaking and slow process that was nevertheless calming. A slab of silicon circuit board got fastened into a vise over a warped tin pie plate. Several careful passes with a blowtorch melted away lumps of solder and inlaid metal, which landed in the pie plate. When it had cooled, the lumps got sold to someone who could separate the metals back into usable materials.

Any scorches (and there were few) were gently wiped away with the cleanest piece of cloth I'd seen in my adult life. Then the piece got clamped into a different device and fed through a foot-pumped saw blade, which sliced it into strips about an inch wide. These were laminated and shaped and riveted into a new handle for a kitchen knife.

The entire process took the better part of the day, and I watched it from beginning to end. Asa said nothing. Neither did I. We sat in silent communion, both deeply appreciative of the methodical procedure. His concentration was entire, which made sense. Not only was he physically hindered, but the nature of the work demanded attention.

For me, watching quieted the stories that bubbled up in my brain, unbidden. What had begun as a means to stay awake, to stave off the fear that comes at night, now plagued me. It was something like staying in a bath far too long. The water'd gone cold, fingers and toes were thickly wrinkled, and it was altogether uncomfortable. Only in this case, the bathwater was undiluted nostalgia, and I felt prevented from leaving the tub by the weight of an unseen hand.

Doggo lay at my feet, quietly farting in the warmth of Asa's room. Apart from the cubbies in the wall, it was eerily identical to the one we'd left behind, only Asa earned enough to keep the methane tank of his stove full. Had I not been ill, I might have even deemed it uncomfortably hot.

I reached down and rubbed my fingertips behind Doggo's ears. He groaned and stretched. I wondered if it'd been long enough and considered asking Asa if Doggo could stay there while I hit up the clinic again. That was when my vision started to darken, from the edges at first. Colour pulled from view, shadows reached up and swallowed the light.

Around the tool he held in his mouth, I heard Asa ask, "Are you okay?"

Then I folded over into my own lap, and I didn't hear what he asked me after that.

THE FLOOR ISN'T COLD so much as hard. When I hit it, the metaphor overwhelms me: rock bottom. There is no further to go. I can swim no deeper through the grotto of my mind's eye. If

I look toward the surface, I can see the light from a thousand pale fires seething into an uncaring sky.

Beside me, by the fire, Olivia whispers, "She's hiding something. It's about Dad." Her lips hang loosely, distorting the rest of what she says into a garbled heap. The letters fall into tangled shapes like piles of autumn leaves.

Doggo sits up and whines. What else could he do? He can't swim. Can dogs hold their breath?

Maybe he's not a dog at all but an otter. I remember watching a video with otters in. They made noises like squeaky toys for dogs and juggled rocks between their paws.

"Why did the otter want to become an astronaut?"

My body starts to shake. A seizure? I do my best to keep my tongue out from between my teeth.

Olivia's mouth starts oozing white froth. Her eyes catch fire and melt down over her cheeks.

"Hey, can you hear me?"

"He wanted to go to otter space!"

"If you can hear me, squeeze my hand."

I'm not even sure I have hands anymore. I reach out, feeling for them with arms like an octopus. An octopus was put in a tank of sharks and ate them when no one was looking. That was a different video.

A thousand miles away, I feel the picture of one human hand holding another. I reach out and grab it.

"Good, good. There you go. Squeeze as hard as you can."

The picture is crumpled into a tight ball. Glossy surfaces rub against one another and make little squeaking sounds, like a dog's toy.

"Do you know your name?" shouts a voice from across a vast undersea chasm. The sound echoes all around, falling like a shower of golden dust.

"You don't even know my name," says someone else from nearby. The voice is cranky and old, put out to be woken up from some fantastic dream.

"Do you know what day it is?"

"Medicine day," growls the voice. "Three days later, we go to pick up two pills. It's not a cure, I just need time to get out. To find her."

Silence stretches like a visible distance. I remember walking down a road that didn't seem to have an end — a wide paved expanse that vanished over the horizon.

Mum's face is haggard. The stresses are too great. Still she turns to me and says, "Keep going, Jesse. We're almost there. If I don't make it, take Olivia with you. Keep her safe!"

She is whisked away by sudden wind, lifted from the ground and folded from sight into the cone of a tornado that spins silently past. Dark currents of grit whirl skyward, but the only sound is my own breath in my ears.

Then I realize I have my hands jammed over them.

"Jesse? Can you hear me?"

"Mum?"

"No."

HAPPY BIRTHDAY, JESSE VANDERCHUCK!
(REPRISE)

MY SEVENTEENTH BIRTHDAY marked our second year Underground. Olivia was coming up to eight. This was long before we moved to the neighbourhood beside the Metzlers. Mum wasn't teaching anymore, so she took work where it could be found. We'd moved out to the westernmost edge of the Underground, beneath the towers of Islington, where she was helping someone set up a tilapia farm.

They were having trouble getting access to water through the usual channels, so there was a petition circulating to allow diversion of rainwater into this gigantic tank they'd found and cleaned out. As much as folks wanted fresh fish, a lot of them were wary of letting the floodwaters in on purpose. They eventually got all the guttering and pumping to a science, but back then it wasn't unheard of to lose a neighbourhood to flooding in a bad rain.

Still, the job kept tokens in the kitty. Mum wouldn't let me and Olivia work — not yet. She had some hang-up about childhood, wanted us to have one as long as possible. While I was fine with limiting the interactions with strangers a job typically entails, Olivia had ants in her pants about earning her own money.

Sometimes I'd take her on short excursions through the nearby tunnels, even to the border of a Heap that leaked out from the bottom of a broken door. We refurbed and sold on the sly, splitting the take. I bought hootch and novels. Until she ran away, I never realized that Olivia had saved every last token to pay for her escape. Maybe if I had …

No. Never mind.

We lived in a camping trailer that someone had lowered into the earth and buried in a hole punched in the wall of a tunnel. That whole area of the Underground reminded me of an old show we used to coax out of a set of tin foil rabbit ears attached to a Sears floor model TV. The title had the name of the creatures in it, something like friggle or fraggle. This area was like that: dank, lit in blue and purple, and always with the sound of distant drips echoing off the walls.

If we had neighbours there, I never met them. For reasons I've never understood, people insisted on stacking themselves like cordwood beneath the remains of Toronto's downtown core. Could've been force of habit, since that's what it had been like before the tipping point. It meant more work in one place, but also more workers in the immediate vicinity. Seemed to me that it just made life more difficult than it had to be. To be honest, I quite liked the breathing room our west-end digs afforded. If only the rich folk had taken up tower space more evenly across the whole of the city.

We celebrated the guesstimated day of my birth with a small party. Mum managed to make a cake but fell somewhat short of making it edible. Still, it got the point across. Olivia broke the sullen silence that had become her personality long enough to hand me a picture she'd drawn on the inner surface of a cracker box. It was us, with Dad, standing in the yard of the farm. The sun was shining and everybody smiled. Mum was conspicuously absent.

Nonetheless, I said, "Thanks, kiddo."

"Don't call me that!" Olivia spat, flinging that zero-to-sixty venom of hers with serpentine accuracy.

I put my hands up in surrender. "My bad! Clearly turning seven makes you a full-on grown-up."

"Nearly eight," she retorted, reddening.

Mum looked up from strapping into a set of green coveralls to say, "That's enough, you two. I don't want you bickering all day while I'm at work."

We both fell silent. Olivia, staring at the floor like it owed her blood debt, stalked off to the bedroom and pulled the curtain closed behind her. She'd spent the last few weeks trying out her skills as a moody teenager and refused to speak to Mum.

"You gotta go right now?" I asked, picking at what was being palmed off as cake. I was just a bit put out that the celebration was so short-lived.

Mum nodded. "In a minute. First I want to see you open your present." She pulled a lumpy parcel of newsprint and brown packing tape from the hall cupboard by the door. It crinkled softly when she set it on the kitchen table. "It's not much, but I hope you like it."

I put on my grown-up voice, the one that knew only the practical concerns of survival, to say, "You didn't have to get me anything. I thought we were saving up for a set of aquaponic grow tanks."

"It's your birthday," she insisted. "Open it up!"

I looked down the hall. Olivia's feet stuck out from under the curtain, her skin dirty through the holes in her socks.

"Hey, Olivia! Come help me unwrap this!"

"Get fucked," she replied.

"Jesus! Watch your mouth, young lady!"

Mum got up to give her heck, but I stopped her. "It's okay, Mum. Just leave it."

"She is ruining your birthday, Jesse."

"Maybe, but it'll be more ruined if you two start screaming at each other. Just sit. I'll open this, then you've gotta get going. You'll be late."

She bowed her head, fuming at Olivia, at her lack of control, at being alone in her role as a parent. "Yeah, okay. You're right." As she sat back down, a mischievous twinkle winked in her eye. "I hope you like it," she repeated.

There was so much tape, it was nearly impossible to open. I pulled and tore and wrenched until I revealed a pair of bright-blue running shoes with an orange stripe up the sides.

"THAT'S NOT RIGHT," I said out loud. My voice came out rough from sleep and disuse. It hurt to talk. "Mrs. Metzler gave me those shoes. I traded them for a coat."

From a distance that couldn't quite be fathomed, I felt Doggo lick my fingers. I reached up and scratched his muzzle. "Hey, buddy! You hungry?"

He started shaking and whining and licked my hand more frantically, like he used to do when I came home from work. When I tried to open my eyes to see what was going on, I couldn't. They'd been taped shut.

"What the hell?" I shouted, feeling at the tape but not quite able to make myself pull it off.

Doggo barked. In response, I could hear bodies rousing outside, muffled by distance and at least one door.

"Jesse? Are you awake?"

My chest tight with barely contained panic, I explained, "I can't open my eyes."

There was a moment of nothing, then a rustle, then the sudden warmth of another human body next to mine. The tape took a few eyelashes with it as it was pulled off. Even so, once my eyes were open, I still couldn't see.

"Wait," said my helper, putting a hand on my shoulder. "It'll take a minute to come back."

The room around me, a bleary smear of colours, slowly resolved into shapes, surfaces. It looked like Asa's, only he wasn't at his workbench. The pot of twelve-year-strong soup sat still and cold on the unlit methane burner. The close warmth I'd grown accustomed to was gone. In the midst of my attempt to pinpoint what was amiss with the scene before me, Doggo's head popped into view and started licking my face.

"Food Bringer! Food Bringer! Food Bringer!" He managed to speak clearly despite his wagging tongue. "You're back!"

"I didn't go anywhere," I assured him, looking around. "Least it doesn't look that way."

My helper turned out to be the medicine woman. She grabbed my chin more than a bit roughly and used it to steer my head as she flashed a light into my eyes and peered into my mouth. "Well, you're alive at any rate. Based on all your fevered jabber, I wouldn't agree that you went nowhere. How's the cough?"

A quick search for the infamous tickle turned up no results, and I said so.

"Clearing up then," she declared. "Fine." She pulled the blanket off me and shoved it into a plastic garbage bag. "Pillow," she commanded, holding out her hand.

I struggled to sit up. My joints were stiff, some exquisitely painful, which made moving slow. Before I could manage to hand it to her, she reached behind me and whisked the pillow into the bag.

"Did you have anything with you apart from that bag? Any personal effects you unpacked?"

My head felt full of something dense and heavy, like wool made of lead. It took a great effort of thought to answer her question. "Um, no. No, I don't think so."

"Good." She shoved my backpack into my chest and glared into my eyes. There were flecks of red and gold in the brown that could only be seen at such close proximity. "Then take this and your fucking dog and get the hell out of here."

I felt like I'd missed something. Between the hefty fluff in my head, and Doggo trying to jump in my lap, I couldn't make one complete thought. The only thing I knew with certainty was that the medicine woman was really angry at me.

"Did I do something? Where's Asa?"

She used a smirk of visible satisfaction to drop a single word into my lap like a glob of molten solder. "Dead."

Though I was still somewhat at sea in the present moment, she went on, "He caught whatever you had, that damned cough. Didn't survive the night. Started coughing at suppertime, and he was dead by morning. Because of you."

"Wait, you can't know that for certain —"

"You brought sickness here! You spent so much time near him — an old man. Your cough became a fever, you blacked out. Asa was taking care of you when he took sick, too. The only reason you're alive is because he paid for the pills, all of the pills, and insisted they be given to you."

She took a moment to collect herself, to catch her breath. Whereas I was still reeling from the idea that Asa died. That it was my fault. Now who will make the knife handles?

"Someone's sent for a constable from the tower to escort you. A hearing was held, in absentia, while you were comatose. They've sentenced you to be banished. You're getting what you wanted."

"What I wanted," I repeated. My system reboot wasn't yet complete.

"You wanted out, didn't you? If only they'd done it sooner."

Another lull, during which I tried to work out if it was because her anger was too great to form words, or just that she resented having to talk to me more than was professionally necessary. Guilt rose up from the floor, flowing around me like water. It felt like sitting in a warm puddle, uncomfortably like wetting the bed.

When my cognitive engine was warmed up enough, I managed to say, "I'm sorry. Did you know Asa very well?"

She didn't deign to look at me when she spat, "Does it matter?"

I felt the need to say something, to eulogize the generosity of this stranger, acknowledge the loss. All I could think of was "Asa was the most skilled craftsman I've ever known. It was a privilege to watch him work. If I could trade my life for his, I —"

"Don't." The medicine woman shook her head. "It's pointless to say things like that, especially when you don't mean them."

"How do you know I don't?"

She just shook her head again and left the room.

Moments later, the constable ducked his head in.

"You," he said, pointing. "With me."

I shouldered my backpack and picked up Doggo. He wouldn't stop licking my face, though I turned my head away so he couldn't lick my mouth.

"Oh, Food Bringer! I'm so glad you're back!"

"At least somebody is," I muttered, ducking out through the low door, back into the land of the living.

RISE OF THE LIVING DEAD

A SPEAR OF PINK LIGHT shot over the eastern horizon first thing. Instead of being struck breathless by its beauty, or even complaining of its brightness compared to the dank shades of the Underground, the thing that came to mind was the pain in my face where I'd been branded a murderer. Having already made the mistake of rubbing the undressed burn and coming away with a slough of crispy skin (not to mention more pain), I did my best to think about anything else. Doggo remained asleep with his snout shoved under my knee. I scratched his ears instead of my face. It wasn't as distracting as I wanted, but it gave my hand something useful to do.

To the best of my knowledge, Doggo'd never been outside before. After the better part of a day and a night, he seemed about as impressed with it as he was with anything else. That is to say, his enthusiasm for outside hinged entirely on whether there was any food to eat, and how much of it he could have. It was an all-you-can-eat buffet of not much.

When I had set out to leave the Underground, there was always some small part of me that thought of it as temporary. A holiday from living hell to which I would return. Maybe I'd find Olivia, or my dad, or whatever other ghost I might try to dig up, and once our unfinished business was concluded, I'd mosey back. If not to the neighbourhood, then somewhere else back Underground. It's not that I liked it so much that I couldn't conceive of leaving it forever, but it'd become familiar. Comfortable. Like a pair of shoddy shoes that smell bad enough to be kept outside the front door but are worn nonetheless. The ones you'd wear to the dump.

I suppose I'd also figured it couldn't possibly be safe to stay topside indefinitely. We'd gone Underground for a reason, right? Just what reason that was had admittedly become a bit blurry. There was still flooding — bad flooding that washed away entire settlements if the sumps went down. There were deviant groups like the ogres, or the variety of polygamous cults that were said to exist in the remote corners of the world below. Was that safer than braving the elements?

Had we hidden out of fear? Or was it shame? If we couldn't see what was happening — if we literally buried our faces so that the fruits of our busy labours fell and rotted above us but were at least out of sight — that surely constituted a kind of safety. Didn't it?

We thought we'd saved the world because we marched willingly into our graves, alive but mortified by what we had wrought. The noble sacrifice of the narcissist. Perhaps all we had saved was our delusion that we were entirely in control for our own demise.

My movement disturbed Doggo enough to wake him. He yawned dramatically, stood up, and trotted over to one of the pillars of the parking structure we'd sheltered in. After a thorough sniff of the perimeter (though what he could possibly be smelling apart from his own scent was a question unanswered), he lifted his leg as high as he could and pissed for some time. He trotted back, smacking his lips.

"What's for breakfast, Food Bringer?"

I shrugged and stopped myself from once again scratching at the branding mark on my cheek — again! Then I hauled myself to my feet and pulled on my backpack. Doggo took the opportunity presented by a lull in the conversation to shake himself from nose to tail.

"Let's go see what we can find."

WITH THE BRAND ON MY FACE, I would never be let back into an Underground settlement. It identified me as a murderer and that I wasn't to be trusted to keep the safety of others above my own. They burned the mark onto my face so that it was difficult to hide or to cut away.

I was branded because a man was kind to me and that kindness had cost him his life.

Whether it was my intention to kill him was irrelevant. The mere fact that I hadn't taken myself into a corner somewhere to die, as any conscientious citizen would, was fault enough. Either stayed in the lift-shaft charnel house or surrendered to a carbon reclaimer for assisted suicide and transubstantiation into stove fuel. Never mind that I would have left the Underground immediately, if only the powers that be had not decided to get rid of the exit I knew.

It seemed to be late summer, but it was hard to tell. Leaves on trees were sparse, though there were also quite a few on the ground. Even the trees they'd imported from warmer places, the ones that were supposed to be heat- and drought-tolerant, looked ill-used by what passed for weather these days. What leaves they did have were yellow, thin, and withered.

The heat of the day was surprisingly tolerable. We even passed standing water as we headed north, up the former 400 highway. Must've rained recently, I supposed. I warned Doggo not to drink from puddles and ponds like those. As tempting as thirst made them look, we went out of our way to find a small creek of running water. My backpack had a fold-away plastic water skin that I proceeded to crumble a purification tablet into then fill with creek water. The water skin went back in the pack while the tablet worked its magic; the pack, I noticed, was quite a bit emptier than I remembered it being.

At Asa's, I'd helped out enough to earn a few spare tokens, which were spent replenishing our meagre stock of supplies. The tribunal who'd found me guilty of murder hadn't seen fit to kit me out with provisions when they banished me. One of them might've taken the liberty of lightening my load for me. Might as well have killed me themselves, the cowards.

The roads were empty, as they'd been on our initial journey to the Underground, but the intervening thirty-five years had not been kind. Grasses shot up through broad cracks so that, to someone unfamiliar with the history of the area, the road would be invisible. Just a different patch of ground here and there, black as though permanently scorched. Branded, like I was.

Buildings were scattered along the roadside for miles and miles and miles beyond the former borders of the big city. Apart from being derelict, the houses in builders' subdivisions appeared sound enough. By contrast, few of the former box stores looked especially sturdy. Frames of steel listed to one side or another, hung with tattered remnants of foam. Signs that had identified these places had fallen. The silhouettes of their logos and lettering had been faded by sun and wind and rain. It made deciphering them nearly impossible, like those 3D optical illusions my mother showed me as a kid.

"Relax your eyes. Stare through the picture," she'd instructed.

Eventually, something would appear but not an identifiable image. More like a cut-out, a shape of the pattern that leapt out of (or into) the page.

One shadow sign looked like an inverted triangle with points or spikes sticking out of its top. Recognition was slow but came eventually.

"Hey, I remember this one," I said aloud.

Doggo didn't answer. He was off in the high grass, finally wise to the existence of other creatures and their butts, desperate to make a kind of canine contact. There was no one else around to hear me. I suppose I'd just felt like talking. Perhaps that night would be time for another story.

The stories had been still since Asa died. Perhaps it was pure coincidence, but the fever had taken a lot out of me when I hadn't had that much to give, and on top of that I'd killed a man. I'd half expected to be haunted by him: to wake by a dying fire in the night and see him looming over me, his good eye glaring down in accusation. The only images that came to me when I recalled Asa were of his hand, his sure movements, his unflappable demeanour. I wondered if anybody had tried to help him, or if he'd tried to make it away from the settlement to die in an empty corner. From the little I knew of him, he wouldn't have wanted fuss.

The situation reminded me of an old billy goat we had kept in our yard for a time, back in Trout Creek. We might've always had him, or maybe we'd taken him on from a neighbour who'd passed. Anyway, he was a grizzled thing, mostly blind and totally skinny. It was the kind of thinness I'd seen in other old animals, where their skin starts hanging off their bones and every movement looks painful.

One morning, I went looking for the old bugger. I'd fed all the animals, apart from the chickens — those were Mum's cross to bear. I couldn't find him. His tether, still staked to the ground, was chewed through, but there wasn't any blood about. Probably not snatched by coyotes then. I moseyed through the yard, shaking the feed in the bucket and calling his name.

"Abraham!"

Must've been a neighbour's original. Our family's naming conventions strayed from the biblical.

"C'mon, Abe! Breakfast!"

I was about to give him up for lost when I caught sight of the frayed end of his tether peeking out from under the back porch. This was a small deck, no more than a foot or so in height, that bridged the gap between the back door and the ground. I followed the trail of the tether to a patch of earth that had been scraped out by a piece of rotten skirting.

Crouching by the broken opening, I squinted into the darkness. There, balled up at an unnatural angle, was Abraham. Slivers of light slanted in from the gaps in the deck boards. He was all twisted so his head bent back across his body. One eye stared open, glaring at me. The other was a bloodied gap. Further examination revealed that he'd caught it on a screw on his way under the porch. His tongue lolled from his mouth. It was grey and dried out, looking more like a dirty rag than a body part. And somehow, as grotesque as the scene was, it made me laugh.

When I brought Dad over to see, he failed to find anything funny about it. Instead, he hunkered down, reached one work-gloved hand into the hole and gave a mighty yank. With a few wet snaps, old Abraham was pulled free. Back into a world he'd tried so hard to escape, it killed him.

That was Dad's assessment, anyway.

"Musta got spooked. Went tearing under here and broke his fool neck. See?" He held Abraham's body dangling by one foot. Apart from the new damage inflicted by his rough-handled rebirth, it was easy to see the loose way his head related to the rest of him.

"Poor thing," I said, or something similar.

Dad scoffed. "Only poor thing about it is that he was kept alive too long for the stew pot. Animals aren't meant to go on and on for the sake of human feelings. They're born, they breed, they're eaten. Law of nature."

His speech ended, Dad let go of Abraham's foot. The sack of skin and bones slumped wetly to the ground.

"Get the wheelbarrow and truck this over the hill by the Barrinows' old place. Mind you're back in time for lunch, and keep an eye for scavengers."

"Shouldn't we bury him?"

"Burying's a people thing," was his reply.

With a grunt, he was gone back to his workshop.

"NOW IS THE TIME for food, Food Bringer," Doggo declared, parking himself in my path. I had to stop so short, I nearly fell on top of him.

"Holy crap! You want me to crush you or something?"

"The snack creatures that run through the grasses are too fast to catch. Use your powers to call them to my mouth."

I crouched down to scritch him behind the ears, but he snapped at me. He wasn't trying to make contact, just warning. I jumped up, anyway, my feelings hurt.

"What the fuck is your problem?"

"I hunger. Now is the time for food," he repeated.

My hands went up in mock surrender. "Fair enough, but if you bite the hands that feed you, how are they supposed to bring food?"

Doggo just stared at me. Either all his goofy friendliness had fled, or it had gotten buried under a thick layer of instincts. Perhaps they'd all tumbled out of whatever cranial storage closet they had been in, overwhelming the sweet simpleton I knew as Doggo.

"Besides," I continued, kneeling to dig through the pack, "if you're so clever, why can't you catch your own food? What kind of wild and wily predator can't even snag a mouse?"

"Mouse?" Doggo leapt to his feet, tail raised in alert, ears perked for sound. "Where's the mouse? I'll catch it!"

There was precious little in the pack that wasn't purification tablets, but nonetheless I took the time for a thorough rummaging.

"I thought you just said mice were too fast for you."

He eyed me suspiciously. "Mouse is a snack creature?"

"Maybe it's good for you to be out here. Old Doggo wouldn't have made that leap of logic."

"I am Doggo. You are Food Bringer." I could see another realization dawn across his goblin face from this statement of simple fact. He humbled himself in a bow, stretching his front legs enough to grunt with effort. Then he lay down, wagging his tail expectantly.

"Food now?" he inquired, all politeness where moments ago there had been sharp demands. Even his voice went back to its normal, goofy tone.

Definitely overwhelmed, I concluded.

I surfaced from my dive into the pack with half a package of compressed krill and the water skin. We took a quick scout inside a former Canadian Tire, finding a camping cook-set in a rotted cardboard box. I took the largest pot and left the rest. The store had long ago been picked for its most useful items, though I found myself strongly tempted by a mountain bike. I left it when I reasoned that trying to use it would be more trouble than just walking. The roads weren't exactly in driveable condition, and Doggo's length meant he would spill out of a basket.

Outside, once a fire'd been built, I dumped the contents of the water skin into the pot and crumbled in the krill. A couple minutes' simmering, and I called it soup.

Doggo had to wait for his to cool, but he seemed happy to do so just knowing he'd eat in the end. All of his macho wild-dog hostility had vanished for the moment. I reminded myself to stay alert for any signs of reversion but in the meantime gave copious belly rubs to reward his patience.

"How about a story while you wait?"

He didn't answer but closed his eyes and made the tongue smacking sounds of a blissed-out pup.

"I'll tell you one, anyway."

Be Just and Fear Not

A woodcutter lived alone in a wood. He'd had a wife, but he'd buried her beneath the front-door step, along with their first and only child.

They'd been taken in the wild cold of the previous winter, while he was carting a load of dried lumber into town. He'd come home to find them by an empty hearth, the babe wrapped close in his wife's arms. The front door had been pushed open wide, letting the snow drift deeply into the house. Whether this had happened by accident or on purpose could not be known.

He'd had to wait for the ground to thaw before he could lay them to their rest.

Now, with winter coming on again, he thought he might leave the wood and take up another trade far away. He went to the magistrate in town and sold his house and its contents for the pittance they were worth. The land, of course, belonged to the lord. The woodcutter kept only his old nag, his axe, and a much-mended tin pot for cooking. Thus equipped, he made off down the road to seek whatever fortune might lay in store for him.

The road wound down through a soft, quiet valley, spending much of its time alongside a lazy river. There was always a gentle murmur of moving water and so many fish that it seemed merely a matter of reaching into the shallows and pulling one up. The woodcutter found himself thinking, "Perhaps I will find a spot to settle here and take up a fisherman's trade."

At the next town, he inquired of the magistrate if they had any need of such a skill.

"Surely we do," replied the magistrate. "Our river knows such plenty for it is protected by a cruel troll who eats any who would dare fish there."

The woodcutter waved this off. "I fear no troll," said he. "Only point me to the fisherman's cottage and I'll take up directly."

He paid a copper farthing for the month's rent in advance and was told where to find the fisherman's lodging. He tied his nag beneath the front-yard tree and hung his tin pot on the front door.

"Now to the river to see about this troll."

The town had not been long without a fisher, since a weir was still set in a curve of the river close by. It was so packed with fish that the woodcutter simply scooped them by the bucket into a wheelbarrow and brought them into town. The townsfolk were so happy to have fresh fish that soon his barrow was empty and his pockets full of coin.

So far, so good, he thought. *And no problem with the troll. Perhaps it has moved on from here.*

He jaunted back to the fisher's cottage only to find his mare was gone.

"No matter," said he. "The creature was beyond her useful life and not long for the knacker. With my new found wealth, I shall buy a chestnut mare whose coat gleams like burnished bronze."

So saying, he went inside the fisherman's cottage — now his cottage — and lay down for a peaceful sleep.

The next morning, he went to do as he had the day before. Taking his barrow to the water's edge, he found the weir had a hole torn in it, so all the fish had swum away.

"No matter," declared the new fisherman. "Once I've filled my barrow and taken it to town, I'll spend my evening mending the weir and set it out by morning."

He rolled up his trousers and waded into the shallows with his net. No sooner had he made his first sweep, filling the net so well it was hard to lift, than the troll rose up from the water. It was covered in lanky black hair and reeked of old meat. A long tail with a tuft on the end hung over its shoulder, and its eyes burned with green fire.

"Who steals my pretty fishy wives?" its voice boomed in the morning stillness, and the fisherman (who used to be a woodcutter) found his legs trembled in spite of himself.

"The fish of this river are your wives?" he inquired.

"Indeed," shouted the troll.

"Surely not all of them?" pressed the fisherman.

The troll raised his hairy, smelly arms up and out and cried, "All of them!"

The fisherman leapt from the river onto the shore and made himself a low bow.

"Ten thousand pardons, good sir! As a widower myself, I would hate to deprive another man of his wives."

Confused by his kind behaviour and gentle manners, the troll lowered his arms. "Then you will cease stealing away my silvered shining brides?"

At this, the fisherman bowed his head. "Alas, I am bound by my landlord to provide him rent for this land and house. To get what coin I need, I know only one trade and that is fishing. Were you to teach me another, I might do that instead and leave your wives alone."

The troll thought on this for several minutes, and the fisherman waited patiently for his reply. It would not do to forfeit his life because he could not remain quiet. In time, the troll replied, "I have but one trade to teach, and that is forging gold from straw. Would this trade suit your need?"

"Indeed it would," agreed the fisherman, who imagined he would soon become a wealthy lord. "Give me leave to plant a field of hay and three months to grow it. When the stalks are high and green, I'll call on you again."

The troll nodded and sank back into the river water.

Now the fisherman, briefly to be a farmer, strolled back into town and told the magistrate what had happened.

"If you'll postpone what I owe in rent, I can grow up a great field of haygrass, which the troll will help me forge into gold. Then I can pay what I owe and more to you besides."

The magistrate, somewhat dumbfounded by the situation, could only nod. It was only later, relating his day to his wife, that she pointed out his folly. "Surely what we must do, my husband, is take the town guard to find the troll and make him tell us the secret of forging gold from straw. Then we may kill him and have the gold and fish in the bargain!"

"Ah, wife! If we but knew where the troll was lodged, the river would be ours again already."

But the magistrate's wife was clever and not to be turned aside from getting what she was after. "Then, husband, wait you until the fisherman calls the troll up. We will learn his tricks in the same moment and dispatch the fiend before he can flee!"

The magistrate thought on this for a time, mopping the last traces of supper from his plate with a crust of bread. "Leave it to a woman," he declared, "to arrive at the plan most steeped in deviousness and duplicity. I will do as you suggest, only we must ensure that word of our scheme does not arrive at the ear of the fisherman. I fear he is too honest for such a trick."

How were they to know that the fisherman was not too honest to plot against a foul-smelling beast like the troll? Yet for all his thought about capturing or banishing the creature, he could not light on a scheme. His stomach soured at the thought of being unable to live up to his promise of overcoming the river's bane, and for three days he could not be roused from his bed.

On the fourth day, the fisherman was to be found in his yard, tilling the soil and preparing to plant his hay. It just so happened that the local lord was strolling down the road dressed as a peasant, as he did from time to time. The lord leaned himself against a tree and watched the fisherman at his labours until the lower man, mopping his brow, took a break.

"How now?" called the lord. "What business has a fisherman tilling the earth?"

The fisherman waved the stranger over and invited him to share his lunch of mean bread and hard cheese. The lord was careful to take little as he was able but enough to seem polite.

"I till this land, good sir, because I may not fish. The foul troll who guards the river has offered to teach me the trade of forging gold from straw, in place of stealing his wives to sell at the market."

"His wives?"

And so the fisherman related the whole story from the wood on the mountain to the moment before they met. The lord, for his part, laughed and wept in equal measure and ended by clapping his new friend on the shoulder.

"Though surely a noble endeavour to trick that which is evil, I fear you are too honest a man to discover a plan on your own. Attend! Down the river from here is a gristmill whose stone can grind anything put to it. Only speak these words:

Mighty and well,
the gristmill turns!
Round and well,
the gristmill turns!
Strong of back,
Single of will,
oh how well the
gristmill turns!

"Now take you that old axe head and grind it well in the magic mill. Take the flour this makes and bake it into a cake in that old tin pot. When the troll comes to pay his call, see that he eats the whole cake. Once inside him, the axe-meal will chop him all to pieces!"

The fisherman barely knew what to say. After thanking the man for his help and his company, he excused himself to get back to work.

"Worry not, friend. You will win the day with a plan like that!"

So saying, the lord-in-disguise took up his merry way and strolled back to his manor house. Inside, now dressed in his finery, he could not stop thinking of the poor, honest fisherman.

I know, thought he. *I'll attend the day of the lesson along with a few of my best guards. Should my friend feel his conscience too strongly to do the troll in himself, I can have my men do the killing for him.*

And should I also learn the secret of forging gold from straw? Surely there is no harm in that!

Meanwhile, back at his cottage, the fisherman could not stop quaking from fear. Not only did he question his mettle when it came to the devious plan, but he fretted the ease with which the stranger crafted such a hideous scheme. *That is a lord's thinking and no mistake. I only wonder how a lowly peasant came to know such intrigue.*

Nevertheless, the fisherman did as instructed. He took the head from his trusted axe — the very one that had served his father so well in his trade — and brought it to the enchanted mill. There he spoke the words and lowered the turning stone onto the iron blade. In a moment, there was no blade at all but a fine-milled flour the colour of iron. He took this up in his old tin pan and brought it back to his cottage. Then he took up a wooden water bucket and brought it to the river's edge to fill it. No sooner was he there than the troll rose up from the running depths.

"I trust you are not here to steal my wives?" His stink was even greater today and was coupled with a foul smell from his mouth.

"Oh no, sir. The grass is planted. I'm only here to fetch up some water for the furrows. Should one of your wives swim into my bucket, I'll be sure to release her back to your care."

The troll seemed satisfied with his answer but was compelled to inquire, "Are you troubled by our compact?"

The fisherman shook his head. "Oh no, sir. I only worry that we may have been overheard and that those who would do you ill scheme against you. When the grass is grown and I call you to teach me, only keep your wits about you for some trickery. As an honest man, I could not live with myself should harm befall you on my account."

The stinking troll was struck by these words and reached into the water by his feet. From the river, he pulled a fine chestnut mare and handed it to the man on the shore. "This is your selfsame nag, made young again by the magic water of my kingdom below. I had planned to eat her but instead am moved by your honesty to give her back."

The fisherman was moved in equal measure and took the horse with hearty thanks.

"I will see you again when the grass is high," he said, taking his leave.

Days went by, and the grass grew taller until at last it was as high as the fisherman's eye.

"To be sure, this is great enough to fit our purpose. I will to the river to call the troll."

What he could not know was that the pair of men sent to spy on him — one from the magistrate and one from the lord — heard this and took off on their separate ways to tell their masters. By the time the fisherman came back, with the troll at his heel, both sets of guards had taken up their hidden posts behind thickets on opposing sides of the yard.

Said the magistrate to his men, "Look sharp and move not until I give the word."

"Follow my lead," whispered the lord to his men, "and attack not until I should give the signal."

When they arrived, the fisherman excused himself to his hearth, where he took up the tin pot in which a cake was baked.

"Here I have a cake, which I have baked to celebrate the fruition of our agreement. Would you eat it now while it is hot, or teach me first and partake when it's cooled?"

The troll considered before answering. "Hot cake is surely the greater treat. But will you not have some with me?"

To the lord's great shock, the fisherman nodded. "To do otherwise," he said, "would be impolite."

So the pair sat at the threshold of the cottage and shared the cake between them. When it was done, the troll stood and made for the yard of grown grass.

"For someone who isn't a farmer, you've done well in your first crop," he admired.

The fisherman could not answer, for his insides were being chopped to pieces by the axe head flour. He groaned, and the troll rushed to his side.

"What ails you, friend?"

"I made a promise to overcome your tyranny of the river, yet found myself lacking in cruelty to kill you for it. I have no family, nor no trade to ply, and all around are those who would upset an honest compact. Therefore I ate of the cake that would have killed you, and so die myself."

On speaking those words, every shred of stinking hair fell away from the troll to reveal a handsome young man. "Thank you, dear fisherman! My brother had me enchanted by an evil witch so that I would be a wicked troll until an honest man should pity me." From his belt, the handsome prince took a skin of water. "Drink of this. It is the healing water that I gave to your mare that made her shed her weary years. One sip will make you live, another will make you young, and a third will make you wiser than the wisest man who ever lived."

So saying, the prince poured one sip, two sips into the fisherman's mouth. Before he could pour the third, the lord's men spilled forth from their hiding place in the thicket. Though the guards stopped short, recognizing the rightful heir, his brother flung himself forward to cleave the prince's head from his body.

At that moment, the lord's sword met that of the magistrate, bouncing away with a loud clang. The lord had some skill, but the magistrate came away from the melee victorious.

When the fisherman regained his senses, he saw the rightful lord looking down on him, while all around were liveried guards on bended knee. Even the magistrate made deference.

To his friend, the prince said, "You are healed and you are young again. Is there another boon you would have of me? In truth I can never repay you. Yet ask what you would, and it will be yours."

The fisherman shook his head and sat up. "What I truly want can never be mine. Instead, I ask only the gift of this cottage that I may live out my days gazing upon the river and knowing what peace can be had."

The prince nodded. "It is done."

Within the hour, a deed was signed, and the fisherman took up his retirement in the little cottage by the river. As for the magistrate, he was pardoned of the murder of the lord and was given a stipend generous enough that his wife did not miss the secret of forging gold from straw.

And so they all lived, as happily as they might, from that day to this.

WINNER, WINNER

"I LIKE YOUR STORIES," said Doggo, licking the last of what I'd dubbed Krill Casserole from the whiskers on his muzzle.

"Thanks, Doggo," I replied.

"What do they mean?" he asked.

"Well, I don't suppose they mean much of anything," I admitted.

He paused to consider. "Then why do you tell them?"

"Because you like them. And I like you." It wasn't a lie, because it had been once true. Thing was I felt compelled to tell the stories. I probably would've gone on telling them even without Doggo to listen, since it was the only thing I knew how to do.

"That makes sense," he said, yawning expansively and putting his head on his paws.

"Hey, buddy. There's no time to sleep. We've gotta get under cover before nightfall."

It was no use. Doggo was out like a light.

I looked out from where we'd perched, partway up the western-facing slope of a steep valley with a creek snaking along its bottom. A fair amount of tall grass grew all around where we sat, but other than that, it afforded a clear view in all directions. I sat up on a nearby rock, gaining enough height that I could see over the grass. We could stay for a few minutes there.

The sun was about two-thirds of the way across the sky, which I estimated gave us an hour or two to find a better place to spend the night. I didn't think that humans spending a mere three decades Underground was enough to repair the damage that we'd done to the climate, but the weather seemed to be holding for the time being. Even if a storm swept across right then, driving us to the valley floor and drowning us in a flash flood, it had been worth it. The struggles, the loss — even the brand on my face.

I figured I might never make it back to the farm, but at least I'd lived like a human being the last of my days. Before this, I'd never realized how soul-crushingly awful it was to live Underground.

Buried alive.

I took a deep breath and soaked it all in.

Just a few more minutes, I thought. *Then we'll make our way back to the road and carry on.*

IN MY DREAM, I wake at midnight, beneath a bloated orange moon that looms near the horizon. Doggo is nowhere to be seen. In my panic to find him, I nearly fail to notice the young woman standing in the waist-high grass. She is tall and looks strong. Backlit by the moon, her face is in deep shadow. Only the merest glint of her eyes can be seen. She's dressed in animal skins and old camouflage hunting gear and holds a spear that looks like it's made from a hockey stick.

"Hi," I say stupidly. "Nice spear."

I'm met with silence. Her only reaction is to shift her weight forward onto the balls of her feet. Some instinct tells me this is not good.

"Want some krill?" I offer, pointing to the pot on a fire I swear I put out hours ago.

She turns. Exposed to the light, I can see she's pulling a face.

"I hate krill," says a deep voice that is rough from disuse.

Against every shred of my will, hope lights a tiny flame in my belly. In spite of its heat, I feel my limbs go dead and cold.

I say, "Olivia? Is that you?"

If it is, I'll never know, because the dream ends there.

I WOKE UP TO SEE it was too late to safely find shelter elsewhere. The sun had set behind us. Though there was still light in the sky, the ground had become too shadowed to move far or quickly. I cursed myself for not having grabbed a flashlight from the Canadian Tire, then thought that even if there'd been any left, they were more than likely all corroded or discharged — well beyond use, anyway.

At least some aspects of scrapping had turned out to be a useful skillset. I could count on one hand the viable batteries that had been salvaged by anyone on the heap. Valuable, sure, but rare enough to not bother looking for. Like a winning lotto ticket, or the Holy Grail.

We could've tried to pick our way back to see if there were any candles or oil lanterns, but I suspected all of those things were also long pillaged by pilgrims headed Underground. There was nowhere to go but onward.

I reached down to rouse Doggo, only to find him gone. Panic rose sharply enough that I bit down on my own tongue, hard enough to hurt but not to bleed. I felt around in the grass for the wetness of blood, the sharpness of broken bone, the softness of a freshly dead body, but found none.

Maybe he'd felt the call of the wild and run away. Off to reconnect with his roots as an Albanian low wolf, hunting snack creatures and failing to lick his butt. Or, more likely, he had felt the call of nature and wandered off to take a dump.

"Doggo!" I called loud enough for him to hear me if he was nearby but not so loud as to attract night-hunting predators. "Hey, bud! C'mere, Doggo!"

I picked up my pack. It'd been rifled but not torn. I didn't think much of it beyond taking a moment to thoroughly and righteously curse Doggo for his gluttony.

"Fucking cock ass shit! I thought we talked about this." To the night, I called out, "Doggo, you greedy prick! Get back here!"

I became heedless of danger. I was well pissed off, and worried about Doggo, and cranky from the rumble in my belly, and angry at the generations who'd spent their time pointing fingers at one another instead of saving the world, and resentful of all the years I'd wasted cowering in a hole.

"Doggo! Jesus H. Murphy, get your furry butt back here now!"

I reached the roadside having only stumbled twice. There was a twitch in the grasses off to my right that I caught from the corner of my eye. Could've been Doggo, could've been a bear. A coyote. A lion descended from the ones released from the zoo. I took a moment to watch, holding as still as I was able. The movement continued unabated, suggesting the clumsy step of an elderly wiener dog rather than the soft stealth of a wild animal.

If only I could whistle. "Doggo?" I hissed, "That you?"

The movement turned to make a beeline for my position. The closer it got, the more certain I was that it was Doggo. Or at least that it wasn't a bear. As it got closer, something about it called to mind a wagging tail and an idiot grin.

"Food Bringer!" crowed Doggo to the deepening night. "I am victorious!" His voice sounded strange, like he had something in his mouth.

"For fuck's sake, Doggo!" I chided him, though I couldn't disguise the relief I felt to know he was okay. "Don't go running off like that."

He busted through the grass looking pleased as punch. His muzzle was dark with dirt — or possibly blood. In his teeth was an enormous rat that was still squirming.

"Now I am the Food Bringer!" he declared, his words somewhat muffled by his prize.

I reached down to take it from him, but he turned his head.

"Look," I told him. "If you're the Food Bringer, that means you have to share."

He started to growl, but it turned into a whine.

"Hey, buddy. It's me. It's okay." I stood on tiptoe to scout the area in what remained of the light. An abandoned car could just be seen up the road a way. I figured we could hunker down in there, use the cooking pot as a fire pit, and roast the rat.

"C'mon. You carry it over there, then I'll cut it up for cooking." The thought raised my gorge a touch, so I added, "I'll even give you the biggest piece."

Doggo seemed happy enough with this arrangement to wag his tail weakly. Still, he was clearly torn between his loyalty to the

Food Bringer and the instinctual drive to hunt, kill, and devour. As we picked our way along the ruins of the highway, I wondered how I could help my furry friend strike a balance between those two extremes.

When we got to the car, Doggo gingerly lowered his kill into my outstretched hand. It continued to squirm a bit, which struck me as odd. Maybe he hadn't made the kill at all but found a bloated specimen chockablock with maggots.

I braced myself for maximum squickage as I flicked open the knife I had been clever enough to look for — and find — at the Canadian Tire. Doggo leapt into the passenger seat and watched hungrily with his paws hooked over the ledge of the open window. *Great*, I thought. *An audience.*

After a few shallow breaths intended to psych me up, I drew the razor-sharp blade across the belly of the beast. For a few heartbeats, I wasn't sure if what spilled forth was better or worse than I'd anticipated. At least a dozen bloody pink jellybean babies kind of oozed onto the hood of the car, which I'd used as a butcher block. She might have been preparing to give birth, or been in the midst of it, when Doggo caught her. That explained more than a little.

I didn't exactly relish the thought of eating the adult rat, let alone boiling up a pot of its blind, hairless babies. So, I decided to give them all to Doggo and make do with their mother. He happily obliged by devouring the litter with lip-smacking relish.

"More?" he inquired.

"You'll have to wait. I'm going to cook up the rest for me. You can have whatever's left."

I anticipated that most of it would be left. Hunger, at this point, had been relegated to a back burner while throat-constricting squick was coming to a simmer.

"Take a nap," I advised Doggo as I stripped the fur from the rat's body. "I'll wake you when I'm done."

Doggo's tail wagged heartily, which made his little wiener swing counterpoint. "I have done well, Food Bringer?"

"Yeah, bud," I assured him. "You knocked this one out of the park."

I'D LIKE TO RECOUNT that something strange and terrible happened the following morning. That all of my teeth fell out, or that I came unstuck in time, or that Doggo turned into a luck dragon. Instead, when the first spears of new dawn thrust over the eastern horizon, I was overcome with the desire to run. A sensation like panic settled over my shoulders, a cold blanket draped on my skin. Only it felt distinct from true panic. A rising energy, yes, but not the brittle judder of a racing heart, of thoughts spiralling out of control. More like a surge. A great wave, building and curling but never breaking. Despite my limited experience of the sensation, it was similar to my memory of lust.

I wanted to run, not away or toward. Just fleet-footed leaping, barely touching the land as I passed. There and gone again; a shadow, a mystery, a ghost. I longed to forget the thoughts of mankind, to step out from beneath the weight of humanity's sins and disappear.

The gentle movement of Doggo's belly beneath my hand as he breathed returned me to the here and now. We were still in the car. It smelled of cold ashes, dampened by a night's exhalations. Once Doggo had crunched the bones and sinew of the spit-roasted rat, no evidence of her life remained. Her only monument would be the steaming pile Doggo was destined to leave shortly after we took up the road once more.

I tried not to put myself in that creature's place, because the past can't be changed. And were it not for her sacrifice, we'd have both gone hungry. Even so, the old dark half pushed its thumb into my empathy centres and I was there, albeit briefly. In the dark, alone and in pain. Maybe not even knowing what was happening to me, only sure that I needed shelter. Safety. And then came this snarling thing of teeth and slobber that reached into whatever hole I'd found. It grabbed me by the middle and pulled me out. Clawing and biting, after one sharp shake, it was all over.

"Thanks, brain," I grumbled under my breath.

Looking down at Doggo, I couldn't imagine that ravening beast, though I knew it was there. Behind his dopey face, his idiot grin, and lopsided ears lay a wolf in wait. Even having glimpsed it, I couldn't quite make it be real.

He was only Doggo, and he was my friend.

The dog breath, though! The combination of exhaled humidity and general stink was getting to me as the air in the car became warmed by the sun. The windows were fogged, so it was impossible to scout the area from inside. There were no manual cranks on the doors, as there had been in my dad's old Datsun truck. There was a leaky sunroof, which we had propped open while the fire was going. Since we'd be moving on, there was no good reason not to bust it off its hinges and crawl up onto the roof. It would allow me to make sure we weren't gonna get jumped by man or beast as soon as we opened the doors.

The air was getting colder day by day, so the wheel of the year was almost certainly turning to wintertime. I wondered what winter would be like, or if it hadn't changed much in thirty-five years. Dampness was pervasive, weighing down the tops of the tall grasses with dew. As the sun warmed this water away, it smelled like my grandmother's kitchen at Christmas — my dad's mother — as she boiled a pot of wheat and honey. I had hated eating the stuff, but the smell reminded me of comfort. Of home.

I scanned the flat ground nearby, then squinted out to where it rose up in monolithic cliffs of pink granite. It reminded me of when the old two-lane of Highway 11 was being bypassed. The new set of four lanes had been cut straight through the stone, which was tinged the colour of rare beef by iron deposits. At intervals, the rough faces were striped by the striations of holes drilled for blasting.

Things looked clear, so I slipped back into the car to let Doggo out. He remained fast asleep, which was odd. I would have expected him to notice my absence and begin licking himself out of worry. When I put my hand on him to give him a gentle shake, his shoulder was hot to the touch.

"Hey, Doggo. You still alive?"

His eyes creaked open. They were kind of lopsided, like he was drunk, and he couldn't seem to focus them. I took his head in my hands. "Hey, buddy, here I am."

"Mmpf," he grumbled as his eyes went crossed and rolled heavenward.

Keeping my tone light, despite the knot of worry snaking through my gut, I said, "You're not looking too good. How d'you feel?"

In reply, he made a series of burps or hiccups, which culminated in him barfing a bunch of bones and rat guts all over the car seat and me. It was the worst reek I could remember smelling. It made me gag, nearly enough to throw up myself. Thankfully, I was able to keep my gorge down long enough to get the door open. Once I got a deep whiff of sweet morning air, I promptly coughed up what little was in my stomach.

Reaching back into the car, I scooped Doggo into my arms. His whole body was shockingly hot and limp as a noodle. Picking him up was like trying to cradle a furry rubber sack half filled with custard.

All I could think to say was "Gonna be okay, Doggo. Gonna be a-okay!"

I assured myself it was nothing serious. Could be he'd just had a bad reaction to so much meat, since he was used to krill and chitin. Or maybe I'd given us both food poisoning from uncooked rat. Only I didn't feel poorly, apart from some lingering disgust, and his fever seemed high. I vaguely recalled reading something about how dogs' heat tolerance was lower than humans'.

He felt so hot to me, I wondered if he was totally done for.

No. None of that defeatist talk, I decided. With much effort, Doggo raised his head from my shoulder and licked my cheek. He only ever tolerated being carried, and face-licking was his polite way of asking to be put back on the ground.

I shifted his weight so his front paws curved around the back of my neck. "Hold on, bud. I saw some cottages down by the water. We're gonna motor over there so we can hunker down till you're feeling better."

"Better. Better," he mumbled, delirious. "Good dog, Food Bringer."

"That's right, bud. You're a good dog."

Doggo wasn't exactly heavy, but he was a good ten kilos of long dog. Scrapping had kept me in decent shape, but the weeks of semi-starvation and sickness had taken their combined toll on my muscles. Every dozen steps or so, my body begged to lay down its burden. To just plain lie down. Then I thought of Doggo, how hot and limp he felt, and how his breath was starting to rasp ragged in my ear. So every time, I sucked in a lungful of cool morning air and willed myself to keep going.

Back when I was in school, I'd joined the cross-country running team. The coach was a sturdy woman from the prairies. Her dark curly hair was most often contained by a red woollen toque with the logo Calgary '88 stitched on the front. She would inform us, "It's all about hustle, folks! You can run fast, or you can run long, but if you don't keep those buns motoring, you'll never cross the finish line."

"Hustle, kid," I breathed as we chugged along. "Hustle, hustle, hustle."

My arms, legs, lower back, and abdomen felt lit on fire when we finally broke through the treeline into the cottage's once-cleared patch of land. Closer to, it looked pretty run to ruin, but the roof was blue powder-coated steel with the merest suggestion of rust at its edges. As long as the walls didn't fall over, it would keep the weather off and the wolves out.

We'd just made it across the yard when I panicked. I thought Doggo had stopped breathing. I laid him down on a partially disintegrated deck long enough to check for signs of life. He'd tricked me like this even when he wasn't sick, because his belly barely moved as he breathed, and he slept soundly as a fricking log. Tension mounted until I felt on the near edge of screaming, frustrated that I couldn't find what I was looking for. Then Doggo looked googly eyed at me as though nothing was wrong at all.

"Hey," I mustered, scratching his head. "Thought I'd lost you."

"Where did you last have me, Food Bringer?" His voice was so quiet, I could hardly hear him over the gentle chatter of the nearby river.

"Yeah. Food. Right. I'll get you settled, then boil up some soup." What I would put in the soup remained to be seen, but that was another problem for Future Jesse. In that moment, I looked for someplace soft to put Doggo and maybe something warm to drape over him. *Is that right? Should I cool him down instead?*

The cottage door wasn't locked. Inside smelled old and empty, like too much dust and not enough life, but otherwise not unpleasant. Nothing had died or taken a dump in there, at least not recently enough to make its olfactory presence known. It was one large room, apart from a closed-off corner that probably had a bed in it, and a much smaller one in the opposing corner along the same wall. A closet, maybe. Possibly a washroom.

In the main room was a sitting area with a wood stove. I gratefully set Doggo down on the seat of an armchair. Off came my coat and I laid it over him. Then I pulled the chair close to the stove and used all the skill at my disposal to set a fire in it. Which was to say not much skill at all. Building a fire outside on the ground is completely different from building a fire in a stove. In a stove, there are settings to contend with, parameters to manage and balance. It's more science than art.

I made sure the flue was open and adjusted the intake choke to its widest setting. Inside the stove was mostly clean. There was no need to dig out a bucketful of ashes first. Then I had only to find some wood to burn. There was likely no outdoor wood pile that had survived this long. I grabbed the hatchet from the stove side and went after the big oaken table in the kitchen area. The varnish on it wouldn't smell too nice once it caught, but I was starved for choice. And even once I got it into small enough pieces to fit though the stove door, I'd still need kindling.

The big evergreen in the backyard, framed by the kitchen window, was laden with pinecones frosted white with sap.

Perfect!

It felt like I was moving in a dream, like I couldn't gain speed no matter how hard I tried. Everything took too long. The process of getting a fire going wasn't more than half an hour, but it seemed like half the day was gone before I took a break with my head against the armchair.

Just five minutes, I promised. Then soup.

Doggo was still breathing. It might've only been in comparison to the heat radiating from the wood stove, but he felt cooler than he did before.

"Hang on. We're gonna get you better in no time."

I rifled the kitchen cabinets first, just in case. Deep in my brain lived the knowledge that there were human foods dogs shouldn't have, but the only ones I could call to mind were chocolate and grapes. And there was fat chance of finding either in any fit state to eat.

"They're probably worst, then." I figured. We'd just have to take our chances, otherwise.

I found a bulging can of minestrone, a couple tins of smoked oysters in broth, and one big can of wet dog food with a bright yellow label.

"Holy shit, it's a Christmas miracle!"

With a bigger pot than the one I'd swiped from Canadian Tire, I could add a bunch of water to the "rich and meaty" dog food and boil the crap out of it. Soup! That way, it'd go further plus get some fluids into Doggo. That was important with a fever, right? Lots of fluids. Something about water, about drinking or swallowing, tickled the back of my brain, but it was neither strong nor specific enough to slow me down.

In a big wall cabinet by the back door, I found a gigantic stock pot. After some physical comedy with a rickety chair, I got it down. I took it to the river at a trot. Once full, I was barely able to lift it, though I managed through sheer will. Everything seemed to be catching up with me at once: my age, my health, my ignorance. On the verge of giving in, the running coach's voice piped up to say, "C'mon, Vanderchuck. Just a few more steps, and we're home free."

The purification tablet packaging was printed with instructions, but they'd been rubbed to illegibility. I could make out something per litre but couldn't tell what the something was, nor could I easily recall what a litre looked like, let alone how many I'd got in the pot. I put two tablets in, then added a third for good measure.

Then I crossed my fingers that *giardia*'s defences against chlorine had become especially frail.

The fire was still going, which, considering my lack of experience in managing such things, seemed downright miraculous. It would need more fuel soon enough, or else I'd be stuck starting it from scratch. I needed another short break before I could think about that. With luck, there was enough heat to boil the water.

Religion was never much of a thing in our house. The nearest church was a town over, in Powassan, and seeing as Mum didn't care much for driving, we didn't go often but she took a few times when I was small. By the time Olivia was born, she only went herself and only by convincing Dad to take us kids for bacon and eggs at the diner across from the church.

Even so, I knew the basics of praying.

It wasn't formal enough or formed enough to give voice. I only put my head down and begged anything listening to help Doggo pull through. Capital Gee God, Odin, Zeus, the Great Forest Spirit — anybody. *There's nobody else but him*, I told them by radiating thought. *And I will not go back to being alone. Not now, not having tasted companionship.* Olivia, my dad, they were just ghosts of maybes. Possibly still alive but probably not. Doggo was there, and real, and I loved that dumb idiot more than … more than maybe anybody, ever.

Please, I begged. *Please don't leave me.*

The intensity of my feelings on the matter was a bit shocking, even for me at that stage of our companionship. I hauled myself up from the floor and staggered into the small enclosure, which turned out to be a small washroom. The cottage didn't have running water, and never had, but a manual water pump stuck up through the floorboards.

My paternal grandparents' place, as well as a few neighbours in Trout Creek, had had such devices. They were usually away from the house, and often as not used as a means of watering animals. I knew enough to tell that with nothing to prime the pump, there was little hope that it would do anything. Still, I tried. On the second or third pump, I felt the catch of suction. It took another dozen pumps, but it eventually coughed icy water all over my shoes.

I grabbed the basin from the counter and filled it. The water was utterly glacial. It numbed my skin as I splashed it on my hands and face. The sensation brought me back to the here and now, like a firm slap to a hysteric. In the mirror, I saw a face so old that it looked like a mask. When I pictured myself, I didn't see a geriatric with the purple-scabbed scar of a facial brand. I saw myself: familiar and fifteen. The Jesse who went Underground, not this resurrected husk. I wondered if the adults I'd known saw themselves similarly. If they held the pearl of their youth as an image of their true selves, or if this was the result of my forced hiatus Underground.

There was no one to ask, so I pushed the question away. Maybe think more on it later.

I chopped up some more hunks of table and brought them stove side. Doggo's face was burrowed into the sleeve of his coat-blanket. Movement. That was a good sign surely. I scritched his exposed shoulder before crouching down in front of the stove door to feed the fire.

Well before the second batch of wood was burned through, the water got hot enough — not boiling but its surface steadily steaming. I pulled the tab, easing off the can lid, and dumped its contents into the pot. The solid slab of chipped meat and gravy made an oozy sucking sound as it exited the can. It flopped into the hot water like a manatee diving gracelessly into a jacuzzi. I used a long-handled ladle I'd found in the kitchen to break it apart, stirring it through, and rinsing the dregs from the can.

Shallow bowls from yet another cupboard, ones that looked like a plate and a bowl had a baby, waited nearby. I figured one of those would be easy for Doggo to get his face into, and it would help the soup cool more quickly than a deeper vessel.

While I sat blowing across the surface of his soup, Doggo began grumbling in his sleep. Better and better! When the soup was just barely warmer than my finger, I gently roused him, peeling the coat away from his face.

"Hey there, kid. Get some of this in you."

He managed to lift up his head. Once he caught a whiff of the stuff, he dove in whole hog, getting more of it on his face and the floor than in his mouth. I had another nagging feeling that I was missing something vital but brushed it aside. In moments, the last drop was gone and Doggo was cleaning the empty plate.

"Hold on, hold on. Let me get you some more."

We continued this way for four bowls before his neck went noodly again. The floor, the edge of the chair, and my nearest pant leg were soaked in soup. And as I pulled the coat up around him, I noticed it was pretty wet, too. I made sure Doggo was getting good heat from the stove. When he was good and snuggled, I got up to resume my ransack of the cottage with a focus on clean, dry linens.

I found stacks of flannel sheets and woollen blankets in the bedroom. The sheets were fine, but the blankets were Swiss-cheesed by moth holes. I took the biggest sheets and trucked them back to the main room.

During my earlier rummage in the kitchen, I'd come across a drawer of hand tools. I went back to it to grab a hammer and some nails, plus a roll of twine. At the top of my reach standing tiptoe on the floor, I nailed the twine in a loop around the wood stove — along the walls and spanning the width of the room, cutting it more or less in half. I used this to hang the sheets, nailing in places where I could, draping them over the string and clipping with clothes pegs where I couldn't. My aim was to keep some of the warmth in and make a smaller space to heat. That would save fuel, stretching what little we had into a virtual bounty.

Back in the bedroom, I chanced on some viable blankets that had been stored in a cedar chest. I brought these back and spread a couple across the floor as insulation. Another one got warmed by my body before being swapped out for my coat as Doggo's cover. I figured I'd need to go outside before bedtime, and the coat was far more manageable to wear.

I walked around outside our little yurt of sheets, making sure all the windows and doors were locked or blocked. Wherever there were curtains, I pulled them closed. Before I latched the front door, I took a jog to the treeline to do my necessaries. There was little to be done since I'd upchucked earlier and not eaten since, but I buried it all the same.

The sun was sinking low behind the trees nearest the road, so it seemed later than it was. There was a level of local gloom that didn't match the lightness in the sky above. Much as I longed to linger, just sucking air, as my dad used to say, a damp chill was setting in. Plus Doggo needed me.

I needed Doggo.

It was hard to distinguish which of those statements was truer.

Back in the cottage, I closed and latched the door. We were as safe as I could make us for the moment. Which was just as well, since I was more exhausted than I could remember ever being. Every muscle and joint throbbed from use. My brain was foggy and ready for sleep. I ducked into the yurt of sheets to settle in for the night.

"Food Bringer," Doggo croaked. His voice was thin, like a ghost of itself. I wasn't sure if I'd heard him at all, or if I just wanted so badly to hear him speak.

I leaned in close, pushing my forehead against his while scritching his jaw. "Hey, buddy. How you feelin'?"

He groaned and rolled over. One foreleg lifted, inviting me to scratch his belly. The gesture was so familiar amid all the newness, of being aboveground, of Doggo being sick, I teared up. Of course, I obliged his simple request. It felt like time for a story, but they were playing coy. Didn't matter. Good enough to be sitting there with Doggo, my best and only friend, warm and safe and dry. We could be back Underground. We could've woken to find we were alone in the world.

We could've died in our sleep and this was Paradise.

Despite any uncertainty, that moment was perfect. I hoped it would last for the rest of our lives as I fell into a gentle doze. Only the story woke me when it was ready to be told.

The Girl Who Followed a Cat

In a faraway land, there was an only daughter whose mother ailed. With no money for medicine, the girl, who was called Millicent, feared she would soon be orphaned. Her father had left years before and not returned. And nary a day passed when Millicent's mother did not curse his name for doing thus.

King's men arrived in the town to recruit lads for the navy. "Stout, strong lads who're not afraid of the sea," they said. "A year's pay in advance for a contract of five. Take home the rest should you live."

Millicent heard these words as she was at the market one day. Like a shot, she was home to their tiny cottage at the town's edge.

"Mother, mother," she cried. "Our prayers are answered! I'll join the king's navy, and you'll have a year's pay on the instant. In five short years, we'll be set for life."

Millicent's mother hung her head. "Oh, foolish child! So like your father. If you're that desperate to be rid of me, just go. They'll not take girls to the navy any more than pigs can fly."

The girl was unswayed. She cut her long hair and took her Sunday best from the garderobe. Then she kissed her mother and was away.

In town, she sold the hair and the dress for a suit of jacket and britches. Once dressed, Millicent rubbed the cloth and her skin with dust from the road. She climbed a tree and got sap on her hands. And she ran up and down the fields to catch some cockleburs and work up a lather of sweat. This done, back she went to the town square to meet the recruiters.

The king's men looked her up and down and seemed satisfied with her pedigree. They asked her but one question: "Have you ever been to sea?"

She replied, "Sure as the love of my mother and father, I have."

They nodded and had her make her mark upon the contract. Then they presented her with a pair of coins — one of silver and another of gold — representing a year's pay.

"Have you a trusted runner?" asked Millicent. "I would take this pay to my ailing mother, only we've fallen out over my enlistment, and she told me not to darken her door the more."

The elder of the men nodded sagely. "All too common, my boy. Worry not, for we'll get the coins to your mam."

That night, Millicent slept in the billet with the other newly enlisted men. The low-ceilinged room buzzed with snorts and snores, grunts and coughs. The girl lay awake, frightened of her decision, and tried to remember her new name. Her father's name.

Crispin. I am Crispin. How d'you do? My name's Crispin, friend. What's yours?

They were a week's journey from the sea, and another two weeks from setting sail. Old salts spent the time barking orders at the new blood, showing them the ropes. One old timer named Galt, bald and brown as a nut, took a special shine to Millicent, now called Crispin. He took great delight in finding fault in Crispin's work or in kicking, tripping, or shoving the lad at any opportunity.

"Missed a spot," he'd cackle, just having pushed Crispin to a freshly swabbed deck with one axe-blade hip.

Two days out to sea, bruised and beleaguered, Crispin sat among the stores and wept. It was cold comfort to know that Millicent's mother was surely on the mend by now. Meanwhile, he looked down the barrel of another five years of torment.

From a gap between casks of salted lemons sauntered a cat. Her beautiful tortoiseshell coat gleamed even in the dimness. She butted her head against Crispin's knee.

"What troubles you, child?" inquired the cat.

Far from being startled that a cat could talk, Crispin poured his heart out to the creature. He told his story and Millicent's, start to finish.

"And now here I am. Five years from my fortune, yet not sure I'll last another five minutes. What am I to do?"

The cat said nothing further for the moment but sat in Crispin's lap, purring loudly. Crispin felt the gentle vibrations wash through his belly and was calmed. Tears ceased flowing and his heart felt peace for the first time since leaving port.

"Worry not, child. I will help and protect you from the worst of things. Consider that you and Galt may have more in common than you realize. Help him understand that helping you helps both of you."

"What do you mean?" asked Crispin, but by then the cat was gone, drifted back between the casks like a wisp of smoke.

Crispin thought long and hard about what the cat had said about Galt. For days, he made no further headway in solving the riddle. Then one morning, he caught Galt alone on the watch. Having little other recourse, the lad up and asked Galt about it.

"Tell me what we could have in common that would make you so bilious toward me?"

Galt stared sharply into Crispin's soft, new face. In that moment, without a word uttered, the riddle's solution. For Galt's eyes, well hidden by his gruff manner and mean looks, were doubtlessly those of a woman. Crispin was struck dumb for several moments. Then he managed to ask, "How? How have you gone so long in hiding? And nobody's found you out?"

Galt shrugged and spat over the railing. "Nothing to find. I'm no more woman today than I was when I walked up the gangplank as a pie-eyed youngster like you. But you're so bad at hiding what you truly are that you'll draw suspicion to us both."

"Then help me," Crispin begged. "Why bully me?"

"Because the best way for two men to keep a secret is if one of them is dead."

THE STORY SUDDENLY dried up on my tongue.

Oh, fuck. Oh, fuck me, rattled my brain.

He's gonna die. I'll be alone again.

What am I doing? Telling some fairy tale to distract from how abso-lutely fucked I am. How fucked this all is. Baked Earth. Tunnel-grub human beings. Me and a dying dog against the uncaring universe.

Fuck, Doggo.

I'm so goddamn sorry for everything.

Not for the first time since settling in, I cursed the cottage's former owners — or whoever had pillaged the place before I did — for not leaving one measly bottle of liquor. I had to settle for a whistle wetting of cold dog-food soup instead.

o you mean to kill me then?" asked Crispin, bracing for a knife to the gut or to bethrown overboard.

Galt's fox-grey eyes glittered in the light of a false dawn. "Tell me first why you're here. Perhaps I'll think it worthy and spare you."

So, Crispin related the whole sad tale, the whys and wherefores of how he'd gotten there. All the while, Galt watched, eyes cruel as stars.

When the boy was done, they stood in silence for a time. Around them, the ship spoke in creaking tones of what it was like to ride the salty swell of the sea. With a grunt, Galt grabbed Crispin by his tunic and pulled him close. Into his ear, the grim man growled, "You may not know it yet, but I do this for your mother."

So saying, Galt pitched Crispin over the rail. The sea swallowed him up with nary a splash and Crispin was swiftly passed by the clipping ship. When it was more than a league away, Crispin (or perhaps Millicent once more) heard a cry that sounded like Galt announcing, "Man overboard!"

The ship was too distant to hear one drowning child's cries for help. So it was quite surprising for that self-same child to hear a voice quite near at hand speaking words of calm. In the next moment, it became clear that the speaker was the tortoiseshell cat.

"Worry not, child. 'Tis as easy to swim as to drown. Only hark me closely and do as I say."

This was a time when most ships kept close to shore rather than make the dangerous journey across the salty desert of the sea. So it wasn't long before the swimming pair sighted land. A short time thereafter, they were pulled up on the strand.

Crispicent (Millipin?) succumbed to exhaustion from the effort of the swim. As they passed in and out of waking, the cat brought them water and small fruits to eat. Thankfully, the tide was high as they arrived so that they were not overwhelmed by rising waters. Thus they stayed for a day and a night.

I TOOK ANOTHER BREAK from telling to go stand by the large front window. Peeking through the drapery, I saw a field of ferns frosted with moonlight. They ended abruptly at the river's edge. Whorls of lazy current drew themselves through water as black as ink.

I contemplated how far I would need to wade into that current before it overwhelmed me. Like a scene from a movie, I watched it happen from outside: the inky water swirled in front of me as I submerged, suddenly seeming to leap into my nostrils, run down my throat.

Wash away my crying eyes.

"Don't, Jesse," I warned myself aloud. "Don't do this. You can't predict the future — you don't know anything. Doggo's gonna wake up tomorrow. We'll spend a couple of days here while he recuperates. Hell, maybe we'll just stay here. Seems nice enough. Who needs to track down ghosts when we have each other?"

The siren song of the river rising in my ears, I closed the curtain and returned to finish the tale.

The cat and the child made their way inland. At length, they found the King's Road. To their left ran its northward arm, which led over the swells of hillocky pasture until it passed through Millicent's hometown. To their right, the road soon plunged into the shadowed tunnel of a dense wood.

"Surely, I should homeward go, for my mother is doubtless worried," said the child.

The cat snorted. "Not only would you deny her your death payment, but you would be jailed for desertion, Millicent or no. Be just and fear not. Take you the southern road, and I'll meet you at the palace."

"Meet me? I thought we might travel together."

"We have. Now we part, later to meet. Remember what I told you."

With that, the cat departed, disappearing swiftly into a field of ripening wheat. Alone, the child took stock. "I cannot be Millicent, for she's a good girl who lives with her mother. Nor can I be Crispin, for he drowned at sea. Who shall I be now?"

Taking a seat on the nearby milestone, the child thought and considered and brooded until the sun was slanted quite low in the sky. Presently, a raucous group of bandits came upon the child so slouched by the roadside. Their leader pulled up his horse and dismounted in one swift movement.

"What have we here? An urchin on dry land, eh?"

The bandits laughed like stones tumbling down a dry river-bed. Their leader scooped the child up and over his saddle. Then mounting the horse behind his prize, he spurred the beast to a gallop and led his gang into the wood.

At the camp, the child was foisted off to the women while the men saw to their mounts, then sat themselves by the fire to drink and sing and laugh. The child was gripped by the chin and pulled to face a sharp-featured woman whose hair was tied in a faded scarf.

"And who are you then? Some little scrap of whore?"

Polite as could be, the child replied, "I'm nobody, ma'am. No name, no home, no fortune. I'm on my way to the palace to meet my father."

The woman scoffed. "And I suppose your father's the king himself?" She threw the child toward a stack of broken pots. "Mend those, and we'll see what use you are, Dogsbody. If they're not done by sunset tomorrow, you'll go into the stew pot."

Dogsbody (formerly Millicent, lately Crispin) fell clattering among the pots, much to the amusement of the bandits' hard women. The pots were in even worse shape, with many worn through or cracked from cheap tinkering. Looking them over well, Dogsbody determined how best to see them mended and got to work. By sunset the following day, all the pots sat out shining, so well mended as to be brand new. Save one, which was missing.

"Where is it?" demanded the drudge. "You've stolen it, have you?"

"Why no," declared Dogsbody. "But I needed metal with which to mend, and so I used that pot for the purpose. It was small and so roughly used beside, I thought it meant to be used thus."

The other women shrugged, leaving the drudge to accept the suit, albeit begrudgingly.

"Fine, fine! Well and good. That challenge was too easy. Come with me."

Together they crossed the camp and went down a short hill into a gully. A stream ran through, beside which was a year's worth of laundry.

"These tunics and breeks were once whitest linen but now are stained and dingy. Get them clean by midday tomorrow, and your life will be spared." So saying, the drudge took her leave.

Dogsbody knelt between the stream and the pile of laundry. At the stream's edge, some soapwort was growing. Using a flat stone to pound the leaves into the linen, the child scrubbed and scraped and finally rinsed every garment clean as the day it was made. These were then hung on the branches of a broad-leafed tree to dry. The way they billowed in the wind made the tree resemble a ship's mast. Crispin, within Dogsbody's breast, surfaced long enough to miss the wild swell of the sea, then submerged once more.

When the drudge returned, she found Dogsbody asleep in a crook of the tree's roots. She kicked the child awake.

"What witchcraft is this? How have you done so well, so quickly?"

Without hesitation, Dogsbody replied, "Only let me away to the palace and I'll tell you my secret."

The drudge scowled but looked up at the freshly cleaned linen.

"Fair enough. Follow this stream until it crosses the road.

Turning south will lead you straight to the palace gate. Now say how you did this."

Dogsbody stood and looked the bandit queen in her jet bead eyes. The child pointed to the soapwort, her glance unwavering. "Simple enough for a child, if you know the trick of it." Before the drudge could clout her about the head, Dogsbody was away. No, Millicent was, leaving Dogsbody and Crispin asleep beneath a tree that was like the tall mast of a ship.

She ran all the way to the palace steps, whereupon she fell fast asleep. In the morning, who came sauntering to her feet but the slender tortoiseshell cat, purring to shame the Devil.

"Tell me, child, what have you learned?"

Millicent sat for a time in silence, absently scratching the cat behind its ears. Then she said, "I have learned that many things are not as they seem. And that a rudderless ship is easily steered off-course. And that if I'm to live my life, it shall be on the terms of my own desires. My mother is no longer my concern, nor my father."

"Ah, me," said the cat. "Would that you could spare one final thought for your father. Do you not wish to see him one last time before making your way in the world?"

"Certainly, I do," replied Millicent. "But to call on the dead to make themselves seen is to invite bad fortune."

"Are you so sure he is dead?" queried the cat, before transforming into her father, though much aged. They embraced, each one weeping tears of joy. When their tears were spent, Millicent's father explained, "Years ago, as I travelled the road to find good work, I was tricked by a pixie into a game of riddles. I won, but the pixie was so enraged by its loss that I was changed into a cat. Only satisfying my heart's question could reverse the spell. And all I desired was to know if my only child would wish to see me after my apparent desertion."

Millicent ducked her head and spoke softly, "Now that we've seen each other, we must part again. I'll not go back home again, but if you would, I know your wife would welcome you with open arms. She has missed you."

"Indeed I shall," said he, and so they parted ways.

TO SAVE, PRESS NINE

BACK IN THE DAY, my dad used to take us hiking in the woods. We weren't going anywhere. Just walking, one step at a time, over hill and dale until we turned around and went home.

These walks were largely silent, bar the occasional complaint about being cold or tired. Those were mostly mine. Olivia seemed content to truck along for ages. The two of them marched in time, though she couldn't have been much older than three when he first brought her. If she did start lagging, Dad would lift her onto his shoulders and carry her.

I can't remember if he did that for me.

Looking back, I can appreciate the meditative quality of going nowhere. The stillness of the woods, the rhythm of footsteps crunching twigs, dried leaves. Occasional silent interactions with woodland creatures. A deer frozen mid-step, eyes pinned to the interlopers, nose working to feel out our intentions. Traipsing through the landscape in spring, in summer, in autumn. I don't think we went in winter.

At the time, though, to me, these walks verged on torture. My mind raced with noisy thoughts and would not be silent. Boots crunching on fallen debris or sloshing through shallow creeks were the only sounds of our presence, apart from the gentle huffing of breath.

Mile on mile, hour on hour.

I guess this was Dad's way of spending time with us, when we weren't "taking the scenic route" on a Sunday drive. Or driving each other nuts around the house.

Sometimes, I dreamed about talking to him. The conversations were as stilted and awkward as they ever had been in real life. In these dreams, I was fifteen in body but fifty in mind. Dad sat still and listened. That was the astonishing part. Not that we were speaking quietly instead of shouting at each other, but that he nodded and said nothing.

I'd tell him about working the Heap. Or about how little I felt when we left him behind to move Underground. Or about how tired I'd grown of the taste of compressed kill. He would listen in silence. He didn't offer the advice I was looking for. He didn't try to fix or opine about anything. His eyes looked thoughtful as I spoke.

That's how I knew they were dreams. Pure fantasy. I hold no ill will toward my father, but there was no way he could ever do such a thing as simple as that: sit still and listen. I don't blame him. Might as well hold the sky accountable for being blue.

MORNING DAWNED THROUGH the picture window. It warmed the light that filtered through the flannel sheets and kicked the dust motes hanging in the air into high gear. Watching them twirl brought a smile to my face, like a reflex. I stretched and turned to wake Doggo.

His body was rigid.

And completely still.

He seemed smaller under the woollen blanket than he was.

There was no fooling this time.

No spark of hope that I was missing signs of life.

His belly was still and sagged emptily when I put my ear to it.

His whole body, underneath the stiffness, had a terrible empty softness.

Whatever resistance that might have remained was gone. Entirely.

It left with him.

My brain eventually turned over, bringing with it that tickling thought from the day before.

Water. Swallowing. Hydrophobia.

Rabies-B.

Sourness twisted my stomach into an impossible knot. The rat. It had to have come from that. Goddamn it, I'd killed us both — me and my stupid dreams. Freedom aboveground! Freedom to starve or to die from eating diseased flesh. I felt suddenly driven to get away from this place. I wanted more than anything to be nowhere at all. To dissolve, to become incorporeal. Every sensation was coming through at top volume, overwhelming my ability to act. To escape.

I needed to move on.

So with no thought beyond that need, I got up and left.

ON THE ROAD AGAIN

THAT DAY, I didn't get far. My muscles still ached from my efforts to save Doggo's life, but I knew that more than I felt it. As I walked, everything went numb. All sensation dropped away and sat waiting at a distant remove. I was ravenously hungry, but I didn't stop. My throat was parched with thirst, and I ignored it.

At the top of a hill, by the side of what had been the road, I sat down. Looking out over where I'd come from, I could just make out the red steel roof of the cottage peeking through the foliage. It reminded me of a game I'd made up as a kid: Spot the Cardinal. Whenever I heard a cardinal's song, I'd spend as long as it took to find the scarlet bird in the green tree. It inevitably took longer than I felt it should have.

That day, the cardinal sang a dirge.

Looking back along my path was like looking into the past. I felt I could point to events that had knotted themselves into the thread of my life. *That one is when I had a family, there's when I had a friend, and here at my feet is where that thread lies badly frayed.* That was when it hit me, all at once.

The loss.

Tears and snot and great wheezing breaths crashed like salty ocean waves over my head. My body felt beaten, my spirit broken. Every scrap of skin throbbed with invisible bruises from the blows life had dealt me. As far as I knew, I was entirely alone in the world, and that knowledge inflicted physical pain.

What is anything for now? I wondered. *What is the point of going on by myself?*

I cried until I fell asleep. If I dreamt, it was of never waking. Or maybe I imagined I would wake as somebody stronger, someone worth saving.

When I woke, I went on. Mile on mile passed beneath my feet, unnoticed. There was scenery, but I didn't see it. I was glad of nothing but the emptiness that now howled in my chest. I went on and on and on until my body collapsed from such ill-use. Heedless of any danger, and unable to do anything about it besides, I slept sprawled out on the road, not far from a sign that told me the population of Gravenhurst was 12,311, and it could be reached from the next exit.

I wish I could say I cried myself to sleep that night, or something equally poetic. But tears didn't come. I wasn't sure they would come again for some time. I'd lost my sole reason for being alive and the fire of that pain could not be quenched with tears.

Another day dawned. I was weak but somewhat restored from my sleep. Driven by habit more than will, I dragged myself to my feet and took up the path once more. The pain in my body was harder to ignore. My muscles felt like stacks of rubber bands that had been twisted until they were over-tight. Some had snapped but most held on, creaking with tension. It was hard to move at all, let alone well.

The road surface was heaved more steeply, with craters where the paving was missing entirely. It was like some giant creature had come and eaten random chunks of asphalt. A rock biter or a tar-eating troll. I tripped and stumbled often. Even fell once or twice. After one such fall, I lay sprawled across the eaten-out road. My vision darkened and my eyes stung. Turned out I was gushing blood from a slash scored into my forehead and it was gathering in my eyes. A small, sensible part of my brain squeaked that I should wash the wound, bind it — if not to prevent infection, then to keep my scent from being detected by animals. I did nothing of the sort.

"You don't know," I insisted aloud. "Maybe a passing mountain lion would like to take Doggo's place. Ever think of that? Pet puma? Companion cougar?" Delirious, I went forward in a crouch with my hand held out in the classic cat coaxing stance. "Here, kitty kitty kitty!" I called to the empty forest. I was continuing on from sheer bloody-mindedness, for no other reason. I had nothing else to do and nowhere else to go. Behind me was a dead end, and the road was laid out at my feet. Walking was slightly easier than killing myself. Took less thought, at least. Just put one foot in front of the other, and try not to fall down so damn much.

PITSTOP

THERE WAS A WATERFALL just off the main road coming into Huntsville. A short chute of frothy water tumbled down a scree of grey granite. Shaggy hangings of algal growth swung green and yellow amid the tumult. It was a tricky pick down a slippery slope to get to its base. There was a small crook of dry land where the creek bent away from, then sharply back toward, town.

Layer after layer, I peeled off my clothing and cast it aside. Shedding my exoskeleton and leaving it to be found as a perfect hollow replica of who I was. Exposing myself. Finding a spot to sit beneath the falling water, I wedged my naked arse between a pair of rounded rocks that were slippery as hell. And I sat, letting the frigid water wash me until my toenail beds went blue. I tried to catch the trails of colour that were surely rinsing off me: black, brown, red. But all I saw was my own rippling reflection, breaking, reforming, and breaking again.

"At least it looks like you can cry," I told that reflection.

In town, I foraged for clothing and for food. At the third house I checked, I managed to find an enormous pair of farmer's jeans, which I cinched to my waist with laces stolen from that same farmer's boots. None of his shirts were viable, but there was a hefty coat of waxed cotton duck that I appropriated. On Main Street, most of the shops had been looted but were intact enough to protect their remaining wares from the weather. A derelict army surplus stood apart at the end of a side street. It had a selection of shirts and shoes still in their packaging. I plundered with abandon.

My search for food was less than successful. I slept in the remains of a theatre — the stage kind, not a cinema — staring at the proscenium and lulled by the grumbling of my empty stomach.

I PASSED BY TOWNS with familiar yet strange-sounding names: Huntsville, Emsdale, Katrine, Burk's Falls, Sundridge, South River. The road bent up and down through a series of highlands, gently curving as it hugged lazy slopes. More red granite, more drilling striations.

One morning, the air distinctly chilled by the changing season, I was woken by my hair being pulled. Snapping up, braced for a fight, I came face to face with a moose, calmly chewing. She'd been cropping grasses near my head, and my hair had grown out enough that she'd caught some by accident. Just behind her, at the bottom of what used to be a ditch, a pair of last year's calves shyly peeked.

I closed my eyes and tried my damnedest to disappear, or at least to stay perfectly still. Moose were always equal parts terrifying and fascinating to me: barrel bodies towering on skinny stick legs, tipped by enormous sharp hooves. Their faces adorable but for their oddly bulbous noses. Growing up in the sticks, I'd been taught better than to do anything remotely threatening around a cow and her babies.

She seemed unperturbed, continuing to crop and chew and consider this strange not-grass thing she'd come upon. Even when her calves crept closer and started nuzzling around my legs and feet, making sure I was in no way edible, she did nothing but watch. A few end-of-season flies buzzed lazily around her ears as they swivelled, scanning for predator sounds.

But not for me. We humans had been gone long enough that they'd forgotten about us.

Were I craftier, or maybe just more opportunistic, I'd have tried to kill one of them for food. I was desperate enough that I didn't think my total lack of weapons to be an obstacle. Perhaps I was starved to the point that, to my addled brain, the notion didn't seem utterly insane. What I did know was that I was so weak that sitting up had become a real chore. There'd be no venison on my menu any time soon.

In time, they moved on. Not one of them so much as glanced back to make sure I wasn't following. I didn't even have energy to be insulted.

HOME FOR A REST

OLIVIA FOUND ME the next day, laid up on the floor of a derelict roadside tavern just south of Trout Creek proper. With effort,
I remembered going for a rummage in the general store across the
street. Certain details stood out. In the back, at the bottom of a
mountain of damp, empty cardboard boxes was a case of candy.
Hundreds of tiny milk carton–shaped packages of pelletized gum,
in grape and orange and cherry. Each white carton bore an image
of its flavouring fruit, anthropomorphized with cartoon faces grin-
ning manically.

Back to the tavern, which I remembered more clearly. The inside of the place was all done in dark pine, heavily varnished so
that it looked laminated in plastic. Walls, floor, tables, chairs, and
bar top were all made of the stuff. It reminded me of the place we

sometimes went for Sunday breakfast when Mum went to church. They served stacks of thick pancakes with real maple syrup.

There was nothing in the taps, so I'd helped myself to whatever dregs remained littered along the bar rail. I put a funnel in the mouth of a bottle of Gordon's that had a couple of shots left in it, filled it with a bit of everything that was left. Then I spent as little time as possible throwing it back. I had passed out from a combination of drink and exhaustion, curled up around one of the bar stools.

Maybe I was attempting suicide, albeit in a delirious and unintentional way. I'd not eaten a thing since … for three or four days, anyway. And that on top of a lifetime of malnourishment. Food scarcity. Starvation. I don't know what I was thinking. Maybe I just wanted to be done.

She stood, outlined by the light from the open front door: broad-shouldered and lean with a serious, square jaw. She had a pack on her back and a newel post held like a club in her hands. She woke me by nudging my tortured kidneys with the toe of her boot.

"Hey! Get up!"

"Mmpf," I protested.

"Who are you?" There was a creak of leather gloves shifting grip on varnished wood.

Through happy chance, I managed to lever myself to sit up in one smooth motion. Perhaps too suddenly. She shifted weight to her back foot and held her club at the ready to deal with any funny business. A sharp inhalation when I turned my head indicated she'd seen the brand on my face.

"What d'you want here?"

"Wanna be left alone. Die in peace."

"I can help you with that."

When I squinted at her, she clarified, "The dying part."

Can't say the exact moment I knew it was her. Something in her voice rang deep bells of familiarity that couldn't be immediately placed. She reminded me of my mother, only with a far sturdier build. Mum had always been slight, which belied her bullish physical strength.

Maybe it wasn't until she leaned on one of the stools, and the light fell on her face. There was Olivia, the petulant teenager clothed in the flesh of a middle-aged woman. A trio of deep lines scored her brow, and her mouth was forged into a straight, narrow line.

"If you're the kind of killer the Underground is making these days, maybe the human race is finally done for."

After a laugh that led to a solid minute of coughing and throat clearing, I was able to retort, "With people like you leaving, how else could things shake out?"

"People like me?"

"Jesus, Olivia. It's Jesse. I'm Jesse."

"Am I supposed to know who that is?"

I felt a moment of cold dread that I was wrong. Maybe this wasn't my sister. Wishful thinking and starvation just made it look like it could be her. Or maybe there was nobody with me at all. At least then I could stop worrying about being beaten to death.

"They took my papers," I mumbled. "How can I prove who I am?"

"Jesse Vanderchuck has a scar from appendix surgery that looks like a snake swallowing an elephant," she said.

My hands went to town, stripping away layers of stolen clothing to expose the very scar. When I looked up to see if she saw it, too, there were tears in her eyes.

"Jesse. You got old."

I pulled my shirts back down and my coat closed.

"So did you. And you're still a pain."

"Shut up, jerk," she said, reaching a hand down to help me from the floor.

I grabbed it. She pulled, nearly falling backward. I guess she expected me to be heavier.

"I was sick with a cough for a couple of months. Best diet program there is."

"That why they banished you?"

Reminded of Asa, all I could do was nod. Thinking of him reminded me of death, which reminded me of Doggo, who was the reason why I was trying to drink the tavern dry of whatever I could find. Without a word, I stumbled shakily behind the bar and went pawing through the bottles for any dregs. Finding the shelves empty of all but broken glass, I headed for the overstock in back.

Olivia followed me, having left her pack and her weapon back in the bar. She watched me for a few minutes as I snuffled like a bear looking for honey.

Incisive as ever, she asked, "You lose someone?"

A single dry bark of a laugh leapt out of me. I started pushing bottles harder than I needed to, and they fell to the ground. Some broke.

"Fuck, Jesse. Getting sick wasn't your fault. And they wanted you to just sneak off and die quietly. Fuck them!" She tried to put her hand on my shoulder, but I shrugged it off. "Hey, geez! You okay?"

I started yelling, punctuating my chant of defiance by smashing bottles. "I can't! I can't! I can't! I can't!" What I meant was up to interpretation, but it was what came out when I tried to convey everything that had happened and how I felt about it.

"Jesse, quit it!"

My hangover, combined with grief and anger and whatever else, made me start retching. Bent double, hands on my knees, I dry heaved hard enough to wrench my back. Urine leaked from my bladder, clamming the crotch of my jeans, but I couldn't stop it. Nor could I stop Olivia from reaching over and rubbing my back between the shoulder blades.

Retches became hiccups. I knew crying would release the tension, but I couldn't find the valve to turn on the flow. My knees wobbled, then gave way. I crashed, shins first, onto a brick floor covered in broken glass.

"Ow" was all I said.

"Fuck sake! C'mere." Olivia got a shoulder under my nearest arm and lifted me up. It hurt too much to put weight on my legs, so I ended up doing a kind of tiptoe shuffle to stay alongside her. She brought me back to the bar and dumped me in a booth.

"Always such a mess," she admonished, shaking her head. "Stay put. I'll be right back."

Lack of food and loss of blood caught up with me, and I started shuddering from shock. When Olivia returned, she dug in her pack and fished out one of those thin foil blankets people used to keep in their cars in case of a winter breakdown. She unfurled it over my juddering shoulders, then set to work on my legs. I guess I passed out, because I can't recall feeling her dig out chunks of glass from my flesh. Nor can I remember the part where I sat up and screamed, full-throated, when she poured disinfectant down my mangled shins. She made sure to tell me all about it afterward, since part of my reaction involved kicking out, which clocked her full on the chin. Wouldn't let me forget it, either.

I do remember coming back to my senses on a wave of cooking aroma. Steamy air and the hot smell of a pot on the boil brought a flood of saliva to my mouth. It disappeared into thirsty flesh, like the first rains in a desert. On the table near my head was a tall plastic cup of water. I downed it in one long swallow, then spent the next minute forcing my body to keep it down. Olivia must've heard me moving around, because she came moseying out of the kitchen to check on me.

"Sit up if you want, but don't try standing yet. Have something to eat first." She bustled back into the kitchen and proceeded to clank and cuss.

It had to be delirium talking when I wondered aloud, "How did I find you?"

"Well, technically I found you. And it wasn't exactly hard."

I waved away her disparaging comments. My arm felt heavy and kind of numb.

"S'not what I meant," I said. "We came looking for you. Didn't think we'd find you, though. Maybe dead, maybe long gone ... seemed like maybe a fairy tale I'd told myself."

My sister returned with a steaming bowl of hot food. She set it on the table, then spent some time methodically peering into my eyes and feeling my forehead.

"Who's we?" she asked.

Instead of the knot of emotion lodged in my throat that I expected, I felt kind of loose. Uninhibited. I replied, "Me 'n' Doggo." Then a pause for consideration. "You dope me?" I asked.

"White willow extract for the pain," she explained, sitting down across from me. "It's alcohol based. I put it in your water. You have a dog? Where is he?"

"Dead," I said flatly and dug in to my soup.

Neither of us said anything while I slurped at the first food I'd had in days. Olivia just watched me eat until the bowl was empty.

"More?"

I nodded. Felt like if I'd opened my mouth, I'd have just burped up everything I'd eaten. Olivia took my bowl back to the kitchen and came back with two. This time, she ate with me.

"You always wanted a dog," she said at last. "I remember that big fight you had with Dad about it. You said you wanted a friend, and he said it was a waste of food."

Her words conjured the ghost of that memory. Dad was especially put out because he'd found out that it took me so long to come back from gathering fuel because I'd been at the library reading. He felt my time was better spent working at home and forbade me from going back.

"Can we talk about something else?" I could feel the near edge of a comedown from the painkiller she'd given me. Kind of cold and thin, like a wedge of ice.

"Well, what else is there to talk about? Seen any good movies lately?"

She had me there.

"Maybe we could just talk about you for a bit. I'm not ready to talk about … about him."

Olivia shook her head, the slimmest hint of a smile crooking the iron bar of her mouth. "Sure thing. Whaddaya want to know?"

We sat and ate and talked. I asked her about her trip north, which turned out to be not all that different from mine. The road was better, and there were more signs of life. It had been spring, so she got more of a soaking than I did. Leastways, she always had fresh water to drink.

"You ever find Dad?"

"Ask me about that later," was all she said about that. "What about Mum? How'd she feel about you leaving?"

"Mum passed away couple years back," I told her. I didn't expect much of an outpouring of grief, considering the two of them got on like oil and water. Even so, I swore I saw Olivia thumb a tear from her eye.

The conversation moved on. Olivia mentioned hooking up with a guy from Temiskaming who'd become some kind of nomadic wild man. He got hooked back and stayed long enough for them to have a couple kids together. When I asked if I'd get to meet them, Olivia said they were gone.

The sun was low when she helped me limp outside to relieve myself. She'd offered to bring me a mixing bowl to use as a bedpan, but I insisted. "I'm not an invalid."

Olivia only shrugged and rolled her eyes.

We spent a moment while we were out there, just watching the sunset and bathing in the twilight. Perhaps not the brightest idea, given that all the most dangerous creatures clock in that time of day. At least, they used to.

"We'll stay here tonight," she said. "I took a peek upstairs while I was making supper. There's a weather-tight patch right at the top of the stairs. Just the one entrance — easy to block off. Not that I've seen a cougar for ages. Folk down the road keep bandits in check, too."

"Sounds good." I replied. "Then what?"

Olivia stared off, squinting into the scarlet-stained sky. An early night breeze lifted some strands of hair that had come loose from the heavy plait that hung down her back. For that moment, she was nothing at all like the little sister I'd known. She was an Amazon: something wildly beautiful and deadly from a faraway land. She turned to me and gave me a closed-lip smile before she said, "Then we go home."

WRESTLING WITH KING NUTKIN

WHILE WE WALKED, I began a new story. Olivia interrupted way more than Doggo used to, so the whole endeavour was frustrating. She poked and prodded and tested. I struggled to keep hold of my patience and to keep my train of thought on its rails. If I didn't know better, I would've said she was nearly as starved for companionship as I was.

"So, there was once a king who ruled over all the squirrels in the wood," I said.

"Squirrels? You've been aboveground for five minutes in the past three decades. When was the last time you even saw a squirrel?"

"Yesterday," I lied. "So, this king was lonely because he had no wife, no children, and no family. He gathered his advisers and told them of his plight.

"'Whomsoever remedies my loneliness shall find himself a duke with a castle and a parcel of land to accompany his title.' The advisers took their leave of the king and went about discovering a solution to their ruler's problem."

We huffed along in relative silence for a few steps before Olivia demanded, "So what happened next?"

"I'm getting to it. Just let me think — jeez!"

She threw up her hands. "Pardon me, my liege. Whenever you're ready."

It wasn't until we'd stopped for a midday rest that I continued.

In the kingdom lived a terrible beast with long matted hair and horns as curved and sharp as scimitars. He heard about the king's lament and so took himself to the palace. "I am good company as any. Let us be friends and spare His Majesty this torment."

When he arrived at the palace gate, the beast was halted by the guard. "You'll go no farther, cur. Begone, back to whatever cesspit you crawled from!"

The beast stood his ground. "I am here to befriend the king and be remedy to his loneliness. I'll not leave until the king himself should turn me away."

You must understand that the beast smelled to high heaven, in addition to being frightfully ugly. And here he stood in the full sunshine. The heat began raising his stink to an extraordinary reek that pervaded the air and assaulted the senses. So the guards wanted rid of him but realized they could not force the creature to move, short of killing him. After a short parley between them, one of the guards summoned a page to relay the situation to the king. "Let His Majesty decide," he explained to the beast.

In a moment, the page returned with his reply. "The king insists that the beast be permitted audience, as any subject of the realm is entitled."

The guards shrugged and allowed the beast to pass.

"THIS ALL SEEMS UNLIKELY," said Olivia, chewing a crispy bit of roast squirrel. "Why would the king want some smelly ass critter up in his throne room?"

I sighed. Squirrel felt a bit too close to rat in my book, so I was munching some pemmican from Olivia's supply.

"It's a fairy tale. They're supposed to be like that."

"Why?"

I took a moment to formulate an answer and to concoct the story's end. The pemmican was slightly sweet, but the cold venison fat gave it a texture like eating lip balm full of jerky. *At least it's not rodent based*, I assured myself.

"These kind of stories used to teach lessons. Exaggeration or unbelievable things made the lessons obvious and memorable," I explained.

"Is that what you use them for? To teach something?"

Her question hit some kind of nerve, and it made me a bit pissed off.

"Can I finish?" I snapped.

Olivia shrugged. "Make it quick. We should get going."

The beast arrived in the king's presence and made his obeisance.

"Stand, creature. Tell me what has brought you here."

"My liege, I come to remedy your loneliness. Let me be your friend, and you'll want for no other company."

The king stroked his beard of white, which came to a point from the end of his chin.

"And how should that be? What does your friendship offer that nobody else's does?"

"I cannot say, sire. Only that I know it to be true."

I STOPPED AGAIN because Olivia had begun to gather her things and kick over the fire.

"Where are you going?"

She looked up from her puttering. "I thought you were done."

"Well, I'm not!"

"Okay, so just tell me how it ends. We've gotta make tracks before dark."

I got so mad I couldn't think straight. Whatever path I'd mapped to reach the ending fell out of mind. "Forget it," I muttered. "Let's just go."

"What's your problem?"

After gulping a deep breath, I found a hard knot caught in my throat. To distract myself into letting go whatever emotions were tied up in it, I pushed my thumb into one of the cuts on my leg.

"Holy shit, Jesse! What's the matter with you?" Olivia tried to get in close to see what damage I'd done, but I shoved her away.

"The fuck do you care? It's fine. Let's go!"

We walked for a good twenty minutes before she tried talking to me again. I'd been leading, though I didn't know exactly where we were going, and Olivia'd been hanging back. Letting me cool off.

"Is this about the story?" she ventured.

I shook my head and swiped at the few tears that had jumped out of my eyes as I blinked. "No. Maybe. I don't know."

Another ways was traversed with only the crunch of boots over rough ground as accompaniment. Then suddenly she caught up with me and pulled me into a hug. Her arms pinned mine to my sides. The strength of her embrace shoved air from my lungs. When she'd finished, she held me at arm's length and looked me dead in the eye.

"I'm sorry I ruined your story, Jesse."

I shrugged and shook my head. "It wasn't you. I'm just out of it. I don't know what I'm doing or why I'm doing it. I thought I knew when Doggo was with me, but since he ... he's not ... What am I for? What good am I?"

"Nothing. Like the rest of us."

She took up the lead on the trail, calling back, "Hurry up! We've got a two-hour walk and an hour to do it in."

DEAR DIARY

SITTING IN MY OLD ROOM, looking out over a backyard I'd known the first fifteen years of my life, I marked how much had changed. It had become an alien landscape. Even though Olivia'd cut back much of what was overgrown, there were two sturdy trees taken root where the pig pen used to be. The deck where Abraham died had been rebuilt. With all the differences in textures and colours, it may as well have been Barsoom.

My cough had come back. Or maybe it was a different one — a surface cough. I'm no doctor. Olivia had me bundled by the fireplace most of the day, but as she'd gone out, I'd taken this sojourn up the stairs. Took the best part of an hour to get there. Apart from the cough, nothing in my body seemed to work. Joints ached and I was tired all the time.

I'd been eating better than I had for the last three decades and change. Olivia brought home meat or fish most days, and she had an entire cellar of dried foods and preserves. Thank goodness one of us watched what Mum had been doing all those hours in a steamy kitchen.

Can't say I'd much of an appetite to speak of, though.

I could not stop thinking about Doggo. Having grieved before, for Dad, for Olivia, and then for Mum, I was struck by how stubbornly he stayed in my mind. I'd turn and fully expect to see him, little furry comma all curled up with his nose burrowed under a cushion. But there was nothing there.

No Doggo. Just an empty space where he ought to be.

I'd tried to talk to Olivia about him, but she wasn't much help. As a listener, she was Dad's daughter. Instead of offering sympathy, or saying nothing at all, she tried to solve the problem of my sorrow by thinking up advice.

"How old was he, anyway?"

I shrugged. "Dunno. He was grown, I guess."

"Any grey around his muzzle? Some dogs go grey."

"Could've been. He had grey in his colouring all over, with black and brown and white."

She thought about that as she set another split log on the fire. A spray of sparks spun up the chimney. "Well, he could've been old and that's why he passed."

"That doesn't make me miss him any less."

"But if he was old, there's nothing you could do about that. It was just his time."

I lay down with my face to the back of the couch. "I don't want to talk about this anymore."

Since I couldn't see her, I could only guess, but I figured she stood up from a crouch, dusted bits of bark and ash from her hands, and glared at the back of my head. In defence, I pulled the blanket up and over — the only proven shield against sister-glaring.

"You're such a raw nerve, you know? Just like Dad said. A tooth that wants to be pulled."

"He's one to talk," I scoffed from my upholstered stronghold. "What's that even supposed to mean, anyway?"

When she didn't say anything, I peeled the blanket back and rolled over to look. The fire was just catching the new log. A blaze of heat surged from the hearth, but I was the only one to feel it. Olivia had pulled a ninja disappearing act and was gone.

"Fuck," I said to the empty house.

OUR TRIP TO THE HOUSE had taken longer than it should have, thanks to the raging infection I got from the wounds on my shins. I was only walking about half-speed. We had spent several days holed up at a neighbour's farm, about two kilometres from our old place. Spitting distance! But I was fevered, and strong as she was, Olivia wasn't prepared to carry or drag me the rest of the way. All of this was made worse still since I kept the infection hidden until its fact was inescapable. Olivia chided me for trying to kill myself and cursed herself for trusting me in the first place.

I had spent large segments of limited cogency trying to remember the name of the family whose farm it had been. "Legat? Le-, Le-, Le-," I droned, intrigued by the feeling of making an ell sound with my tongue. "Something starting with Le, right?"

Olivia grunted, dropping a load of split logs on the living room floor. "How should I know? I was six when we moved away. People weren't properly introduced to me."

"Doesn't … doesn't it say on, like, a mailbox or something? Farm people allus … allus make those cutesy signs for the front porch, with the names on?" My ability to think was drifting away from me again, so I had to hold on to hear her answer.

She came over to feel my forehead and to tuck the blankets more securely around me. I moaned that it was too hot. "You have a fever, dummy. If you're not covered, you'll get a chill. Stay put and drink some water."

Sudden panic overrode every circuit in my brain.

"This is how!" I gasped. "This is how I killed Doggo! It's wrong! I've got rabies-B … Please don't let me die!"

"Shh! It's okay. I'm not gonna let you die. We've got medicine to make you better, and I know what I'm doing. Unlike some people I could mention."

She meant it as a joke, but I didn't laugh. Humour was too far away to see clearly, and all I could think were soft pink thoughts.

"Levesque," she said. As I sank deeper into delirium, I felt her stroke my hair and pat my cheek. "The family's name was Levesque. There's a sign by the road."

When I came back from my jaunt to the land of Fever Dreams, I was alone. I could hear the sound of wood being split from out in the side yard.

"Levesque," I muttered to myself. "That's their name."

❖ Cold Hands and Warm Heart ❖

In a land that knew only winter lived a boy and a girl. They weren't related but loved each other as brother and sister. Their families lived in a broad river valley, separated by a broad expanse of well-kept woods.

The girl's family burned charcoal, while the boy's hunted for meat and skins. Even so, in the deepest part of winter, the boy's family helped harvest wood for the burner. And in the warmer months, when the forest creatures were fatter and moved about more, the girl's family assisted by setting and clearing snares.

The pair saw each other nearly every day, though the journey between their houses was several miles. Every day, each would invent some excuse to run an errand or do a chore that required taking the path through the wood, and so they would meet in the middle. Together they ran through the forest, laughing and playing and singing, until their chores ought to be done. Then each would help the other complete the needed task before taking off for home.

Though they both loved their parents and blood siblings, they loved each other best in all the world. One day, they made vows to one another to never let anyone see them parted. The boy used his knife to cut the tip of his finger.

"Let me do to you likewise. We'll mingle our blood so that our bond will be made, and none can tear it asunder."

The girl consented but winced when he made the cut. Together they held their fingers over the same spot in the snow and let the blood drop out.

"There! Our bond is made so that God in heaven cannot break it."

She worried at his blasphemy but smiled all the same. The boy held out his handkerchief so that she might staunch the cut with it. She in turn gave hers to him.

"Keep the cloth close to your heart," she said. "And don't let the blood be washed from it."

The boy nodded, then looked to the sky. "Oh my! Look how low the sun hangs. Let us now do our work and return home so that we'll not be missed."

This they did, then bid each other farewell at the roadside as they did each day. The girl took off directly for home, carrying the bundles of kindling she was sent out for. The boy, with his satchel stuffed with edible roots, dawdled along the path. He packed a ball of snow between his hands, then rolled it down the road to see how large he could grow it.

As he went, he came across a carriage stopped on the path. Travellers along the road were rare enough, but this was clearly some noble or other. The carriage was fine, its sides decked with carving, but its grand wheels had gotten mired in the wet snow. The driver of the carriage, a stout bearded fellow who was no taller than the boy, took note of his company and waved him over.

"Boy! Do you come here and help me. This wheel, being well mired, is too great for me to unstick by myself. Take hold, as will I, that together we might lift it clear."

The boy examined the situation and shook his head. "I'll do you better than that, sir. Let me but fell that sapling yonder and cut you a pair of skis. We'll bind them to your carriage wheels that you might glide across the top of the snow, the better to make your way from the valley."

The dwarf clapped his hands and laughed heartily. "Well and good! You're a fine, smart lad and no mistake. Let us make haste and get done. My lady within grows colder and crosser by the minute."

In a short time, the tree was felled and split down its length into two sturdy yet flexible skis. These they endeavoured to lash to the carriage wheels as speedily as they might. They were nearly done when the lady shouted from within.

"Are we not gone yet? What use have I for a driver who leaves us stuck so long?"

"Do but patient yourself one moment longer, my lady," said the boy. "Our fix is nearly done."

The lady thrust her head from the carriage door, eyes of red glaring from skin the colour of the snow itself. Her lips and locks were of the same shining black hue, and on her brow sat a crown of diamonds like ice. She caught the boy with her stare, and he gasped at its force.

"Who dares speak to me so, as though I were some crabbing housewife? Know you not who I am?"

The boy fell to one knee and bowed his head. "Indeed not, my lady. I'm but a humble know-nothing who has seen aught but the trees of this wood. I beg your forgiveness for my ignorance!"

The lady reached down and lifted the boy's chin to peer into his face. Her hand was cold as the air of the wood and stung his skin at her touch. The boy was fair to look on and well fashioned in body. On seeing this, the lady's manner softened. She ducked her head coyly and smiled sweetly to him.

"Fret not, my chuck. I've forgotten already. Only I wish you would hurry, for I'm quite frozen through."

The boy was being drawn in by her spell, yet the handkerchief in his breast pocket whispered to him, "Beware, beware! Remember you your vows!"

Shaking his head, the boy looked to the low-hung sun. "I will do as I promised, then must hie me home, for the hour grows too late."

The lady pursed her lips. She'd committed to taking the boy to her palace in the mountains and would not be turned aside. "Once you've finished, I'll have you in with me. You'll warm your hands by the burner, and together we'll drive you near your home. I could not let you go with not this least reward."

Though the handkerchief burned at his breast, the boy consented. After all, he was so late and the way so long, it would be an hour before he reached his home on foot. What harm was there in accepting a ride? To refuse such gratitude was surely uncouth.

"Very well," said the boy. He right away bent himself to the task and, with the driver's help, soon had the second ski fixed. No sooner was this done than the driver was helping bustle him into the carriage to seat himself beside the lady. At her feet was a bronze brazier into which she placed lumps of charcoal and lit them.

"Were you sitting this whole time without heat, my lady?"

"Hush, boy, and join me beneath this fur. You must truly be frozen through from your labours."

This he did, and they took off down the path of the wood. Through the carriage window, he shortly saw the lit windows of his own home. Yet wrapped in the lady's fur, close to her body, he'd become colder and colder until his body was frozen solid as a statue. The only part of him that moved still was his heart, warmed by the bloodstained cloth of his vow.

"Fie, fie!" sighed the cloth in a voice not unlike the girl's. "Love be damned in the face of bewitchment."

On and on they sped. Day became night and night warmed back into day, until at last they reached the lady's castle in the mountain. It was carved of black granite blocks, mortared by thick frost, and glazed over with ice. In the courtyard were a dozen statues carved of blue-tinged ice. All of them were comely youths, none unlike the boy himself. Some reached out, others stood with heads bowed, their tears frozen rivulets upon their cheeks.

"Here is your new home," crowed the lady. "My garden of pretty boys now sees its crowning jewel."

The dwarf hauled the boy roughly from the carriage, yet he felt not a bump. His whole body was stiff and numb. He could no more move a muscle than he'd ever been able to fly. His only thought was of his foolishness and of his beloved sister. He feared of never seeing her again.

As he wept and prayed in the prison of his own mind, the west wind swept into the courtyard and whispered past his ear. "Fear not, child," it crooned. "I will send for help."

So saying, it reached into the pocket over his breast and fetched out the bloodstained cloth. Up and over, tumbling round and round, it was tossed on the breeze, out and far away from the wicked lady's palace of ice.

Up and over, round and round, the lace-edged square flew far and away, until it was hung up on a twig in the yard of the girl. She'd gone to meet the boy only to find him missing. She went to his home to ask if he ailed, that she might bring him bone broth to fortify his recovery. She arrived only to find his whole family despairing, for he'd not returned from the wood.

"Did you see him? Do you know what became of him?" For though the youngsters thought themselves quite clever in their deception, both sets of parents were well aware of their meetings in the woods.

The girl did a small curtsy, shaking her head. "No, I don't. We parted when the sun was low, and still I made it home before suppertime, though my house was the farther."

"Oh, child! Go thee home and fetch thy father and mother. Perhaps if we all go our ways through the wood, we will find where he has gone."

She curtsied again, then was off on her heels, running the shortest path through the wood until she came again to her own door. She burst in and told her parents what had happened, all in a great flood of tear-soaked words.

"Oh dear," said Mother.

"Well, well," said Father.

Then the pair soothed their daughter. They banked up the fire and set her by it, cloaked with the best furs and woollen blankets in the house. Then they packed themselves some provisions and bundled up warmly against the cold.

"Stay here, and we'll to the boy's house, there to begin our search. Mind you keep the fire stoked, and do not open the door before our return."

The girl leapt up. "But I would come with you! I must help find my beloved brother!"

Her father was firm. "You will remain. What if he has gotten lost and arrives on our front step with nobody home? Stay and keep watch. Should he come, you may let him inside. Only him and no one else."

She relented, and they left.

After the first hour, the girl was sure she heard some scratching at the door. Frost coated the front window so thickly that she could see nothing through it. So she unlatched the door and peered outside. What should she see but a small white flag flying from a twig. No, not a flag — a lace-edged handkerchief! Heedless of the cold, she ran out into the snow to fetch it. Sure enough, it was stained with blood. It was the very one she'd given to the boy, that he'd tucked so well into the pocket by his breast.

"How has it arrived here?" she inquired.

In reply, the east wind slithered close to her ear. "My cousin, the west wind, has blown it here. Climb on my back and I will take you to his house that you might ask him whence he came by it."

Without her coat, her stockings, or her boots, the girl mounted the east wind's back. No sooner was this done than they were away, high above the forest treetops. Instantly, the girl felt her skin go painfully numb. She shivered violently yet clung hard as she might to the back of the east wind, and to the bloodstained handkerchief she still held.

They flew fast and they flew far, until at last they flew over the horizon, to the home of the west wind. He was crouched by his hearth, brewing a cup of tea and having a terrible time of it. Therefore he greeted his guests sharply, "What do you want? Can you not see the trouble I'm at?"

The east wind replied, "Is that any way to greet your cousin? And see, I've brought you a guest."

The girl slid from the back of the east wind and went directly to the teapot. There she set about fixing a fine tea. Her hands moved swiftly and surely, until she presented the winds with a brimming cup each. The west wind sipped his cup with caution, only to find it tasted so well he could barely believe it.

"Ho, ho, ho!" he gusted, nearly blowing the girl over. "What brings you to my home, other than your fine tea-brewing skills?"

In silence, she held up the bloodstained handkerchief.

"Ah! It is you who seeks the boy. He's in the clutches of a wicked lady who lives in a castle of stone and ice. I will tell you how to rescue him. Only what do you offer me in return?"

The girl, so humble and polite, curtsied and said, "My lord, I would offer my hand in marriage, to stay and make you tea, if I but knew my beloved brother was safe and happy."

The old west wind sat back, stroking his beard. While he considered, his cousin took her leave. "I've places to blow and ships to push across the wide oceans. Take care, young lady, and know that my service is yours to call upon."

She thanked the east wind well, who was then up, away, and gone.

"My cousin is soft-hearted. I will take up your offer of marriage, for surely that was the finest tea ever brewed. To find your boy, you must travel to the wicked lady's castle. It lies high in the mountains, between a pair of crags like the tines of the Devil's pitchfork. My back is too old to carry you there, but likewise is the way too long for you to walk. Therefore, I will give you loan of my horse. He will carry you swiftly there and just as swiftly back, for I will tell him of our engagement. Should you try to steal away home with your lad, the horse will find you and bring you to me."

"Fair enough," agreed the girl.

"As for the means to free him. You have the handkerchief you gave him?"

"I do," she replied.

"Simply weep into it three fresh tears, then place it back in his breast pocket. This will warm his heart and break the spell that holds him fast."

"What if the wicked lady should come upon me?"

"If she should catch you, she'll turn you into a hen and feed you to her dwarf. But she'll not catch you if you wear this fur of mine. It will make you invisible to her eye and keep you warm on your journey besides."

She accepted the fur be placed around her shoulders, then took his hand to help her mount the horse.

"Grip tightly onto his mane, for he travels very quickly."

This she did.

"Go swiftly and return directly. Already I long for another cup of that fine tea!" So saying, he smote the horse on his flank, sending it off like a bolt of lightning.

Moments later, they stood together outside the wicked lady's courtyard on the mountainside.

"I'll wait here," said the horse. "Hurry and save your boy, for my master expects us back soon."

At the horse's words, the girl fell to her knees in tears. "Oh, why have I made that promise to marry that old west wind? As sure as I want my brother to be free, I also long to see my family again."

The horse was moved by her lament and asked her, "Have you still the cloth stained with your own blood?"

She reached into the pocket of her smock and pulled it forth.

To this, the horse said, "Once you've waked his heart with the first cloth, weep four tears onto the second, and use this to bathe the boy's eyes. Not only will he wake then but will recognize your face, which he would not do otherwise. Take his hand, and you'll be whisked off home. There you may take proper leave of your family that you won't pine for them when you're wed. When this is done, I will come for you and bear you to my master."

The girl threw her arms about the horse's neck and thanked him well. Then she crept into the courtyard to free the boy. Into the lace-edged square, she wept three tears and tucked the handkerchief into his breast pocket. On the instant, a blush of pink warmth rose up his neck and across his face. Then into the second cloth wept she four tears. She brushed this over his left eye, then his right. When they opened and lit upon her, he cried out from joy and caught her up in an embrace.

The moment before they disappeared, the wicked lady stood at her door and saw that the boy was released. In her frustration, she screamed so strongly that she brought the whole castle down upon her head. Deprived of life, her spell on all the other statues was broken. They stood milling about the courtyard while the boy and girl were whisked away to their own homes.

By the hearth of her parents' house, where the pair wept for the lost boy and their own lost daughter, she suddenly appeared. They ceased their lament and embraced her warmly.

"Do not be too joyful, for I cannot stay. I've sold my freedom for that of my brother and will be married to the west wind. I came only to say goodbye and that I'll be well cared for."

Her mother wept again, while her father nodded his head. "A deal struck is a deal kept. You must surely fulfill your promise."

No sooner had he spoken than the horse landed on their front step. The horse, seeing the sorrow on her parents' faces, was once again piteous toward her.

"My child, lay the west wind's fur across my back. I'll take it to him and say that you were caught by the wicked lady. In your haste to warm the boy, you draped the fur upon him. Thence were changed into a hen and eaten. He will sorrow but let you alone."

Again, she thanked the horse whole-heartedly. In repayment, she told the horse how to make such fine tea.

"At least the west wind will have that of me," she said.

"You're a good girl with a noble heart. The man who has you for his wife is well blessed."

The horse was away in the blink of an eye. Then upon the step appeared the boy. On his face was a look of purest ardour.

"My sister! Without you, I'd be yet frozen, far from my family — and from you. How can I ever repay you?"

"I am repaid already, for my brother is home."

They embraced for a long moment, then made a plan to meet the next morning in the wood between their houses.

FAMILY TIES

WHEN WE REACHED HOME, I was still a bit gimped from my legs, though I was walking more or less like an able-bodied human being again. The moment we got to the long drive from the road, I felt like a pin in a map to mark a point of origin. Home. Trying on the word in my mind was similar to digging an old sweatshirt from the bottom of a forgotten drawer: comfy and kind of smelly.

It was also a bit like recognizing someone familiar who's wearing a disguise. The edges were fuzzed over with wild growth of strange plants. Even so in the full daylight, I could see the mailbox and the fence post I'd carved the word "fuck" into when I was mad at Dad. I pointed it out to Olivia, chuckling at the foolishness of youth. A thought occurred. "That reminds me: Did you ever find Dad?"

Olivia's expression darkened. She didn't look angry so much as sad, but anger wasn't absent. It made me uncomfortable enough to start babbling.

"It's just, you said you'd tell me later. Back at the tavern? I think. The days have kind of blurred together, and I can't really make out what was a dream and what wasn't —"

"You talk too much" was all she said, lifting a tangle of vines so I could limp under them.

On the other side, I stopped walking and took her by the shoulders. "You don't have to be weird about this. All cryptic and shit. You can just go ahead and tell me. Did you find him or not? It's okay if he died. He would've been, what, seventy-something now?"

She stepped away from me, my hand sliding off her. When she turned to look at me, her expression was soured by bitterness. "No, Jesse. It's not 'okay' that he's dead. You're all weepy for your dumb dog. You don't know what grief is, okay?"

Olivia stormed off, leaving me surrounded by hip-deep tangles. I went after her, but the way was slow going. I caught up with her at the door to Dad's workshop. She was holding the door handle like she'd fall down if she let go. Her knuckles were stark against a paling tan, and her face was grey.

"Jeez, Olivia —"

"Is this okay, Jesse?" she asked, her voice trembling. "You're older — you tell me."

She yanked the door along its rail. The wheels, so weathered and ungreased, shrieked their way over the rust-scabbed rod for about a foot before one jumped off completely. Before she could rage-hulk the door into the bushes, I stepped forward and put a hand between her shoulder blades.

"It's good enough," I reassured her.

Most of the windows were smashed out of the frames, so the only obstacle for the daylight was the growth that had crept up the wall. Through this filter of leafless twigs, there was enough to see by. I poked my head in through the gap of the open door. For the most part, it looked like Dad's workshop always had: plywood-topped tables made of two-by-fours lining the walls, pegboards with the outlines of tools drawn on.

"A place for everything, and everything in its place." I breathed deep as I took it all in. Smells of sawdust, lightly dampened by the exposure of an uninsulated building, and of something else. A strange tang crept in at the nose and lingered on the tongue.

That same breath was knocked out of me when I finally saw it. When I did see it, I was at least as shocked that it took so long to register as I was by the sight itself. An old oak office chair on casters sat to one side of a heap of bones. There were some rotting threads of denim and flannel mixed in, but most of the clothing was long gone. Directly above the bones was a dusty length of double-thick nylon cord tied into a blue and yellow noose.

"Fuck."

"That's right, fuck. Mum took us away from him, and he killed himself. How 'okay' is that?"

"Jesus, Olivia …"

"It's true! Just look — look at what that bitch did to him!"

I caught my breath. There was something that finally made a terrible kind of sense. "Olivia," I said, "I need you to listen to me."

She turned away to head for the house, so I put a hand on either side of her face and pulled her back to me. "Listen! Mum said something to me before she died, something that didn't mean much until just now."

"What?" she growled, swiping my hands away, though momentarily relenting.

"Leaving didn't make Dad kill himself." I had to stop for a moment, taking a few swallows of cold air. Before I went on, I looked Olivia in the eyes. "We left because Dad killed himself."

THE DAY MUM DIED was a lot like any other day Underground. We'd moved to a double residence across the hall from the Metzlers a couple months after Olivia left. The closet I came to call home was on the Metzlers' side of the hall, two doors down.

The tilapia farm was still on shaky footing, and with only the two of us, upkeeping a whole camper didn't make sense. Cost more than we could earn to maintain, that was certain. I'd gone looking for work and found the Heap downtown. Mum followed shortly after, and we set up shop.

At first, Mum had done some reconditioning on the better things I came across at the scrap. For a small amount of labour, we could sometimes double what a thing was worth in trade. A bit of elbow grease or a dot or two of solder could fix what was broken. We got solvent from a woman who collected food scraps from all the neighbours, fermented them in a five-gallon plastic bucket, then distilled out the white spirit using an old chemistry set and a fan run by a stationary bicycle. Like Mrs. Metzler, she was cheerful and broadly built. Prairie stock, Mum said. The phrase offered vague notions of Eastern European immigrants posed before fields of head-high wheat. An image from a history textbook.

The solder was reclaimed much the way Asa went about it. A thin Japanese man of indeterminate age lived in a dead-end culvert toward the southern edge of the neighbourhood. He traded us for textiles or for glossy magazine paper.

Like I say, we'd been settling in. Stella and my mum got on well enough to be sisters. Fought like it on occasion. They'd disagree about something and get their dander up. Days passed under the grim pall of silent treatment, until Mr. Metzler would come stumping up to our door to invite us to dinner. Just like that, all was forgiven.

Mum seemed to find the cycle comfortable, if not comforting. When she came back from a row with Stella, she wore the same dark expression that Olivia did when she was truly, exceptionally pissed off. But it was gone within the hour, or by morning. Like a cloud foreboding rain, it was impermanent.

They'd had a fight the day before she got sick. It was a bad one. I'd heard Mrs. Metzler shout, "And don't you dare come back, you goddamned ingrate!" The statement was punctuated by a dented can hitting the wall beside our door. It was a 'shine cup, glass being expensive and hard to come by and plastic too delicate for high-octane juice. Mum stepped on the thing with her boot, crushing it flat, before coming inside.

"Sounds like she's in one of her moods again," I offered.

Mum snorted and stomped off to her bed, drawing the curtain closed. I shrugged and went back to my book. The cover was worn so I couldn't make out what it was called, but it featured a young man named Paul and a planet entirely covered by sand.

"You finished cleaning that batch of salvage?" Mum inquired from within her nest of blankets.

"Yeah. Why?"

"Take 'em down to trade and don't let them fleece you like last time. Ten tokens, at least."

I sat up. It was well past suppertime. Not that the post would be closed, but I usually did a drop off on my way to the scrap. "You mean in the morning?" I asked.

"I mean now, Jesse. Right now."

In all my time, I'd not heard her voice as it was then. Not angry, not sad, not exactly. A bit tired maybe, but mostly resigned. That's what I came to realize, anyway. Point is, it made me want to stay. Something in that voice spoke of danger. At the same time, it was a voice that brooked no argument.

"Up and at 'em, Vanderchuck," I muttered, gathering the salvage into an old canvas hockey bag.

Before I left, I hung by the door. I wanted to say something, to ask her if I could stay instead, or if there was something else I could do. Make a cup of tea. Anything but leave. Nothing came out. All the words crowded together, jamming in my throat, leaving me mute.

Just beyond the edge of this held breath, I thought I heard her crying. My face flushed red and I took off. Being in proximity to another human being's strong emotions felt taboo. I'd do the trade, come back, and she'd have herself together. Maybe I'd be able to sweet-talk a dram of what passed for wine in the Underground. Take out a loan on some cake. A treat would make everything better. It was what Dad would've done.

I was back in no time, with a pair of molasses cookies carefully folded in a clean handkerchief and tucked in the breast pocket of my overshirt, and ten tokens jangling in my jeans. Once I'd explained things, Reg at the post said I'd owe him the rest, but he was doing me a solid on account of my mum being poorly. Soon as I stepped through the door, something felt amiss. I'd expected silence, but the silence of sleep or possibly of muffled sobs. The texture of this silence was all wrong.

"Mum? I'm back. I got cookies."

I hung the hockey bag up by the door and crossed to the curtain hung 'round Mum's bed. After a long, uncomfortable moment, I knocked on the bed frame. There was a groan from beyond the curtain. Then a wet, spluttering cough and a laboured breath. A cold fist of panic tightened around my stomach.

"Mum, you okay?"

Pulling the curtain aside, I saw the soles of her bare feet. They stuck out, blotchy pink and white, from beneath a stack of blankets. They kind of tensed and arched downward as the lumpy pile of bedclothes was lifted up. At the other end of the bed, her neck crooked at a painful angle, Mum's face shone pale and slick from the covers. The whites of her eyes were webbed red with straining capillaries.

After far too long, it finally dawned on me that she was having some kind of seizure. I rushed to the head of the bed, trying to remember any first aid. I noticed I was kneeling in cold vomit. That indicated this had been happening for a while, maybe since I'd left.

"Hey, Mum. It's me. I'm here," I said as soothingly as I could muster.

Her body jolted again, back arched like a strung bow, fists clenching and unclenching, eyes rolling back. They made contact but didn't see me. From her throat came tiny creaking noises. Part of me knew I should get somebody to help. Mr. Metzler or the barber — the closest we had to a doctor, or more accurately a surgeon. A child's superstition kept me by her side instead. Because I also knew, with a child's certainty, that the moment I left would be the moment she died. I stayed, and I held her hand, and I waited for it to be over.

When the tremors stopped, I edged to the pump and filled a bottle with water. Never took my eyes from her the whole time, which meant I spilled at least as much as I got in the bottle. Then back at her side, trying to prop her up.

She was pale and grey, her skin clammy with cold sweat. I put the bottle on a shelf above the headboard. Then levering one arm and shoulder under her back, I lifted her so I could shove balled up pillows, clothing, and blankets until she was nearly sitting up. Her lids drooped over eyes that wouldn't focus, and a thin thread of drool leaked from lips that hung slack. Gentler tremors rippled through her arms and legs, like a marionette whose strings were being jiggled.

"Oo … Ool-ah …"

I wasn't sure if she was trying to speak, or if the dance of tremors was just shimmying through her throat. I held her head as I tipped the tiniest sip of water into her mouth. When she seemed to swallow that without choking, I poured a tiny bit more.

"Do you think you could eat something?" I fished the cookies from my pocket. Thankfully, they'd stayed in the hankie, because they'd gotten smashed to pieces at some point. Mum tried to pick up a lump of cookie, but her muscles were still feeling their oats and wouldn't obey. Frustration began building in her eyes.

"Hey, it's okay. Let me." I found a piece big enough to pick up but small enough that I couldn't see her choking on it. "Open wide!"

That went well enough that I gave her a bit more. Some more water, some more cookie. After a while, her arms and legs fell still.

"Feeling any better?"

Mum squeezed her eyes closed tight and nodded. She even managed to pat my arm with a hand weak enough to belong to a ghost.

"Okay. Lie back here and try to rest. I'm just going across the hall for a sec. You feel a spell coming on again, you just —" I paused, looking around. My eyes landed on a multibit screwdriver with a handle of smoky black plastic. I picked it up and folded Mum's fingers around it.

"You feel like you're gonna seize or spew or anything, just use this to bang on the bed frame. Or throw it on the ground or something. Make a noise, and I'll come running. Got it?"

Another nod.

"Good stuff."

I stood up. The tokens jangled in my pocket. Two would get the stalest of dry rations, another two got an override for extra water or fuel (not both). That left six to pay the sawbones to come, but none for treatment. Assuming he could do anything but shrug and advise me to pray. As though reading my mind, Mum tugged at my pant leg and pointed to a rusty coffee can on a shelf in the kitchen. When I peeled off the red plastic lid, there were seven more tokens inside.

"Ssssaving them fo-or your birthdaaay," she croaked. When she smiled, half of her mouth pulled into a grit-toothed rictus while the other half stayed slack.

I made myself smile back, swallowing the horror and dread rising like bile in my throat. "They'll be plan B, then. Just relax. I'm going to have a chat with Mr. Metzler." I put the coffee can back on the shelf and hustled out of the room. Every step felt further weighted by a burden of illness, until I was sure I was bent double stepping out the door.

Once in the hall, I straightened. Free of the room, of that twisted version of my mother's face, I was tempted by a giddy impulse that told me to run. Run far, run fast, run away. Several deep breaths were enough to walk me back from the edge of that cliff. It was another minute before I felt composed enough to approach the Metzlers' door.

"D'you know what fucking time it is?" His face appeared like a big, beefy moon, with only a dim light in the room behind him.

"Who is it?" called Stella.

"Vanderchuck's kid," he called back. To me, he said, "What d'you want?"

Clearing my throat, I said, "Mr. Metzler, I think my mum's sick."
Then I threw up on his door.

"WHAT'S THE POINT of all this, Jesse? I thought this was about
Mum's deathbed speech. So say it already."

"I'm old, Olivia. And that's not how memory works. Shut up
and listen."

SHE LINGERED FOR NEARLY two weeks. Seizures wracked her
body with increasing regularity. The barber came and witnessed
one. Then he shook his head and advised us to send away for a
proper medic, if we could afford it. I replied that if we could afford
a medic, we wouldn't have wasted his time.

Our neighbourhood barber was typically surly at the best of
times but never more so than when performing his sawbones
routine. Mum had said it was a reference to an old television
show that her sister watched all the time. Instead of giving me
what-for, he clapped me on the shoulder with something that
seemed like sympathy.

"Keep that sense of humour, kid. You're gonna need it down here."
Then he left.

They all left. I was alone with Mum for days. She'd developed
a cough that made it hard for her to take in food. No sooner was
the empty spoon pulled from her mouth than its contents were
sprayed out by a fit of growling wet coughing. As a result, she lost

a lot of weight, even in that short span. I could carry her in my arms to and from the tin washtub in the kitchen. It was little more effort than carrying Doggo.

One morning, I just sat beside her bed, my head on the mattress. I was running low on will, we were running short on tokens, and the neighbours were running short on charity. Mum's breathing sounded like lengths of corroded chain being hauled out of a swamp, all loud rattles and damp slapping.

And I felt like I was standing at the foot of a tall dam made of salt and it was dissolving. Eroding. I didn't know how much longer it would hold back the tidewater. I only hoped it was long enough to see this to the bitter end.

This. Mum's death.

I was just waiting. Maybe we both were. Counting down the clock, alone together in our dingy little room for two. Sitting there, half dozing, I was woken by her hand gripping mine. It was strong enough to hurt. I sat up.

"Hey, what's wrong? What's up?"

She sputtered for a moment, getting frustrated at herself and making it worse.

"Calm down. Take it slow."

Mum closed her eyes and took two deep, deliberate breaths. When she opened her eyes, the pain in them hit me like an actual slap in the face. Some instinct made my body shrink back, but she held me fast by the hand. Pulled me closer.

"I was wrong," she said. Her words were slurred, but I heard her clearly in spite of it. "We shouldn't have come here." Tears welled and dropped from those tortured eyes. My petty complaints were shamed to insignificance by the exhaustion I saw in them — years of toil and sacrifice, of compromise and ingratitude. I saw all of this, and I watched it rise up and disappear like smoke.

Her grip tightened another notch. This time, I gripped back.

"And I'm sorry about your dad," she said. "I should've let you say good-bye, but I thought you were too young. I didn't think you'd understand." The end of her sentence was pinched and twisted by a rising fit. She turned her head so she wouldn't cough into my face. When the fit was over and she turned back to face me, the pillow and her chin were smeared with bloody sputum.

"Fuck! Fuck, fuck, no," I sputtered. I wanted to get a cloth to wipe her face. I wanted to hug her and beg her not to leave me all alone. I wanted to apologize for any and all bratty teenage transgressions of which I was guilty. At the same time, I would not — could not — let go of her hand.

"Mum, no."

"Tell Olivia, when you see her." With her free hand, she reached across and brushed my hair back from my forehead.

WE WERE STILL STANDING in the ruin of Dad's workshop, a little ways from each other. Olivia hung her head and picked at a loose tail of yarn that hung from the end of her mitten.

"Don't do that, you'll unravel the whole thing."

"Shut up."

I guess the story took longer than I'd thought it would. The sun was high enough now to throw most of the room into shadow.

"We should bring in some firewood. Or something. Right?"

She said nothing. My story had woven a spell to make her six years old again: stubborn and silent in the face of strong emotion. I tried the only counterspell I could think of to rouse her out of herself.

"Hey, Liverwurst."

"Don't call me that!"

It worked. I grinned. "What're you gonna do, tell on me?"

The joke was dark, but it broke the tension. We ended up collapsing on each other, our faces wet with tears of release, our ribs aching. It might have been the first good laugh either of us had had in years.

"I'll grab some firewood," she said when the laughter had faded. "You head inside and chase out any raccoons that might've got in."

I feigned surprise. "That a regular problem?"

"Regular as a cow on a high-fibre diet," she replied.

WATCH OUT FOR THE ICY PATCH

IT WAS GETTING DARK and Olivia wasn't back yet. We'd hit the depths of midwinter and it was horrendously cold. I wasn't worried exactly — there were times she'd be gone for days — but the prospect of being alone right then was unpleasant. There was an unshakeable funk on my shoulders. Being sick, being lonely, being old, and ruminating about the past. Everything had just kind of mounted up. Pair that with a dose of cabin fever, and it was a perfect storm of suck. At that moment, I wanted nothing more than somebody to play Scrabble with. I settled for chucking another log on the fire.

"Don't be sad, Food Bringer."

I started. Hearing voices was not a good sign. Especially voices that belonged to the dead. Holding still, I listened hard for the least signal that Olivia was nearby, playing a prank in incredibly bad taste. Nothing but the wind creaking around the roof. At times, it gusted up hard, blowing across the top of the chimney to make a deep hooting sound.

When I concluded I was alone, I let go of the breath I hadn't realized I was holding in. From close by my ear, Doggo said, "Can I get under your blanket? It's cold and scary out here."

Before I could stop myself, I leapt up off the couch. The blankets fell to the floor. I shrieked to an empty house. In reply, the wind continued its jug-band solo across the chimney.

"Don't do this," I begged aloud, but barely. "It's not fair. He's gone!"

"Who's gone, Food Bringer?" His voice was so close, it seemed to come from my ear. Not inside, exactly, but not outside, either. "Is it time to eat?"

On the verge of breaking down completely, my haunting was interrupted by a loud bang from the back door being kicked open. Creaks and heavy thumps on the floor were followed by the damp thud of a fresh kill landing on the kitchen table.

"Jesse?" called Olivia. "If you're awake, come help dress this buck."

The whole house was dim. I'd lit no lanterns or candles, so the only light came from a few slanting rays that reached through the kitchen window. Before Olivia closed the door behind her, I could see past her shoulder that it was starting to snow.

"Thought you were off on one of your wanderings," I said, lighting a hurricane lamp we ran off refined animal fat. The flame burned lower overall than it did on kerosene, but the glass chimney kept it protected from the drafts that pervaded the old house.

In reply, Olivia gestured to the carcass she'd slung on the table. "Would've been quicker, but my aim was off. Hadda follow this one over hell's half acre till he tired out, so I could finish him off."

She tossed her hunting knife into the sink, its blade dark with blood, along with her similarly stained mitts. Then she continued methodically divesting herself of no fewer than seven layers of clothing, down to a sagging set of trapdoor long johns the colour of an old dishrag.

"I heard Doggo," I blurted. I was desperate for reassurance, to hear her dismiss the fancy as the sickness talking. That there was nothing to worry about.

"What, like walking around the house?" she asked, to my disappointment.

Mild shock at her indulgence held my tongue for a moment. "No," I explained. "Talking. To me. Like he's alive."

She looked at me askance. Oh, now she was gonna get skeptical.

In response, I got indignant. "Don't give me side-eye. I'm serious."

Olivia crossed the room, put her hands on my shoulders, and looked up into my face. "Jesse, I've been meaning to say this for a while. Listen to me carefully: dogs can't talk. Okay?"

"Doggo could talk, Olivia. I heard him all the time."

"What about other people?" she asked.

"What do you mean?"

She sighed and guided me into the living room. She was silent as she sat me back on the couch and bundled the blankets around me. Then she crouched by the wood stove and stoked up the fire.

"'What about other people' as in did anyone else hear Doggo talk? Did they comment or say something like, 'Holy shit! A talking dog!'?" She picked up the poker and jostled the partially burned logs into a better configuration.

I scrunched down into my woolly cocoon on the couch. The conversation was beginning to make me uncomfortable. Much as I might've questioned my sanity from the safety of my own head, it was decidedly unmooring to hear someone else do the same.

Neither of us spoke for a time. Meanwhile, the wind blew up a hootenanny that only ended when Olivia damped down the flue.

"Well?" she asked, finally.

"No, not really." I had to admit. "Not as such. That I can recall."

"When you heard Doggo talk to you for the first time, didn't it strike you as odd that a dog was talking?"

I sat for a long while without answering. Of course it had, but then I'd dismissed it as some fluke of life in the future. Just something that happened, like phosphorescent forests of fungi or the instinct to check a stranger's hands for weapons.

"This is dumb," I said. "He was just a talking dog in a post-apocalyptic world. What's the big deal?"

Olivia shook her head. "I get it," she said. "For a while, after I found Dad, I heard him. Not just his voice. I heard him walking around the house. That weird frog croak thing he used to do in his throat."

There was another one of those pauses that seemed to plague our conversations. She got up and sat on the other end of the couch, burrowing her feet under the edge of my blankets.

"I was alone," she explained. "I was afraid. I'd spent a few weeks trying to find this place, dodging bandits, getting lost. Because I didn't know where I was going exactly. I had to look at maps, when I could find them. Ask directions when I came across somebody and hope to God they didn't try anything. I only had the name of the town, and lots of folks who might've known the way were either dead or gone Underground. Getting to town got me close. Not everyone I met was helpful. Or kind."

She exhaled through her teeth before going on. "So I finally got here, but I didn't go in the workshop right away. I only went in to look for some tools I needed, and then … Jesse, I felt so guilty. *We left him, we left him*, I kept telling myself. I got so mad, I almost burned the whole place down. I was about to, just torch it and move on. That's when I started hearing him. And I couldn't."

"Maybe you should have." My words fell heavily as stones into a still pond.

Olivia shrugged. "I'm just saying I understand. I don't remember much about how things might have been before, so maybe I'm used to being afraid. I heard him for a while, and then I stopped. Maybe you'll stop hearing Doggo when you stop feeling guilty about his death."

"But I heard him when he was alive. Maybe I'm just crazy. What if I'm crazy, Olivia?"

She laughed. "You think this world is sane?" Then she reached over and started rubbing my back, between the shoulder blades.

"That calms you down, not me."

"It calms everyone down," she replied, brooking no argument. "Anyway, even if you're crazy, just promise me one thing."

I tried not to, but my eyes slid closed and I let myself relax. "What's that?" I muttered.

"Don't axe murder me in my sleep, okay?"

I nodded slowly. "Got it. Only axe murder during waking hours."

"You're such a shit," she told me.

"It runs in the family," I replied.

ANOTHER FINE MESS

"THE CHARGE IS RECKLESS endangerment of a community by ailment and communication of disease resulting in death. The truth of this charge has been proved to the satisfaction of this court, and you are found guilty. The sentence of banishment without parole will be carried out immediately."

The scent of cooking meat was enough of a rarity that it was acrid even in my memory. Or dream. Or whatever this was. The knowledge that the meat was my own flesh was something I tried to keep from my conscious mind. Being kicked out of Underground permanently was bad enough. No need to make things worse by upchucking on the brand-wielder's shoes.

I did throw up, but that was later. Doggo and I were alone beyond the city gate, which was no more than a derelict access hatch behind one of the towers. The door slammed in our faces with an echoing metallic clang. And that was that.

Like an idiot, I scratched at an itch on my face. On my newly burned and branded face. Instead of relief, I felt a round patch of wet emptiness as the barely formed scab came away in my hand. The emptiness filled with stinging pain when a drying breeze blew across the wetness.

That's when I threw up. Doggo was thrilled.

"Oh, thank you, Food Bringer! Your miracles are truly great!"

Disgusted, I nearly served up seconds. Instead, I managed, "Don't mention it, Doggo. Seriously, please don't."

For hours after getting the boot, I sat in silent self-pity. Doggo joined me once he'd finished ridding the world of my stomach contents. He licked his chops heartily, then sat down for an enthusiastic crotch cleaning.

"This is a big tunnel, isn't it?"

"It's not a tunnel, Doggo. We're outside."

He scratched at the corner of his eye with one outstretched back claw. "What's outside?"

"It's where we've been going this whole time. Where my sister is. I think."

"Oh. Good."

We sat in silence a moment longer before he continued. "When is she coming by?"

I picked up a handful of gravel and started skimming stones, one by one, through the tall grass.

"She isn't. We have to go find her. If she's still alive."

Doggo rolled onto his back and lifted his front leg, giving me the side-eye stare of full submission. It was a look he used when he was about to say something he thought would make me mad. "Then, Food Bringer, why do we sit here?"

THE DOOMSDAY BOOK OF FAIRY TALES

Much as it pained me to admit, he had a point. Who knows
— without the simple questions of his tiny brain, we might never
have got going. Maybe I would've just sat my stupid ass down in
front of the Underground gate, locked forever behind me, and let
myself get eaten by a mountain lion.

The sun was about two-thirds of the way across the sky.
Everything was bright and difficult to look at. Still I scampered
up onto an old wrecked car so overgrown with vegetation it was
practically buried. From there, I could get a read on the direction
we needed to go and where we might set up camp. North-ish from
our position was a set of concrete walls jutting out of the grass. It
looked close enough to reach well before dark.

As I got myself down from my perch, I noted how easily and
well these skills came back to me. Long-dormant instincts floated
up from some forgotten well to bob on the surface of my brain.
Beneath the throbbing of my face, I was almost proud.

"Let's get a motor on, bud. We've got a fair stretch of ground
to cover."

Doggo leapt to his feet, tongue lolling, and trotted after me,
close at my heel.

CALL ME MUAD'DIB

THE WEATHER HAD CHANGED over thirty-five years. Winter still came, and it was harsher than ever, but it only lasted a month or two. Either side of it, what used to be spring and autumn, were seasons of powerful winds and torrential rains. Rivers and lakes filled up, turning brown hillsides green overnight. Then when the rains dried up, the winds tore away the dead and dying leaves, twigs and trees, blowing seeds far and wide.

But summer was the worst season of all. Hot doesn't fully encompass what it was like, nor does dry. Winter was cold, sure, but there was nearly always another blanket, a spare sweater, a log on the fire. Not to mention that water was plentiful, albeit frozen. Summertime was like the whole area got teleported to a desert.

Strange new succulent species unfurled from the roots of trees that went dormant for the dry season. They rolled their dusty green spear-shaped arms skyward, like reaching tentacles. When droughts reached their worst stages, we'd milk those alien plants for their stored water.

Everything became uncomfortable and gritty. There wasn't a drop of water to waste on washing ourselves or clothing — not that we wore much more than personal modesty dictated. Six months of the year was eaten up by this torment, where food was scarce and there was only so much clothing to be taken off.

Olivia was used to the weather. But then she'd been at this longer than I had. I'd grown old, I reminded myself, and set in my ways. She had no hang-ups about things which were necessary for survival. It wasn't that I wanted to be a prude. By the same token, I wasn't that keen on seeing my sister in the altogether, no matter how practical it was. As a concession, she made a cover-up she'd wear in my presence.

My first summer outside was a slap in the face. I'd faced the relatively mild autumn, followed by a frigid but survivable winter. Even the stormy spring had a certain thrilling charm to it — like a moody mate who stomps through the house, then weeps before gently embracing you. The transition seemed to happen overnight, too. We went to bed in springtime and woke up on Arrakis, the desert planet. I told Olivia I half expected giant armoured worms to break through the surface of the earth.

"What are you talking about?" She squinted at me, machete poised midchop into a cactus stem.

I ducked my head, abashed. "You were never much of a reader."

She shrugged. "Didn't see much point. And it's not like we could afford to keep books just for reading."

Fair point.

We got ourselves into a rhythm of waking early to drink and gather food, then sleeping through the hottest part of the day, waking again shortly before sunset, then sleeping through the night. We moved as little as possible and conserved everything. Water was sipped. Food wasn't chewed and swallowed; it was gently and slowly mumbled until it disappeared.

While dozing, I found myself thinking of the year-round cool of the Underground. The tunnels gently breathing. Moisture sweating from walls of concrete, steel, or rammed earth. It wasn't pleasant, but it was better than the hellscape. As I mused, my thoughts would return to the lift-chamber hospice. Intrusively, the smell of that place would suddenly well in my nostrils as though I'd been physically transported there. Sometimes, I could even hear the crunch of a sheet of milky plastic as I turned my head to cough.

Doggo was conspicuously absent from these daydreams.

Toward the tail end of the season, what used to be September-ish, when the heat was merely intolerable, we'd start a garden. We'd hack down a patch of land over a series of sweaty and exhausting mornings. The dry grasses were packed into pucks and treated with animal fat and tree resin for fire starters. Then we'd turn over the soil by cutting a series of thin trenches and collapsing the sides down into them. It wouldn't do to expose too much moisture to the air — the topsoil would dry up and blow away. To help prevent this, we'd spray the earth down with a mixture of aged urine and compost tea. We did this several times over a course of days until the soil was nearly black.

Finally, one evening, we'd plant the patch. Olivia had seeds, dried and sorted from previous seasons. Under her direction, we'd divide up the patch and sow according to need. Corn amid beans so they could grow together, the vines climbing up the stalks. Large leafy things went around the roots to shade out weeds and keep in moisture. We'd put some seeds lower down with other seeds on top, phasing growth through the short season. Then we'd set snares around the perimeter of the patch. The urine we'd used for fertilizer kept most pests away, but the braver ones would do for winter meat. Rabbit jerky makes a decent stew.

BUT THAT FIRST SUMMER morning stole my breath away. It was aggressively hot, and the change of weather had been so immediate that I was utterly unprepared. Before nightfall, I'd suffered heatstroke. Twice.

"You need to sit down before you kill yourself," advised Olivia.

Being too delirious to speak, I could only nod in agreement.

My clothes were soaked through with sweat, though my body had reached a point where sweating was no longer an option. Instead, I quaked with fevered chills, my teeth chattering like a novelty toy. Olivia had to peel away the layers of sodden fabric, hanging them up as they came free. When they were dry, they were almost solidly stiff with salt. With my skin exposed, she wiped me down with a mixture of water and vinegar. Then she let me sip at an infusion of wintergreen that cooled my parched insides.

When my mind wandered back to sense from its time away, I vowed, "One of these days, I'm gonna take care of you."

"Shut up and keep still" was her reply.

I tried to sit up but was instantly overcome by an intense spinning sensation the moment my head lifted. After fighting back an accompanying wave of nausea, I went on. "No, I mean it. I'm the eldest. I should be the one who knows stuff, who guides you through the world."

She helped me into a more upright position by wedging her rucksack under my shoulders, then gave me another cup of tea to sip at. With barely a breath between, she said, "Shut up. And stay still."

YEAR AFTER YEAR, summer continued to sneak up on me. I'd fall into the trap of being lulled by spring's syncopated rhythms. Then one day, I'd get slapped awake by ghostly hand made of white-hot bricks, its shape roughly described by a shimmer in the air.

In the run-up to the tipping point, there had been talk of sending people to Mars. The idea was that once we ruined our first planet, we could just move to the next one over and start ruining it. The notion, like all notions intended to solve our many problems, sparked endless debate. And so the result was no action at all. No result but sore feelings and bruised egos.

With summers as they'd become, we might as well have colonized Mercury. I'd read that because it was so much closer to the sun, its surface was hot enough to melt aluminum. There were summer days here on Earth when I thought how lovely it would've been to hop over to Mercury to cool off. Dip my toes in some molten aluminum.

I told this theory to Olivia one drowsy afternoon at the farmhouse.

"There's no point being bitter toward those people now," she said. "They're probably all dead, or will be soon." Leave it to Olivia to sum things up succinctly.

She was right. This was the world we had ended up with. There was less of a chance to make a new start on another planet than there had been. It was up to us to keep on or to die trying.

Still, I could've done without the fucking heat.

Another Crack at King Nutkin

The king of the squirrels pined for want of company. No wife warmed his bed, nor did any children scamper and play throughout the palace. Day on day, he sighed in his throne room until his advisers became quite vexed.

"If we do not find a friend for the king, he's sure to waste away for want of companionship."

King Nutkin agreed and begged his court to search the kingdom high and low.

"Whomsoever becomes my friend shall find himself in possession of hereditary title, the land it provides, and all ensuing gifts therein. Even if he stays but a day, I would know the blessing of companionship before I die."

Thereupon all the court set about casting the word far and wide: a friend for the king was a duke for life and all his lineage. Many lined up outside the castle gate. Few were seen. Fewer still had any hope of being gifted the king's favour.

Things continued in this vein for some time, until finally every creature in the kingdom had been to Nutkin's court. Save one. Here it was: a great shambling beast covered in dirty hair that hung limply from long limbs. This horror came knocking at the king's door, yet knew nothing about His Majesty's search nor of the royal decree. It came only seeking succour from its suffering.

"Please," it begged of the guards. "I want only some food and a night's lodging, for I am utterly alone in the world."

"No doubt, cur," said the first guard. "I dread even to look upon you."

"And I to smell you," chimed the second.

Their laughter only subsided when they noticed the creature's tears falling upon the polished gate stones. It was pitiable enough that they summoned a page to fetch the grand vizier.

In the tradition of grand viziers everywhere, this one was long and lean and scheming. He was a stoat with his whiskers waxed into a drooping mustache, and he wore long robes of woven thistledown. Approaching the beast at the gate, the vizier raised his nose heavenward, spying 'round its side with one tar-drop eye.

"What have we here?" purred the stoat. "Some derelict with hand outstretched, I wager."

The first guard ducked his head. "Begging your pardon, Your Grace. This … errr … creature said it's alone in the wide world and wants only some food and some company."

By this, the vizier took it that the beast had come to fulfill the king's decree. The vizier saw his chance to usurp Nutkin and succeed his throne with his own line. Surely the very sight of this creature would drive the king to madness, if it did not kill him outright. In an instant, the vizier was all smiles. He reached out to the beast one delicately clawed hand, saying, "We are honoured that you have come, friend. We were despairing that the king should never find a friend in this wide world. I suspect you are just the one to salve his loneliness and save the realm."

The beast was far too retiring to correct such a splendid courtier, so it simply took the hand it was offered and followed in silence.

I SPENT THREE DAYS in deadlock with this tale before I gave up. Olivia had gone out. The old farmhouse creaked around me like I was a hermit crab carrying a garbage can.

Who am I even telling these to? I demanded of myself. *Why bother wasting my breath? What little I have left.*

"What happens next, Food Bringer?"

At least that time, I had the presence of mind to be shocked that a dog was talking to me, even if it was only because he was dead.

BRIEF REFLECTION

I THOUGHT I FELT old years ago, but I feel agedness gnawing through me more and more. When I picture myself, I no longer see that long-lost twenty-year-old face looking out from an elder body. I don't see any recognizable face at all. All I see is a shrinking, shriveled self, sitting up or splayed out in front of me. Growing tired of the passing years. The place where a face would be is too shadowed to discern features. Indistinct. Empty.

A dark hole staring out of a broken mirror.

POST-APOCALYPTIC DRINKING GAME

OLIVIA AND I WERE lying down in the shade under the stairs. The day was brutally hot, even for summer. Doing anything more than we were would've resulted in being forced to the ground by an invisible hand made of scalding noonday concrete. We were taking turns sipping water from a long leaf of spineless cactus.

"I've been thinking about my kids," said Olivia, out of nowhere. She'd mentioned them before but infrequently. Two had made it through childhood. Only one to adolescence. The lone survivor had gone east with her dad to find the ocean.

"She could have her own kids by now, if they found anyone out that way." Olivia drew out a pause, sipping some cactus. "If they survived at all."

"Why didn't you go with them?"

"I had to stay here and find you," she joked.

I went to laugh but didn't. Instead I felt my stomach bottom out, my skin go clammy. My forehead broke with fevered sweat and my chest rattled, weighted by the iron chains of disease. In my ears, I heard the close crinkle of thick plastic sheeting. This terrible reverie was broken by Olivia nudging me. She proffered the cactus leaf, which I took with gratitude.

Then she continued, "Seriously, though, I didn't want to go just in case you came back. I knew chances were slim, but I couldn't leave. Just in case."

She reached for the cactus, so I handed it back. "I find it hard to believe that you like me more than your own kid," I confessed.

"And I find it hard to believe you survived so long on your own. When you're not bellyaching about something, you're falling down sick or injured. Frankly, you're a mess." Another sip was followed by a short laugh. "It's possible this cactus juice is fermented," she said. "I'm feeling a bit light-headed."

Getting up on an elbow, I felt the merest wooze of tipsiness. Shifting near enough to get a whiff off the leaf, it was unmistakably boozy. "Whew! As the older sibling, I feel it necessary to confiscate this contraband." I reached across to take the leaf.

In response, Olivia gave my shoulder a half-hearted shove. "Piss off and find your own," she insisted.

"C'mon, it's no fun drinking alone. I know from many, many years' experience. Just heartache followed by hangover. At least if you drink with somebody, you've got someone to suffer with the morning after. Give it here!"

When she finally passed me the leaf again, I caught its pungency. Must've been too tired, or too thirsty, to notice it at first. It smelled herbal, slightly peppery. The taste was sharp and sour on the tongue and burned pleasantly down the throat. "I think you're right. We should get more when the sun goes down. We'll get shitfaced tonight."

Olivia didn't reply, not even when I passed the leaf back to her. I settled back, accepting the dense quiet, and started to fall into a doze.

"I think I'm gonna go try to find them." She said it so softly that I nearly didn't hear her at all. The wild fermented hooch humming in my ears probably didn't help. I realized it could be the kind that makes you go blind — only time would tell. Having gone some time since last being drunk, the stuff was hitting me fast and hard. I wrangled the leaf back from Olivia before it sank in that she'd said anything.

"Hm? What's that?"

She sat up. Her back was straight. Backlit from the world beyond the stairs, she made a silhouette of determination. "I said I'm gonna go find them. Go east. See if they made it."

"What, right now?" I asked, snorting at my own cleverness and squeezing the last of the cactus juice down my gullet.

"Fuck sake, Jesse," she said, tearing the leaf from my hands and throwing it away. "I'm serious."

"That's no reason to be wasteful," I chided.

"I already tried, once. I was on my way. But something distracted me and I had to turn back home."

Before I could coax a reply from my addled brain, Olivia'd gotten up and out from our shelter. The heat was still insane, but it always bothered her less than it did me. She'd grown used to it after a couple of decades. Through the haze of my decent buzz, I found what I'd wanted to ask.

"Distracted?"

Nailed it.

Olivia was in the kitchen now, banging pots around. Looking for something, I guessed. "I had everything with me. A route plotted out. Maybe not the most efficient, but it followed roads. Mostly flat land, near old settlements for resources …"

The rattling and rummaging stopped. A ringing sound of metal against metal lingered in the air, like the peal of a stainless steel bell.

"So what went wrong?" I asked, clueless as ever.

There was a deafening bang, and for one hideous heartbeat, I convinced myself it was a gun shot. Then Olivia's face appeared out of the blinding brightness beyond the stairs. "I found you. This old, pathetic fart blitzed on skunky liquor, more than half starved. And I recognized you from the start. You look just like him. Except you're skinny like her. You needed caring for. I couldn't just leave you, but I …"

Something clicked, the way it sometimes does when you're drunk, letting me say what she didn't want to. "Couldn't take me with you." Even though I said it myself, it sounded cold.

Olivia shook her head. When her hair had been longer, it had more colour. Shorn for summer, it was almost completely white. She looked as old as I felt, despite being nine years younger. The world had moved on, but it hadn't gotten less cruel.

"I can't," she said in a raspy whisper. "I can't take you with me."

The reality of that statement was sobering. My mind, ever helpful, went entirely blank. I nearly heard a cold wind whistling between my ears. "Oh" was all I could think to say.

My sister sat beside me so she could cradle my head in her lap. Suddenly, she wasn't an annoying little sister but somebody's mother. She stroked my hair and crooned a wordless melody. When her song ended, I felt a tear run down my cheek. It wasn't mine.

"Hey, don't worry about me. I'll be fine," I lied. The thought of her leaving me here alone terrified me more than I could put into words. But even I wasn't selfish enough to say such a thing out loud.

Olivia wiped her eyes. "If it was that easy to not worry about you, I'd already be gone. And it's not like I haven't tried. Every time I was ready to leave, you went and got sick. Or hurt. I was starting to think you were doing it on purpose."

I nodded, still riding the falling edge of my unintended binge. "That's the kind of needy shit I'd pull. Wouldn't put it past me."

That got a laugh. It also got me evicted from her lap as Olivia stood up, dusting her palms together. "Okay. Time for some actual water. Maybe treat ourselves to a wash, too. Whaddaya say?"

Leaping to my feet as dramatically as I could, "I say to heck with washing. Let's hit the mudhole out back of the Stephensons' place."

She laughed again. "You mean the stock pond?"

"That's rainy season talk!" I scoffed. "It's a mudhole, and by now it's probably at its most soothingly muddy."

"It's probably long dried up, but even if it isn't, how will we get the mud off again?"

"Sun-baking, as our ancestors did." I grabbed her hand and led her toward the door. "C'mon, I hear it does ah-*maze*-ing things for the skin!"

For the next hour, we were kids again. The heat faded into the background of a romp in the thick silty muck. We rolled around, we threw mud clumps at each other, and we laughed more than we had in years — possibly ever. We gave each other the best possible send-off. I didn't know when Olivia planned on leaving, but once she left, we'd never see each other again.

There wasn't really anything stopping me from going with her. I could've found her map and made a copy. I could've secretly followed behind her, dogging her steps toward the east coast without telling her. Then I could've met her family, if she ended up finding them.

Such fancies were foolish for two reasons. First, she'd figure out I was there, one way or another. She'd either sense my presence or find me taking a dump in a patch of poison oak. At that point, I would become the burden she feared: slowing her down, obligating her to care for me. Second was that she did not want me there. Simple as that. Her family — the father of her children, her surviving daughter, and any other additions thereto — was not mine. The sphere of her family unit was uncontaminated by her past, free of its weighty baggage. It was almost wholly of the world beyond the tipping point. I had no rightful place in that world.

And I was not invited.

That should've made me sad, I guess. Instead, I felt something more like acceptance. An entire generation buried itself alive to make way for the birth of that new world. Those ways and ideas were underground with the people who held them, and that seemed to be for the best. We of the old world had fucked up. The least we could do was leave the kids alone as they got on with things. Who wanted some meddling old coot peering over their shoulder while they tried to live their lives?

Our muddy ablutions completed, we lay down on the grass in the partial shade of a skeletal maple tree. I remembered when these trees used to get huge, with trunks so big you couldn't wrap your arms around. On that day, I'd have been pressed to find ten to make such a bundle.

The sun was setting, but we were mostly dried by then since the heat remained sweltering. It'd cool off quickly once the light had gone. We lingered a few moments longer. Neither of us wanted to be the one to say, "Let's go home."

"It really is okay, Liverwurst," I said. I had to work to get the words out through the thick mask of dried mud around my mouth.

"Oahnalleeat," she replied.

We laughed at how silly we sounded, then spent a minute excavating our faces.

"I hate that nickname."

"I know. Why else would I use it?"

When the top curve of the sun dipped below the distant trees, we knew it was time to go. Still neither of us moved. We held on until the tension became unbearable. "As the eldest, and therefore most responsible person here, I declare it's time to get our asses home," I announced.

When I stood up, stretching and flexing, a shower of dried mud flaked away from my skin. It felt especially pleasant in the cooling air. I reached my hand down to help Olivia up. She hesitated before taking it. Together we walked across the field to the back end of our family's property. Where the lots met, there used to be a line of wooden stakes, their tops sprayed fluorescent pink. They were long gone, along with the concept of owning land.

"That was a good idea," observed Olivia.

"Thank you," I replied.

"I guess everyone has one sooner or later."

THE TROUBLE WITH STORIES is that they begin and they end. Lives certainly follow this pattern: one is born, one dies. Life as a whole does not. There are no happy endings, because nothing ever ends.

Nevertheless, I tell stories. I weave them out of the ether, out of threads stolen from life's tapestry. Strands of the Fates, spun and snipped, slip golden through warp and weft.

And when I'm gone, what becomes of them?

I'll never know, because my story will be over by then.

The Curse of Forgiveness

There was a girl who was raised by wolves. Though she was a fierce hunter and rough in manner, she grew to be the most beautiful woman ever born. She roved the forests and ranged over the hills, rarely staying still for very long.

Her mother had named her Willow, after the slim bending trees that grew near water. As is the way of things, Willow took after her namesake. Her limbs were long and lean, flexible yet strong.

One day, she met with a hunter in the woods. He was setting traps to catch wolves, under contract to some farmers in the nearby valley. They blamed the wolves for stealing away their sheep, and he could sell their pelts in the market besides.

Willow had a knapped flint at his throat before he knew what was happening.

"Take your traps from here, and you'll leave with your life," she warned him.

"If I take my traps away, I'll be branded for breaking a contract. And if that weren't enough, I'll be out the earnings for it and the pelts. How will I afford to keep my life should I give in to your demand?"

She thought on this for a moment, then released him. The moment she stepped into his sight, the huntsman was smitten, for her beauty was quite overwhelming.

"Who holds your contract?" she asked.

"The farmers in the valley," said he. "They say the wolves take of their flocks, and they will not have it."

Willow stood up straight and tall. "No wolf worth his hide would hunt a lowly sheep for his supper!"

In this way, she was quite intimidating. The huntsman cowered and apologized. "My lady, I know only what they tell me. The sheep go missing and are never seen the more. They blame the wolves and so hire men like myself to kill them."

"Killing wolves will no more solve their problem than will casting wishes down wells. If I can find the culprit of this crime, will it satisfy your contract?"

He wanted to say he wasn't sure, but he thought about the feeling of the flint against his neck and reconsidered. "I suppose it must," he admitted.

"Then this I will do. Wait here for me. The wolves will bring you food to eat and protect you until I return. Only know that if I am not back by sunset on the third day, you must run for your life, for it means I am dead and my control of the wolves ended."

The huntsman only nodded dumbly.

Willow took her leave, carrying no more than her flint knife and a spear across her back. She climbed high into the hills above the valley, looking for any trace of the sheep thief. Finding none, she descended to the farmers' settlement.

"Perhaps if I hide myself here, I will catch sight of the culprit and thus make an end of his mischief."

She sat herself in a dense thicket at the edge of a pasture where the sheep had huddled for the night. No sooner had she settled in than the ground began to shake. From the treeline beyond came a great ugly troll. His nose was like a burlap sack stuffed with turnips, and his tail was tufted with greasy, matted black hair.

Into the field he strolled, bold as brass, and took up a pair of fat sheep — one beneath each of his hairy arms. Then back up the hill he strode, careless that he might be watched.

"Now I have him," declared Willow, stealing up the hill in the giant's footsteps. She trailed him to a copse which hid the mouth of an enormous cave. Inside a fire burned brightly. At the rear of the cave was a pen full of sheep, to which the troll added his newfound spoils.

"Soon I'll have the lot," said the troll to himself. "Then I'll drive them over the hill to my brother, where we'll have a great feast of mutton."

Willow kept herself hidden until the troll lay down to sleep. Then she stole forth, meaning to cut the beast's foul throat and have done with it.

Though she was quiet as a summer breeze, still she made some sound to wake him. Before he could spot her, Willow ducked down behind a great boulder on the floor.

"Who goes?" demanded the troll, peering into the darkness.

"It is only the summer wind," she replied. "I meant to blow you sweet smells of night blossoms that you might dream well."

"That's all to the good," said he. "But must you be so noisy?"

"Let me sing to you," said Willow in the wind's voice. "The song will lull you into the deepest of sleeps so that no noise might wake you — not even the clap of thunder."

The troll considered this, for though he was very tired, he feared his sheep might be stolen should he sleep too deeply. "How do I know you don't mean to steal my flock?" he queried.

"I swear on the North Star and the South Pole that any thief shall wake you. Fear not!"

"Very well," grumbled the troll, settling his head back on the ground.

When his eyes had closed, Willow sang an enchantment she had learned from Old Mother Owl. It cast the troll into a deep sleep from which he could not be wakened. This done, she crept up to the place where he lay and cut open his throat with her wicked little knife.

A great gout of blood washed out of his throat and over her legs. She went to a wooden trough of water that stood by the wall and washed herself clean. Only, her feet were stained a dark red that could not be budged by scrubbing.

"Old Mother Oak, why are my feet stained so?"

From beyond the cave mouth sighed the answer, in a voice like a wind through treetops. "The taking of any life in this way leaves its mark. Your sin will stay with you all the days of your life."

"Is there no way to cleanse it?" she begged.

Again came the soughing reply. "Make atonement to the family of the dead. If you do this before the birth of your firstborn, the mark will not be passed to your child."

She vowed to make atonement to the troll's brother, though she could not think how. In the meantime, she took the troll's tail as proof of his guilt and drove the sheep back to the farmers' lands.

When Willow returned to the place where she'd left the huntsman, he was asleep, surrounded by her entire pack.

"Hunter," she called, waking him. "Take you this tail as proof that a troll took the sheep, and tell them the next trapper they send into these hills will not be so lucky as you."

The huntsman sat up and took the tail with gratitude. "I thank you for sparing my life. I have nothing to offer you in return, but would ask you to be my wife. Let me care for and shelter you all the days of your life that I might make up my fullest gratitude."

He spoke so well, and was comely enough besides, that Willow consented. "Only leave me a year and a day to prepare my trousseau. When you come back, I will marry you."

The huntsman nodded and hurried away to collect on his contract. When he was gone, Willow fell to the ground and began to weep.

Her elder sister sat at her side and offered comfort. "What ails you? Were you hurt on your hunt?"

The girl threw her arms around the wolf's neck and burrowed her tear-soaked face in its fur. "Oh, sister! I have killed a creature outside the hunt and am marked for my sin. Look only at the red stains on my feet. If I cannot make atonement with the troll's brother by the time my hunter returns, my transgression will mark my children also. Yet I know not how I might amend myself. What shall I do?"

Her sister replied, "Sadly, dear heart, I know not." After a long silence, she continued, "Dry your tears and climb upon my back. Together we will go and find Old Mother Pine where she lives, far away. Perhaps she can tell you what you need to do."

And so Willow crouched closely on her sister's strong back and wound her fingers into her sister's mane. The great she-wolf leapt forth over the hills, across the fields. On and on she ran, while beyond and below them all the world sped by.

Then at last, they traversed the horizon. Over the crest of light they went, into the kingdom of the rising sun. Every surface was touched with gold; the air itself was gilded. No sooner had they entered than a brace of guards in golden livery appeared at their side to lead them into court.

There, resplendent on his throne, was King Sun. He had the rough, ruddy beard of a farmer with a face to match — broad and friendly as the day was long.

"What do you seek in the land beyond the horizon?" said he.

Willow, lacking manners, replied, "We seek Old Mother Pine. Does she not reside here?"

"But for your impertinence, I'd have told you straight off. Since you've no manners toward a king, I set you this task: go to the lake at the southern border of my kingdom. Take this net of angel's hair and use it to catch the largest carp in the lake. Bring this fish to me alive, and I will tell you all you need to know."

When they had quit the palace, the wolf scolded Willow. "How came it that you know not the way to address a king?"

"Ask my mother" was her reply.

Together they went to the southern tip of King Sun's realm, where there lay the lake. Willow took the net from her shoulder and reached it into the water. No sooner had she done so than a great fat carp leapt into it.

"Are you the largest carp in this lake?" Willow asked the creature.

The fish boasted, "To be sure, I am!"

"Then you're with me," concluded the huntress, who flopped the carp onto her sister's back.

Her sister said, "We must make haste to return so that the carp will remain alive. Climb on my back and hold the fish tightly. I will run my fastest to get us there the sooner."

Willow did as she was told, climbing on her sister's powerful back and cradling the fish's slimy body to her breast. The pitiful thing stared at her with one rolling golden eye as it gasped for breath.

With one great leap, they were gone. In half the time it had taken them to get to the lake, they were back before King Sun in his golden palace.

"Have you the carp?" he demanded.

"I have," replied Willow, holding forth the very fish.

It gasped slowly now, for it had been out of the water a good long while. Swiftly and softly, King Sun came forth and kissed the carp. Thereupon it transformed into a slender youth with a golden robe.

"Father?" spoke the boy. "I had the strangest dream …"

The king caught up the boy in a hearty embrace.

"My son! My son! He is returned to me!" To Willow, he said, "For this boon, I will tell you whatever you wish and give you half my kingdom besides."

Humbled, Willow ducked her head and spoke gently, "My lord, I have no desire for wealth or land but only to know where Old Mother Pine resides. I must ask her how I can atone for the sin of murder."

"If anyone knows the answer, surely it is she," replied the king gravely. "Yet I know not where she lives. Seek you the Sultan of the Moon, for he shall know better."

As the sisters turned to leave, the king bade them stop. "Take as your gift this cup that is always full and this boodle that is never empty. They are trifles, to be sure, but may prove helpful on your journey."

Willow and her sister left the kingdom of the sun. They travelled many a weary day and night until they came to a place where the sky was black at midday. Everything, every surface was gilded with silver.

"This is surely the Sultan of the Moon's realm," said the she-wolf. "Now remember your manners. We wolves are more beholden to the Sultan of the Moon, for he is our ruler. He'll brook no inso-lence from the likes of you."

Willow nodded and said nothing.

There was no escort for them this time, only a parliament of owls whose number grew and grew the closer they came to the pal-ace. Until at last when they arrived, all over the whole of the castle were perched owls of every kind: stark white, speckled brown, and downy grey.

They stepped inside in silence and went up the main hall into the court room. Here were perched a dozen more owls, each the size of a man. They wore helms of worked silver and carried hal-berds at their sides. On the throne sat a great fat man whose face was round and red as a harvest moon. He beckoned the pair come closer.

"What seek you in the silvered Sultanate of the Moon?" he asked. His voice was low and melodious as the ringing of silver bells. A poor match for his hideous girth. He was so sorry to look at that Willow quite forgot herself once again.

"We seek Old Mother Pine that she might help me cleanse my sins. Know you where she lives? Only say if you don't for we haven't much time to waste."

"That's a tart mouth you have, girl, to speak so to a sultan! For that, though I would have told you what I know, I shall first set you a task that might teach you some manners."

At Willow's side, her sister sighed. "My lord, I reminded her to keep her tongue not ten paces from your door. On behalf of all wolves, I beg your forgiveness."

"As you like," replied the fat sultan, his several chins quivering. "Just know that for her misstep, you will all be punished. When my face shows full in the sky, no wolf shall rest. Running and howling, you will make obeisance to me until time itself is ended."

"Indeed, my lord," said the wolf.

To Willow, he said, "There is an orchard at the northernmost end of my realm. On the trees there grow the rarest fruit in the world: soul plums. Find the tree which grows the fattest and roundest of these fruits and gather them all in this birchbark bushel. Take care to pack them well so that not one is bruised! Bring this fruit to me unscathed, and then will I tell you what you wish to know."

Willow looked about to speak but held her tongue at her sister's gesture. They bowed their way to the back of the court and there took their leave. As they stepped over the front threshold of the palace, every owl there perched leapt away into the night sky. It looked very much like a fall of snow in reverse.

For days and nights, they travelled north through the Sultan of the Moon's realm — though for how many, it was hard to say for the sun did not show his face here. The appearance of night remained unbroken and unchanged.

At last, when she could abide no longer, Willow's sister demanded to know why she could not be civil even to the lord over all wolf-kind.

"Did you learn nothing?" she demanded.

"Ask my mother" was the reply.

In time, they came to the orchard where the soul plums grew. The rows of plantings stretched to the horizon in all directions; they hardly knew where to begin.

"Oh, sister!" moaned Willow. "To find the finest tree in this orchard will take ten lifetimes! I have less than a year's time to make amends to the troll's brother and keep my betrothal. Perhaps I should give up and live out my days with the wolf pack. What do I care for some human hunter? Or the idea of sin?" She fell to the ground, unable to stop the tears that fell from her eyes.

When she was quite finished, her sister replied, "The tears you cry are reason enough. You were raised by wolves, but you are not wolf-kind. You must go your way and live among your people, for the good of yourself and our pack. Come now. Let us ask for help."

To the nearest tree, the she-wolf bowed deeply. "Oh, noble soul plum tree! Will you tell me please where my sister shall find the greatest of your siblings that she might pay her respects? She is soon to be wed and would have a blessing of good luck."

The soul plum tree shook its leaves proudly at being addressed with such kind words. "Why certainly, my child. Our queen, the comeliest of trees who bears the finest fruit to be had, grows at the top of yonder rise. Only follow the shaking of our branches; we will show you the way."

This they did. As they passed by, the trees quivered and shook so that the sisters knew the path, even had their eyes been closed. And there, apart from the others at the peak of a gentle hill, stood the Queen of Soul Plums.

"Are you the tree that bears the fattest, roundest soul plums in all this orchard?" Willow asked.

"I am," admitted the tree.

Then quickly as they might, she and her sister plucked the tree bare of fruit, packing it gently into the birch-bark bushel. Yet they weren't fast enough, for the tree soon cried them out for thieves. In response, from a distance came a great flapping of wings. Soon, a piece of the eastern sky detached from the blackness into a massive flock of ravens. Silver light glinted off their beaks, their glossy wings, and their clever eyes.

"Hurry and climb on my back. Hold tight to the bushel so I might run with all haste back to the Sultan of the Moon's court."

Willow did as she was told. No sooner was she upon her sister's mighty back than they were away, flying faster than the birds that chased them. In a trice, they could see the white-marble spires of the palace reaching above the trees. And above their heads, soaring silently, were the owls. They met the raven army head on, and there fought a bloody battle.

In the confusion, Willow and her sister were able to reach the palace in safety. Once inside, Willow stepped down from her sister's back, clutching the birch-bark bushel as firmly as she might without crushing the fruit within. She did not notice that one of the fruits had fallen out as they flew, lost forever to the dense forests of the Sultanate of the Moon.

Together they entered the sultan's throne room. Upon the throne sat a man of inhuman thinness. Had he not been dressed in the billowing sags of the fat man's clothing, Willow might have taken him for an impostor. Where before he had waxed in fullness, he now waned.

To the Sultan of the Moon, Willow bowed deeply and held forth the bushel basket. "My lord, here are the fruits you had us fetch. They have come at a great cost, for we were chased the whole way back by the raven army of the orchard, who even now are beaten back by your owls."

"I see someone has been teaching you manners" was the sultan's replied. "The better for you. Now take the whole bushel and cast it to the floor with all the strength you can muster. I would do it myself, but I am at my weakest."

Willow did this, and all the fruit in the basket smashed to the cold marble floor in a spray of grey pulp and red juice. From the midst of the mess sprang a handsome woman in a dress of fine-wrought silver lace. Her silver locks were held high in a snood of silver chains.

"My darling wife!" declared the sultan. "You are returned at last, delivered from that evil curse which trapped you."

The sultana turned to her husband and went to his arms. "My loyal husband, it is so good to be myself again." And so she was, though the little finger on her left hand was missing. This was because of the plum that had been dropped while they fled.

"Think no more on it," said the sultan. "I would happily give my own small finger — the whole of my right hand, in fact — that my wife should be at my side once more. Tell me again what it is you seek. I will give you that, and a boon besides."

Willow bowed deeply again. "My lord, we seek Old Mother Pine where she lives, or else the way to atone to the troll's brother for the sin of murder."

"Atonement takes honesty, and I know only lies and secrets. That said, you may find Old Mother Pine where the west wind blows. Of any creature on earth, surely she can tell you what you seek."

Humbled and bereaved, Willow turned to take up her long journey once more.

"Hold! Would you decline my offer of a boon?"

"No, my lord, never. But I know not what to ask for. I have travelled half the earth and more besides in search of this answer and have learned little, save how to address kings and sultans. If you would grant me a boon, I beg you choose one you think best."

The sultan and his wife looked kindly down on the noble creature before them, yet hardly knew what to say.

At last, the sultana stepped forward and laid her hands on the girl's shoulders. "This poor child of two worlds! Take with you this braid of my hair, that it might serve you well on your travels. Take also this ruby ring, which can light a fire without spark or tinder." Then she laid a kiss on the girl's brow with lips that burned icily. "Were you my own child, I should be so proud of you to undertake so long and perilous a quest. Go your way and find what you seek."

The sisters bowed their way to the back of the court and took their leave of the sultan's realm. At the border, they came upon the old west wind, who was quite out of breath.

Willow asked her sister, "Might we offer him a ride upon your back to take him where he's going? After all, we are headed in that direction ourselves."

The she-wolf obliged, and together they offered the elder a ride.

"Why certainly," agreed the west wind. "How kind of you to think of one less fortunate. Whither do you go?"

"We seek Old Mother Pine, the better to learn how to wash away the stain of sin."

The old man declared, "Why, she is my neighbour! For your kindness, I will make your introduction to her."

When they arrived to the barren place the west wind called his home, he was as good as his word.

"Good lady," he called to his neighbour. "Here are a pair of wolf-kin who would have your guidance. They were kind enough to help me home when I found myself quite blown of breath. Do help them as best you can, and I will be much obliged."

Old Mother Pine nodded her boughs, and to the pair addressed herself. "Kindness and good manners are always rewarded. What would you have of me?"

Willow made a deep bow and showed the stains on her feet. "To help a man and to save my pack, I killed a wicked troll who was stealing sheep. Now I am cursed to bear the stain of sin and am doomed to pass it on to my children, unless I make atonement to the troll's brother. Please do tell me what way I can make him forgive me."

Old Mother Pine shook her boughs and sighed through her needles. "One cannot make forgiveness any more than one can force joy. Go unto the troll's brother and ask him what he would have of you. Do as he asks and do it well. Only arrange with him beforehand what tasks will satisfy your debt, or else he'll never let you go."

"Thank you, good mother. I'll take your leave, for I've not much time and many long miles to travel."

"Dear heart! Let me grant you this small boon. Walk beneath my right-hand boughs and you'll find yourself at the troll brother's doorstep."

"Thank you again," said Willow and stepped forward.

Her sister stayed behind, unmoving.

"Are you not coming with me?" asked Willow.

I'M WRITING OUT this story, since there's nobody around to tell it to. The walls, the floors, the ceiling — wherever I can find blank space to scrawl on.

When I wrote that line, I felt like I'd been punched in the gut. Olivia left.

There's nobody to invite me to join them on an adventure, on a journey home. I'm all alone again. I'm starting to think it's my natural state of being. Right up until my sister trudged out of sight down the slope to the road, I'd had some hope. The tiniest bright spark that she would turn around and ask, "Are you not coming with me?"

She didn't even look back to wave. With the happy buoyancy of a ship cut free of its anchor, she was away and gone.

I look at the charcoal in my hand. That hand is stained and marked and thin. So much older than the forty years since I stood on the strand, witness to the expansive enormity of life itself. So very much older than I feel. A moving skeleton veneered in leather.

Every activity I engage in is done on autopilot. I gather food, I eat, I maintain my shelter … for what? There's nobody left but me. And I'm not sure I'm worth saving.

I lift my eyes to look out over the backyard. Beneath a hump of growing things hides Dad's workshop. He's still in there. Well, his bones are.

"What are you thinking about, Food Bringer?"

"Ah! It's nothing, buddy. Just a cramp in my hand."

Doggo's disembodied voice seems to come from an ancient stuffed toy. It's from the Fall Fair that used to happen every year on a patch of ground where the borders of several small towns conjoined. The prize for some kind of game. Maybe ring toss? It's supposed to be a dog, I guess. It has huge cartoon eyes made from glued-on felt and a big red felt tongue that doesn't quite attach to the line of stitching meant to be its mouth. Its fur is patchy and it's filled with tiny foam beads that crunch when you squeeze it. The poor thing looks little enough like a dog, let alone Doggo, but it's better than when he seemed to talk directly into my head.

"What happens next? In the story?"

The toy doesn't move, but I can almost see Doggo's dopey little face looking up at me while he wags his tail hard enough to shake his whole body. It's equal parts disturbing and comforting.

"Okay. Yeah, right," I mutter. "Where was I?"

"Are you not coming with me?"

Another cold gut shot hits me, followed by the sensation of being lifted up off the ground.

"What did you say?"

ister, what's wrong? Come, let us go home to-gether. I would bid you good-bye before I take myself to the troll brother's service."

"I will not move until you explain yourself. You say you were taught your rude manners by your mother, yet she is my mother also. I know she taught us well how to mind ourselves. So tell me how you learned differently."

Willow crouched by her sister and embraced her well. "Oh, sister! I meant not our mother but my mother — the human woman who bore me into this world. Before ill fate befell her, she whispered that I should bow to no man by virtue of being told to do so. Therefore does my back remain straight and my knees unbent."

When she had spoken thus, they kissed and made apology to each other. Then the sisters walked together beneath the upraised bough of Old Mother Pine. One moment, they were at the end of the world where the west wind lay his head. The next, they were near enough their own home to see familiar fields and woods from the mountain's far slope.

"Darling girl, I must leave you and go back to our pack. Just remember to make your deal well and serve the troll as he would. Then come and bid us farewell before fulfilling your betrothal." They embraced one last time before the great she-wolf leapt away and was gone.

Willow stood truly alone for the first time in her life. She drank deeply of the cool mountain air. Perhaps, instead of atoning, she could simply run. Away down the mountain to a land where she was not known. There would be no troll brother, no huntsman to keep her. And if her feet were stained ever more, then so be it.

Before she could take a step, the great door in the mountainside that she'd taken for a boulder swung widely, silently open. There was a great intake of air, as though the slope itself inhaled her scent. From its candle-lit interior came a low voice, "Who comes to my door this day? Who smells of sin?"

Quite against her will, Willow began to tremble at the sound of that voice. It was not so loud or so harsh as his brother's. In many aspects, it was a pleasant voice. Yet there was in it a tone of threat that could not be hidden.

She bowed deeply to the empty doorway. "My lord, I am your brother's killer. I come to atone for his murder."

There was a series of great rumbles as giant feet struck the ground. Then the troll's brother appeared in his doorway, twice as tall and thrice as ugly. In his melodic voice that so contrasted his look, he said, "And why should I grant you such a thing as forgiveness? You, who have killed my only brother, should be killed in your turn."

"If that is your wish, I can only honour it. But first shall we not share a meal and a draught of good wine? Killing is distasteful business, so I would sweeten its blow even a little."

Her words and good manner convinced him to stay his hand.

"Very well. Come inside so we might sit by the fire."

They went together inside, only to find the fire had quite burned out.

"Damn and blast!" cursed the troll.

"Allow me," offered Willow.

She stepped forward and, using the ruby ring, quickly had a fire roaring in the hearth.

"What witchery is this?" the troll inquired.

Willow held up the ring for him to see. "It is an enchanted ring, given to me by the Sultana of the Moon. With it can be lit any fire."

"I would like to have such a ring," he admitted. "In the autumn of my years, it grows ever harder to spark the tinder."

"Well, when I am dead, it can be yours," said she. "Now let us eat and drink."

The troll lifted her from the ground so that she could stand on top of his enormous table. There she pulled a cloth from her magic boodle and spread it out. All across it were arrayed fine dishes of succulent meats and sweet fruits. Then taking the troll's goblet, she filled it from the never-emptied cup. From it, the troll quaffed the best vintage he'd ever drunk.

"Why, this is marvellous! Tell me how you've done it."

"These trifles?" Willow ducked her head modestly. "They are but simple rewards for serving the King Sun. Upon my death, they will surely be yours."

They ate and drank, though Willow was careful to be moderate in both. Soon enough, the old troll grew sleepy with meat and drink and, with a great crash, fell with his head upon the table. His snores were so loud that they shook the walls and floor.

With all the stealth she could muster, Willow crept 'round the sleeping troll. About his neck, she looped the hair braid also given to her by the sultana. The other end, she tied well to the stone mantelpiece that hung above the hearth.

This done, she went beside the door and shouted, "Foolish lout! You'll not kill me!"

Startled from his slumber, the troll leapt to his feet. The braid around his neck caught him, pulling him sharply back so that he was laid out on the floor. At the same time, the mantle stone was yanked from its mooring above the fireplace. It fell down upon the troll's head, killing him in an instant.

No sooner was he dead than Willow's hands became likewise stained with red. All around her kicked up a swirling wind, from which came a voice. "A sin repeated is damnation doubled! Go your way knowing that there is no atonement that can wash you clean. Any child of yours will be marked as a demon, cursed to live its days in wicked solitude." She knew the voice to be Old Mother Pine. In her words, Willow could hear the depth of her disappointment.

Quitting the troll's abode, she travelled back to the land of her people. As she passed, no birds sang. She saw no squirrels, nor rabbits, either. Her only company was the sound of creatures fleeing her presence, the feeling of many pairs of eyes watching her at a wary distance.

Willow at last came to the clearing where her pack often gathered. It was empty, though she could sense her brothers and sisters watched her from nearby. Unable to bear her loneliness, she fell to her knees and wept. "I am truly forsaken and without friend in this world! Better the troll had taken my life than to live without comfort!"

In time, she dried her tears and moved away from the clearing. At her back, she could hear the wolves filing out of the trees to watch her leave. She didn't go far but found a spot where she would wait for the huntsman. It was not long before he arrived. The moment he caught sight of Willow, he was upon her, lifting her in his arms in passionate embrace.

"Every day was like a year of its own. How long have I waited to clasp you so? But, dear heart," he asked, "why do you cry?"

"I weep for joy, my love, for you are here and we are together at last. Let us away and be wed!"

"Would you not bid your family good-bye?"

"It is already done," she replied.

Away they went, arm in arm, to live as well as they might.

"DON'T YOU MEAN 'happily ever after'?" asks Doggo.

I want to reassure him that yes, that is what I mean. I mean that every story ends happily, or at least it should. I want to say all this and more, but I'm too busy crying to answer him.

ONWARD AND UPWARD

MY AUTOPILOT starts to wind down in the absence of anyone but myself. And what am I? Besides old and tired and lonely, what is Jesse Vanderchuck?

Empty. Out of time.

Yes, that seems almost too apt: out of time. One foot is stuck in a past that cannot be reclaimed, while the other foot tries to step onward into a future on a planet become alien. There is nothing left of the "good old days," except me.

At some point in the distant future, should humans live on, someone will turn over the stone that covers the Underground. Maybe some people will still live there, gone pale and boneless as worms. That's what comes of trying to recapture a thing that is long gone and was maybe never yours in the first place.

Damnation.

A DAY DAWNS, like any other. It's mild and fine with a vast blue sky settled on the hills like an upturned porcelain cup. I could almost believe it's the old days. That Mum and Dad are downstairs, and that I'll soon be called down to breakfast. That Olivia's in the room down the hall, tucked under the dormer eaves in her window bed, still sound asleep.

Sleep's been rough the past little while. I keep dreaming that I'm in the Underground, that I never left. I'm by the elevator shaft surrounded by rough breathing, wet coughs, and the crackle of aged poly sheeting shrouds. Sometimes I'm tending to those who're too sick to move. Sometimes others are tending to me. When I ask where Doggo is, they shake their heads and move on.

I look out over the backyard. The slumped form of the workshop taunts me. It's a burial mound now, having lost its status as a building to the entropic effects of time. Seeing it there, looming over the place between the yard and fields, sagged walls and broken-spine roof softly draped in grasses and vines, goads me to act. Some part of my brain lights up the way it would to see a beautifully made bed piled high with pillows and blankets of purest white.

God, when was the last time I saw actual white fabric?

"FOOD BRINGER?"

Doggo's ghost trots along behind me as I rattle around the house, pacing the restlessness out of my bones. He left the dog plushie at some point. It's hard to remember how long ago, since days have started blending together.

There's a mania to my actions. I could feel adrenalin jitters in my hands as I packed a bag for hunting. Then I set it down and now can't recall where I left it.

"Food Bringer." His voice is lower in pitch, with a tone of command it's never had before. I'm still distracted but nonetheless ask him, "What? What is it, Doggo?"

He sits on the kitchen floor and wags his tail. It makes no sound as it passes through the flaking linoleum surface.

"What do you want, buddy? Show me."

He hesitates before rising with an inaudible creak and ambling to the back door. Sitting again, he casts a glance over his shoulder.

"Outside? You wanna go outside?" I'm talking like there's an actual dog that actually needs to go to the bathroom. The insanity of this doesn't escape me, but it doesn't bother me, either. Not anymore.

I undo the bolt and grab a doorknob that feels electrified. It sends a tingling jolt singing up my arm and straight into my head. Until it's over, I can't think. Or see. Or sense anything. As it ends, all my systems come back online one by one.

Rebooting.

Doggo is still sitting at my feet, staring at the bottom corner of the door, willing it to open. His focus is so complete that his tail is still and straight as an arrow. He doesn't seem to have noticed my ... episode. Seizure?

I pull the door open and he's gone. Doggo leaps over the threshold and disappears into the daylight. I do my best to catch sight of him, but all I can see is the occasional rustle of tall grasses, which is all but certainly the wind.

The empty stillness of the house is deafening, or maybe it's the aftermath of my fit. In dumb shock, I begin to close the door. There's a thump, past which I can't budge the door. When I try to push it closed, there's a ghostly yelp.

"Doggo?"

The faintest outline of a doggy shape is sketched in the air between the door and the jamb. He backs up two steps to sit on the porch and looks up at me.

"Are you not coming with me?" Doggo asks.

The jolt of cold that seems paired to that phrase drives into my solar plexus like a fist made from ice and leaves me deprived of air. A catalyst. A trigger. It means something more than what it's asking.

"Where are we going?" I ask once I'm able to draw breath. The kind of question you ask because you think you might know the answer, but you don't want to know. You know?

Doggo seems to know this, too, and continues to sit in silence. Waiting for my reply.

When I can push words from my mouth, they sound heavy and resonant. The tolling of a distant windchime that hung from the corner of Grandma's porch. "I'm not ready." Some part of me is still convinced I mean my hunting bag. Where the hell did I leave that thing, anyway?

"Aren't you?"

The question doesn't come from Doggo or from me. At least I don't think it does. Everything's fuzzy, and I start to think that maybe that seizure was more serious than it seemed.

"Jesse. Let's go."

Speed is vital. As with suicide, you have to keep yourself distracted long enough to go through with it.

Look at the sky as you climb the bridge railing.

Think about how small the distance is between a trigger at rest and a trigger pulled.

Never mind that you're looking down the barrel.

The mania of the morning is gone. In its wake, I feel hollowed out and brittle: an eggshell around a void. The best solution seems to be following my feet. Like autopilot, it's a thoughtless process. Look only as far ahead as needed to avoid tripping or stepping off a ledge. Go until movement becomes unthinkable.

Repeat.

SLAPSTICK

I DON'T HAVE A GOAL in mind, other than to leave. It's several hours in before I decide to establish one. It may be arbitrary, but so is existence. None of us asked to be here. While some see that as reason to abdicate responsibility, I always saw it as a dictate to help. Or at least not be an asshole.

Try as I might, imagination fails to produce even the shadow of a goal. Maybe, I muse, it's because I'm not really here. If I was reborn at the ocean's shore, perhaps I died when we went Underground. This is just the ghost of Jesse Vanderchuck, rambling through the woods of what used to be Northern Ontario, telling stories to nobody but air.

Maybe everything that has happened since leaving the Underground has been a figment of my imagination.

The road is an intermittent companion. It was made to wrap around natural features, whereas I am compelled to push straight through. I'm heading more or less west from home. If I walk long enough, I'll fall into the ocean. Wouldn't that be poetical?

My ambition is too blunted to contemplate such a lofty goal. I'll come across a derelict Tim Horton's before too long — maybe that's good enough.

I WAKE ONE MORNING to see the peak of a small mountain brightly lit by the first rays of dawn. It's on the far side of a nameless town beside a lake. I'm nearly sure I know the name but cannot trust these scrambled eggs I call a brain, and the road sign by the highway exit is long gone. All that comes to mind is the name of the lake. Nipissing. I only recall that much because the kids in class all thought it was the height of comedy that a lake had "pissing" in its name.

The surface of the water glows in the rising light, so that it looks gilded. I watch its gentle shimmer, circled by flocks of gulls, until I'm interrupted by the growl of my stomach. I've been hunting for food since leaving home, with middling success. Never did find that bag of gear. Nor did I have presence of mind to bring supplies. Just Jesse Vanderchuck of Very Little Brain.

"And Doggo" comes a whisper in my ear.

He comes and goes. Thought he was gone for good two nights ago when he took off in the midst of a dramatic retelling of my last day with Olivia. Our relationship is very different, now he's dead. There's no need to protect him, to care for him. He's just a bit of company, which is why I'm pretty certain he's imaginary.

Not that he seems to know that.

"Is it time for food?"

I unfold my legs and rub some feeling back into them before trying to stand up. A lesson hard learned that I'm not as young as I used to be. We trek along the broken road until we come across the biggest grocery store I've ever seen. Like all of them, it's been picked over, but there's almost always a lonely can of lima beans for a hungry old beast like myself.

The lake is closer here. We take ourselves down a trail to a sandy patch of beach. I sit and eat my beans. Doggo snuffles in and out of some low-growing bushes.

That's when I decide that what I really need to do is climb that mountain.

Who knows why? Because it's there, because I have nothing else to do …

I make a deal with myself that if I make it to the top of that mountain without dying, I'll stop. I won't move from the place I park myself, and that'll be that.

Maybe I'll self-mummify like a monk, and years later some other fool who feels the need to climb a fucking mountain will come across my body — cross-legged, at peace — and shit their everloving pants from here till next Tuesday.

Hell, kids today probably don't even know what Tuesday is.

OR LONESOME NO MORE

IN MY DREAMS, I am safe. I wake up in a strange place of warm sounds and sweet air. Everyone I see is radiant with health. They laugh simply because of how wonderful it is to be alive. Food and drink are plentiful, and we partake at every hour of the day because we can.

I make love, in this dream, to anyone who'll have me. I don't understand why anyone would, since every reflection I see shows that I am a mildewed skeleton draped in rotting rags. A sexless monster that hungers for warmth, for safety, for companionship.

When I wake, it's always colder than I think it should be. Doggo, when he's around, flickers in and out of existence. I can only hear him if I try really hard. Even then, he sounds like a mistuned radio: a stream of patchy chatter, punctuated by stabs of static.

I eat through my meagre supply of lima beans in stages, weaning myself off food. Next I'll do the same with water but not until the climb is finished.

The way isn't especially hard. Or perhaps it is, but I take my time, conquering it step by step. I am something inevitable, approaching the mountain as inexorably as a glacier. I feel enormous and unstoppable, which is how I know I am also right.

Over the ripples of smaller hills, dipping down into valleys that flow with countless tributaries, connecting thousands of lakes. As I go, I must angle to the north. Gaining latitude is akin to travelling back in time. Semi-arid plant life of the present day gives way to more temperate flora. The maples and pines of my youth, the dark-green leaves that colour the tales I spin, they surround me. A wind blows down the slope ahead of me, heralding cold rain.

"IT'S NOT ALWAYS ABOUT YOU," Olivia wrote in her letter to Mum. "You did things, took actions, because you thought you were in control. But the truth is you needed that control to feel less small. So you took it. You stole us away like some kind of monster and left my father — your husband — to fend for himself. And I hate you for that."

Those words, and many more like them, were thrown with the intent of revealing some great truth. A semblance of justice. But in the end, they read like what they were: the angry words of a hurt little girl who missed her daddy.

Bits of that letter could've been aimed at either of us, Mum or me, but she got the brunt of Olivia's ire. I guess it makes it easier if the blame isn't spread too thin. More like shooting a laser than a shotgun. You hurt fewer bystanders and more certainly wound your target.

I'm thinking of this as I stir the embers of a fire with a length of broken hockey stick I all but tripped over. The tape around the handle is hard and dry, flaking off in places. Whatever branding was once painted on it is long gone.

Everything I knew is long gone. How can I know if I'm still alive if there's nothing familiar to measure my existence against? Who's going to be impressed that I still remember all the lines from *Rocky Horror Picture Show*? Who'll mourn the lack of Jesse Vanderchuck in the world?

Then I recall that it's not all about me. Stir the embers. A flash of sparks shoot into the air and are almost instantly gone.

Too cliché?

I CATCH AND EAT a rabbit beneath the light of a full moon. The wild ones taste of the grasses they eat. Not like the ones we kept for meat. They were enormous things, sturdy yet terrified of everything. In stew, they were tender as anything. A bit like eating silk — if silk were made of meat.

Gaminess aside, I eat the whole thing, down to gnawing the bones. I'm supposed to be abstaining from food. Preparing for my ascendance from mere mortal to mythical creature. Then the tummy rumbles start, and a feral instinct to survive takes over my body and mind. Next thing I know, I'm mowing down on undercooked rabbit beneath the silvered leaves of a sugar maple, like a wolf from a fairy tale.

The next night, a brace of fat squirrels donate their bodies to my survival effort. They're so docile, it's more or less a matter of walking up to them and doing them in by hand. In no time at all, I've become a dab hand at snapping tiny necks.

There are one or two moments when I bitterly mull that Olivia's missing out on my capability. She could have had someone like me helping her out, but she didn't believe in me. Not like I do. Except that it took a literal year for me to work up the courage — the desperation — to quit that house and strike out on my own. A big part of that was self-doubt. I didn't trust myself to keep me alive any more than Olivia did.

AS I WALK, I look for another story. Nothing will allow itself to be conjured from the ether. Everything here is too real. Literal life and death. I get started once or twice, then nearly die from tripping over a tree root or putting my faith in the wrong sapling for stability. To say nothing of the giant footprint I stumbled into, nearly drowning in the water puddled at its bottom.

It's no use. Whatever magic had found me is gone. Fled, like everyone else.

Doggo's diminished to a faint wiener-shaped sketch that trucks along beside me. It waits, wagging a ghostly tail, for me to recover from every stumble. It rustles through the ferns as it walks. But it does not speak.

One benefit of this trek is that I've stopped dreaming of the Underground. Though the last time I did was a real nightmare. Milky plastic draped over my face, crinkling with each ragged breath. I felt like I couldn't move. I tried to speak, to tell one of the attendants that I was still alive, but could make no sound come from my throat. Only a thick gurgle from fluid-filled lungs.

They took me from the hospice room to a place lit by deep-sea biolume ropes. The sound of soft machine breaths whispered from a vent shaft. And there were shapes hulking in the half-light. Strange inhuman shapes. They lay on tables and stretched up to the ceiling. Every so often, there was a low groan, as if an old man was settling into his favourite armchair. I was set down on a table. I felt something cold and sharp drawn down my abdomen. It didn't hurt. When it was done, I only felt wet. Exposed.

Shuffling. People in respirators and gloves lifting gelatinous globs from white plastic pails and putting them on my chest. My belly. No, not on. In.

Real as anything, I could feel the globs slide into open flesh. Numbed by disease but not unfeeling, they oozed into the crevices between shrivelled organs. Took root in the fertile bounty of my earthly self.

Haven't dreamt of the place since. Thank God.

IT'S A TRICKY proposition to keep track of time these days, but I think it's close to a week before I'm in the foothills. I only know I've come close to my goal because I can no longer see the mountain, unless I look up. Close to, it's certainly taller than it looked at a distance.

My resolve is steeled. This is my mountain, and I will conquer it — come what may.

Were I younger, it might have only taken one day to climb that slope. As it is, I take my time, one foot after the other. It's less a matter of making straight for the top than of taking a series of shallow switchbacks. Parts of the climb are steep enough that I have to wedge my foot between the roots of a tree and the ground to keep from tumbling down.

I spend the night tied to the thickest bole I can find. No fire, no supper. Before I pass out from a potent combination of hunger and exhaustion, I swear I see a pack of wolves being led by a proud, red-headed woman walk past me. When they've gone, bits and pieces of tiger-striped fur peek out from behind every tree trunk, stone, and bush. Facing east, I wake when dawn's first rays stab into my eyes through closed lids.

There is no pause for food here. The growling beast inside, demanding to be fed, is cowed by the peril of the climb. Besides, it's not like there's a ton of critters just lounging around on the side of a mountain or anything. They stick to the flatter ground, like sane things.

What am I doing this for? Am I trying to prove something? If so, to whom?

These questions and similar ones swim through a mind growing ever foggier from want. I see their sides flash out of murky water, like the scales of a wish-granting fish. The one time my dad took me fishing, we went to Wendigo Lake. It was small and flat, almost perfectly silent, tucked away off a back road, surrounded by a fence of evergreens. The water was clear but deep, tapering sharply from brown to black.

A fish would surface to catch a fly, and that's all we saw. Hours and hours of silent communion in a place that might just as well have been on another planet. Then at some hidden signal, we packed up and went home.

AT SOME POINT between the gnawing hunger and desperate thirst, I look up from a rocky patch of dirt to see the vista that spreads out before me. Behind me, the sun has risen high enough to shine down from overhead. Purest white light glints off glossy foliage, spread like a textured green blanket across the slope. Here and there, large boulders hunch their shoulders up through the trees. Far below, a wide lake covers the flat land from foothills to horizon. It shines white and blue.

For a moment I could believe it was the ocean. Gulls wheel above the shore. The wind drives little white-capped waves as it blows across the surface. It smells entirely different than saltwater, though. Soft and smooth. With an undertone of decay?

There's plastic sheeting over my face.

I can't — I can't breathe!

Help me!

A hand on my shoulder sparks panic in my heart. I'm alone on a mountaintop, so whose hand is that? Looking up, I see the kindly face of the woman who's been caring for me. Every breath is like pulling air from water. It burns with effort.

Without words, she tells me to calm down.

"Where's Doggo?" I manage to gasp through the pudding in my lungs.

She shakes her head and leaves again.

IT'S QUIET WHEN I come to. The sun is setting over the lake, burning the tips of the waves red and gold.

"Red sky at night," I say aloud.

There are no trees here at the top of the world. Low scrub brush digs its toes into lean soil, hunkered against an unjust universe. I reach over and pat the spiky twigs that shoot out the occasional glossy green leaf.

"The struggle is very real, my friend."

The place where I sit seems darker than the rest of the world. The world of the sunset. And even that world is being dimmed, minute by minute. Eventually, we'll all end up in the same darkness as one another. Alone in company.

"It's okay," I say. Maybe to Doggo, though I've not seen him for a bit. Perhaps he went back to the house. Or back Underground. I wouldn't blame him. It's tough out here.

Maybe I'm saying it to myself. And I'm startled to discover I believe it. I'm not lying or joking or martyring myself. I'm just here.

And it's all okay.

ACKNOWLEDGEMENTS

I'D LIKE TO THANK the Brampton Festival of Authors for creating the opportunity to connect with publishers. Also, everyone at Dundurn: Scott Fraser, who took the time to chat at BFOA and who liked the first thirty pages enough to ask for the rest of them; Rachel Spence, who thought enough of my manuscript to pitch it for publication; Sara D'Agostino, for patiently walking me through the contract signing process; my editors Jenny McWha and Julie Mannell; and Stephanie Ellis, Laura Boyle, and Elena Radic.

I'd also like to thank Peter Rowley for the use of his professional's eyes, the kind staff at Second Cup 324 Bloor Street West for letting me spend far too much time putting in "office hours" for the price of a coffee and muffin, and, of course, my husband and dogs, without whom I wouldn't be here.

ABOUT THE AUTHOR

EMILY BREWES grew up in the wilds of North Bay, Ontario, where she learned to be afraid of nature, especially bugs. Her writing career exists to spite her second grade teacher, who accused her of "getting help" on a creative composition that was perceived as being "too good." Many years on, Emily attempted National Novel Writing Month several times, one of which produced *The Doomsday Book of Fairy Tales*. She lived for some time in Toronto, where she learned to write wistfully of Northern Ontario's rugged beauty and haunting landscapes, but she has since moved to Kingston, Ontario.